11 SL

D0403412

AUGUSTUS REX

Also by Clive Sinclair

Augustus Rex

A NOVEL BY

CLIVE SINCLAIR

ORIGINAL DRAWINGS BY
YOSL BERGNER

ANDRE DEUTSCH

for Fran & Seth

First published in 1992 by
André Deutsch Limited
105-106 Great Russell Street
London WC1B 3LJ

ISBN 0 233 98768 1

Printed and bound in Great Britain by
WBC, Bridgend

PROLOGUE : 1912

"The future of Strindberg stimulates and baffles curiosity," observed the omnipotent *Encyclopaedia Britannica* with typical gravitas, blissfully unaware that at the very moment of publication his intestines were already efflorescent with cancer. Ah, but *I* knew! How? Was I his private physician? Hardly, my dears. That honour fell to his son-in-law. Let us just say that I had *access* to various medical reports, including those of Dr Petrén of Lund who, unimpressed by talk of Benike's worm, clearly suspected malignant encrustations. I knew what that portended, being well-versed in the skills of diagnosis and prognosis, as I have to be in my line of work.

Why have you turned so white, my dears? Do you fear to dwell upon the inherent weakness of your flesh? Does the consideration of death hold too many terrors? Ah, I understand, you think I am an undertaker. Silly things! You should see me shiver when I cross the path of one of those shadowy morticians, all astink with the odour of embalming fluid. No, my job requires me to reach the moribund patient's bedside *before* the patron saint of every grave-digger, the Angel of Death, has had time to deliver the coup de grace. You could call me a travelling salesman, of sorts, specializing in a single merchandise.

What is most likely to tempt the dying? That's right,

1

my dears, I peddle second chances. Some turn out to prefer death, of course. Others get it, whatever their predilection. Believe me, I understand the disappointment they feel as they draw their final breaths. There is nothing more frustrating, for one such as I, than to enter a sick-room full of expectation only to find the Angel of Death, already successful, with a post-coital smile on his smug face. "Necrophiliac!" I cry. Nor am I far from the truth. Who put *mor* into a*mor*ous? The Angel of Death, called Azrael but known by most as the Don Juan at the gates of doom.

He is a handsome brute, a cold-eyed seducer; a creature of instinct whose main function is to lead the dying to their final orgasm, assist them to let go, to finally shake off the self. He is the winged harbinger of a process that is one hundred percent natural . . . unlike me. It shames me to admit it, but there have been times when I have paused on the threshold of a room in order to watch my rival at work through the keyhole.

Forgive me, my dears, the memory of those humiliations has caused me to forget my manners. I beg you to show indulgence toward one whose breeding is not all it might be and permit him to introduce himself! His name is — *my* name is Beelzebub, Lord of the Flies. Look, I don't entertain false illusions about myself, I know that most people run a mile when they hear the boom-buzz-boom that announces my arrival. To tell you the truth I wouldn't blame you if you did the same. My looks are not pretty, like Azrael's, nor is my character admirable. I would run too, if only I could. Unfortunately I possess a particular talent much appreciated by my master; I can catch souls. No, it is more than a talent, it is a gift. I was therefore spared a tedious apprenticeship among the moribund hoi-polloi and, from the outset of my career, was only despatched to obtain the immortal souls of the very great. My deeds would be less criminal, would even be *excusable*, if my master actually sought these noble beings (these Nobel prize-winners) for the sake of their company, but he neither had nor has developed any interest in their conversation whatsoever; he wants them only because of their *names*, because of their value to his eternal opponent. In short, I must sell the best minds of every generation a bill of goods.

When it became public knowledge that August Strindberg was in a bad way I was immediately shown his case history and told to prepare myself for the journey to Stockholm. Let us get something straight, I may be Lord of the Flies, but there are none on me. I knew all about Strindberg and his works long before I consulted his entry in the *Encyclopaedia Britannica*. As a matter of fact I was something of a fan. So why did I agree to conspire against him? How little you mortals know! There are some commands (as distinct from commandments) that cannot be disobeyed. Especially those of my master, whose sanctions are immoderate. To be frank, I am in thrall to a brute with no more mercy than a fatal disease. It pains me to confess to this want of courage. I'd much rather present myself as a cultivated soul, whose particular skills have been perverted by force of circumstance, but for once in my life I feel inclined to tell the truth and the truth is that they have not. I am what I am. The responsibility for my actions is mine alone. Why do I decline to exculpate myself with the time-honoured words, 'I was only obeying orders'? Because, while accurate, they avoid the uncomfortable fact that I enjoy my work immensely. This means that I went eagerly to Stockholm, as required, but with a bad conscience.

* * *

While still a healthy man Strindberg had predicted that he would breathe his last on 14 May 1912. In order to prove

3

him wrong I had to make sure that the Angel of Death was otherwise occupied on that day. So I told him that Edvard Munch was on his last legs. Why Edvard Munch? Well, the Angel of Death has a penchant for artists, though he knows nothing about art; what he knows is that they have a talent for self-destruction. This ignorance has led to many spectacular blunders.

Allow me to introduce Marc Chagall's own account of one such, which gives you a good idea of my rival's rather dramatic working methods. "A square, empty room. In one corner, a single bed, and me on it. It is getting dark. Suddenly the ceiling opens and a winged being descends with a crash, filling the room with movement and clouds. A rustle of trailing wings. I think: An angel!" The Angel of Death thinks: This man, Chagall, is still full of years. Embarrassed, he tries to make an inconspicuous exit, but fails. "After rummaging about all over the place," continued the astonished artist, "he rises and passes through the opening in the ceiling, taking all the light and the blue air away with him."

Franz Kafka received a similar visitation. "Towards evening I walked over to the window and sat down on the low sill," he wrote in a diary entry dated 25 June 1917. "Then, for the first time not moving restlessly about, I happened calmly to glance into the interior of the room and at the ceiling . . . The tremor began at the edges of the thinly plastered white ceiling. Little pieces of plaster broke off and with a distinct thud feil here and there . . . a bluish violet began to mix with the white; it spread straight out from the centre of the ceiling, which itself remained white." Finally the ceiling broke apart to reveal "an angel in bluish-violet robes girt with gold cords" who sank slowly "on great white silken-shining wings." The Angel of Death saw the malign scars on the tips of the young writer's lungs, which looked like the clipped wings of a fallen angel, but he also saw that the tuberculosis was far

4

from its fatal denouement. Two months later, prompted by Kafka's first pulmonary haemorrhage, Professor Pick confirmed my friend's diagnosis. Thereafter the Angel of Death kept a fatherly eye on Franz.

As planned, the credulous fellow was on a wild-goose chase while Strindberg lay adying in his room within the Blue Tower, which overlooks the intersection of Drottninggatan and Tegnérgatan. I decided to make my entrance from the balcony where The King of Poets, the People's Strindberg, had ventured for the last time the previous January to acknowledge the torchlight procession in the street below. "There must be thousands of people down there," he had mumbled to his daughter Anne-Marie. She had squeezed his hand. "Happy birthday, papa," she whispered, as one of the brass bands struck up the *Marseillaise*. Tears filled her eyes, but these may have been occasioned by the icy blast, there being a complementary drip on the end of the playwright's red nose. "Long live Strindberg!" the workers exclaimed as they paraded past the ailing scribe, ruddy banners billowing in the easterly wind. Their champion was sixty-three, and had only four more months to live.

Enter Beelzebub, the people's hero, to the rescue. Strindberg was clearly sinking fast. His poky room reeked of disinfectant, but not even the strongest of fumes could have concealed all the olfactory evidence of corporeal dissolution. Hence the flies that congregated upon his stinking sheets. I had arrived in the nick of time. A woman in uniform kept a vigil beside his bed, like a Jewess in silent prayer at the Wailing Wall, though she brought no solace to the irascible invalid. On the contrary her obstinate adherence to such an uncomfortable wooden chair seemed to irritate him, so much so that the sting was temporarily restored to his tongue. "Nurse Kistner," he murmured, "go to bed, there is no need to worry about me, I am no longer here!"

5

"If you are not here," I asked after the nurse had reluctantly taken her employer's advice, "tell me, where are you?" I can usually count on the element of surprise, the buzz-boom-buzz effect; but Strindberg, being a man of the theatre and well used to uncanny entrances and exits, was harder to impress. "Beneath the waves," he replied calmly, as though the devil's emissary were an everyday visitor, "at the bottom of the sea." "Am I a fish?" I asked. "No," he conceded. "Then you are not at the bottom of the sea," I concluded. "But I am badly holed," he replied. "My body is finished. All its innards are in revolt. It feels ready to burst, though there is precious little left of it. I am not sorry. I always suspected that my soul, my mad soul, was not fitted for confinement in such a pathetic vessel."

My immediate task was clear; I had to prevent Strindberg from jumping ship. "It may be a poor thing," I agreed, "but without it you'll be press-ganged into the diaspora of lost souls that howls in the fog outside the pearly gates. Be advised, my friend, heaven is full; even with restricted entry it resembles nothing so much as a London slum." Strindberg looked at me curiously.

"Why do you use the word *diaspora*?" he demanded, ignoring my warning (and the subtle nod to his favourite English author). "Are you a Yid?" "No," I replied, "but the Jews named me." "Named you what?" he asked. "Beelzebub," I replied. "Aha," he said, "I know all about you. The Philistine *baal-zebub*, lord of the insects, turned by the punning Israelites into *baal-zebul*, lord of the dunghill. If I may say, you do not come smelling of roses. Have you read *The Roots of World Language* or *Ancestors of the Modern Tongue*? In them I prove, quite conclusively, that Hebrew, the sacred tongue, is the mother of all other languages. E.g. Idaho, *yehuda*. Minnesota, *minasoth*, a place of refuge. Canada, *kam*, a market town. Ad infinitum. A funny people, the Jews; even on my death bed I do not know whether I love them or hate them."

7

Archimedes said, Give me a lever and I will move the world. Strindberg, in his excitement, managed a comparable miracle. He raised his emaciated frame upon his elbows so that he was, in effect, sitting up. His hair, white and sparse, was damp with the strain. "I'm cold," he said. So I draped a frayed dressing-gown around his shoulders. "My clothes do not fit me any more," he said, "not even this." He was correct; in his brown-check robe he looked like a scarecrow. "Now help me walk to the piano," he said. It was on the other side of the ill-lit chamber, against the far wall. I ferried him through the chiaroscuro, through the waves of daylight that squeezed between the cracks in the closed shutters. He was as weightless as a teacup. "Hush," he said, "mustn't wake Nurse Kistner." Then, to my amazement, he proceeded to pick out *Nearer my God to Thee* on the keyboard of the Steinway. His face, fitfully illuminated by a guttering candle, flickered like a fading photograph. "Are you aware," he said, "that the orchestra on the *Titanic* insisted upon playing that when the ship went down? Look at me. The *Titanic*, c'est moi."

"I am Beelzebub," I said, "my breath can melt icebergs. You do not have to die." "I've told you already," he said, "I pray to be released from this undignified corpse." He tapped his noddle. "Only my mind is worth saving," he said. "That alone, being homogeneous with the supreme intelligence, will be absorbed into the godhead, as was the *Titanic* by the mighty ocean. I yearn for death." "How can you, a great artist blessed with many more unwritten masterpieces, dispose of your destiny so easily?" I demanded. "My enemies have worn me down," he replied. "I am weary of the fight. Like Prospero I hereby renounce my magic." "I am offering to restore it," I said. "And in return," said the dying man, closing the piano lid, "you'll doubtless roast my immortal remains until the last trump."

"I'm surprised to hear such propaganda from Strindberg,

of all people," I said. "I make an offer of celestial gener-osity and by way of gratitude I am pelted with fire and brimstone. Believe me, sir, hell bears no resemblance to the prophecies of your clerics. And even if it did would you choose to spend eternity in their company? Or would you prefer the society of Lucifer, Descartes, Newton and Pascal, our guiding lights? Do not look so surprised. If Pascal had truly been on the side of the angels would he have informed the Archbishop of Rouen that a certain Père St Ange was entertaining some speculative ideas on theological points that were not strictly orthodox? It seems that while he found it shocking that men who were in the right should not be tolerated, he found it even more shocking that men who were in the wrong should be.

"I freely confess that hell has its bonfires, but its general appearance resembles that of a well-tended garden; one that has been cultivated, with no little effort, from the tangled forest of human emotion and misbehaviour. It is true that anti-social insects – ah, I mean instincts, of course – and unruly inclinations can never be bred out of the species entirely; but just as the good gardener binds his honeysuckle and wisteria and forces them to grow along pre-ordained routes, so we control hysteria and similar manifestations with constant watchfulness and rigorous re-education. We see our society as a microcosm of the whole, a reflection of the universe which is – though it is often forgotten – ruled by hierarchical, regular and eternal laws. In short, we believe that truth is objective, that order descends from the higher to the lower, that humanity is raised above the animal kingdom by virtue of reason, and that the duality of mind and body symbolizes this distinction. Although you are welcome to take up residence immediately we do not necessarily encourage it, for we have no wish to over-populate hell. Rather our long-term strategy is to colonize the world by persuading carefully selected clients to stay put. You should therefore regard hell as the homeland to which you may retire when you consider that your life on earth has been properly fulfilled."

"Are you asking me to believe that hell, far from being a place of punishment, is the ultimate rationalization," gasped Strindberg, "the final reduction of life to its scientific principles? Forgive my scepticism, Mr Beelzebub, but I think you are trying to sell me a bill of goods. There is no smoke without fire. Of that I am convinced!"

Before you also dismiss me as a fraud, my dears, spare a moment to consider my position. I am a realist. I know that I cannot expect people to flock to hell as if it were the French Riviera. I must be able to offer something more – and, believe me, I do. Those extra years are no con. We do not have many virtues in hell, but patience is one of them. That being the case I was not offended by Strindberg's rebuff; indeed, I expected it. Most of his peers have similar reactions. However much humanity's great thinkers may prattle on about order, no one but the most deracinated of individuals really desires it; deep down, in secret places accessible only to torturers, lurks a greater dread than disorder; boredom, the fear that dares not speak its name. Therefore when Strindberg, exasperated by my persistence, cried – "Are you deaf? Did you not hear me when I said that I was finished with this vale of tears?" – I did not believe him any more than he believed me. I recognised the world-weariness of a man eaten away by cancer and responded accordingly, concentrating upon the practicalities of life rather than its theories.

"I remain unconvinced that you really consider spiritual intercourse to be superior to the bodily kind," I remarked. "And so I am going to set you a simple test. Do you remember what Harriet Bosse said to you when you were still courting?" He remembered. Tears rolled down his wasted cheeks. "She asked God to bless you for having written the line: 'I felt like Faust regretting his

10

youth, before this masterpiece of a woman child.' Well, I can give you everything that Faust received. And more. A new dawn and a new Harriet." "No," he said, shaking his head.

I was beginning to weary of his obstinacy. "I may be deaf," I snapped, "but I have not been blinded by the church's calumnies. What do you think you will see when you are eventually granted admittance to the celestial sphere? God's green acres? Ha! Heaven is a cess-pit. And why? Because no one is prepared to do a minute's work up there. In heaven they think every day is the sabbath. Its characteristic sound – the flip-flop of fat feet – is echoed by its very name: *hea-ven*. Compare it to *hell*. Did you know that there have been occasions when that bell-like toll was sufficient to revive the comatose? Ding-dong hell. Listen. Hell. *Hell*. How desperately the tongue tries to free itself from the closed *h*. Fortunately, *e* (for escape) comes to the rescue. And down the double *l* you slide. To freedom. Now look at the word. Hell. The bar across the *h* is like a prison door, blocking you off from the essential pleasures of life. *E* is the key. And *ll* is the tunnel, the tunnel of love, open, unbarred and bottomless. Consider the alternative; nevermore to touch a female body, nevermore to smell womanly perfumes. No new Harriet, no new dawn. Instead you will choke upon the finite stench of your own putrefaction." I had not used le mot juste; the whole of my carefully constructed argument was condemned by the careless placement of a single word at its end.

"The alchemists believed that putrefaction was the sine qua non of ultimate wisdom," he replied, "they looked upon the grave as a womb, wherein would begin the renaissance of man." "They were wrong," I fibbed, "without the body there is nothing." Above my head I heard a rustling and, raising my eyes, saw that the ceiling was beginning to glow, as though it were suffused with ultra-violet light. "Alas, you do not have long to make up your mind," I

11

said, "the Angel of Death is fast approaching. It is, I am assured, a pleasant thing to expire in his arms. Give the word and I will leave you to his tender mercies." I made ready to depart, hoping against hope that Strindberg, now that his final appointment was at hand, would change his mind.

"Wait!" he cried. "It is true that I was weary and ready for death, but your cunning words have reawakened my appetite for life. Help me, Beelzebub, I am no longer prepared to forsake all earthly delights. What must I do? Help me!"

At that precise moment, as the clock on the mantlepiece struck four, the ceiling of Strindberg's bedroom parted and the Angel of Death was manifest. "It seems that my ability to assist you is at an end," I observed. "The Angel of Death is as beguiling as a snake-charmer. In his presence I am powerless. Poor Strindberg! You now belong irrecoverably to the dying, who do not have free-will, who have no choice but die." "No!" cried Strindberg. "Take what you want, take my immortal soul, but give me life!" "I'll see what can be done," I replied.

The Angel of Death has turquoise eyes, which burn like arctic ice. In order to win a reprieve for Strindberg I knew that I would have to avoid their disabling fire. I concentrated instead upon the golden buttons of his tunic. "I was here first," I said. "Undeniable," replied the Angel of Death, "but I am here now, and unless this gentleman has unwisely signed one of your contracts I mean to have him in a matter of minutes." *Gentleman*! Then he didn't know in whose house he was, a particular hazard of his roof-top entrances. Nor was Azrael likely to recognise his host, now that his face was covered with nothing but a butter-coloured membrane. I took heart. Meanwhile, the Angel of Death plucked Strindberg from the piano stool and returned the ragged bag of skin and bone that bore his name to its bed. "This is a man whose time has come," he announced. "Listen," I said, "compromise on this nonentity and you'll meet no opposition the next time a celebrity nears his end." "For example?" he asked. "The Great Caruso," I replied, relying upon the angelic passion for grand opera. "You've got a deal," he said.

I hurried over to my client, who was growing colder by the second. I propped him up against his pillow. "You must make a new will," I informed him, as though I were some solicitor's articled clerk. "To what end?" he asked. "Here is pen, here is paper," I replied impatiently. "Now write the following: 'My body must not be dissected or laid out in state, only shown to my relatives. No death-mask can be made, no photographs taken. I want to be interred at eight in the morning, to avoid any curious bystanders. I do not want to be buried in a crypt, much less in a church, but in the new cemetery; not in the section for the wealthy, however.' Got it all?" Like Samson, that other cuckold, Strindberg somehow managed to recapture his demonic energy at the last. I saw that he had transcribed every word; nor had he forgotten that all-important addendum, his signature. "Look," I explained, "you are too far gone not to die. To do otherwise would be to humiliate the Angel of Death." "So you failed?" he asked. "On the contrary," I replied, "I have arranged for you to be spared his most fulsome embrace. You will not *actually* die, but merely enter a state of suspended animation. No warmth, no breath, shall testify, thou liv'st; each part, depriv'd of supple government, shall, stiff and stark and cold, appear like death; and in this borrow'd likeness of shrunk death you will remain for a generation or more. Until your acquaintances have all followed you to the grave. Then, *providing your instructions have been obeyed to the letter*, I shall raise you up."

And so it happened. Strindberg died at 4.30 that afternoon. In the words of one of the few people considered close

13

enough to attend the corpse, "the pale face on the white pillow had a strange expression that is hard to forget, a beautiful, almost impish little smile." I think you know why, my dears.

PART ONE : 1961–1965

Not the *Titanic*, but the *Wasa*. You are perhaps wondering what the *Wasa*, the flagship of Gustavus Adolphus that went famously to the bottom of Stockholm harbour on its maiden voyage, has to do with the posthumous playwright. Those of you who are better educated than the Angel of Death may recall that the belligerent monarch was the eponymous subject of a Strindbergian epic; a good guess, but that coincidental connection is not the significant link between the sunken galleon and the earth-bound scribbler.

No, to discover the real bond we must look to the ancients. It was Anaxagoras the Greek who, seeing in a minute atom the infinite universe, first applied the principle of analogy better to comprehend the otherwise inexplicable. Likewise did Trismegistus the alchemist declare that the chemical processes of his alembics were similar to those of the sidereal laboratories. "All is in all," he wrote. "Everywhere analogy infers the same laws." From analogy to identity is but a single step.

Thus when Swedes in their thousands congregated at the maritime fringes of Skeppsholmen, Kastellholmen, Beckholmen and Djurgården on that memorable day, 24 April 1961, to witness the *Wasa* break surface and emerge dripping from the muddy depths, I saw only Strindberg.

15

He, doubtless, would have ascribed the *Wasa*'s miraculous state of preservation to a trinity of lucky threes, since the vessel was submerged for exactly 333 years. Actually, what kept the *Wasa* more-or-less intact was a unique characteristic of the Mare Balticum; the *teredo navalis*, an aquatic termite that devours water-logged wood elsewhere, likes a lot of salt on its supper, and therefore keeps away from the brackish Baltic. Does this mean that it was another quirk of nature rather than the black arts that kept the coffin flies, *sarcophaga carnaria*, off Strindberg's flesh? Have we to thank Sweden's cryogenic soil for his imminent resurrection? What do you think? Would a little clue be of some assistance? Very well. I am known as the Lord of the Flies, my dears, not only because I *attract* the loathsome insects, but also because of my ability to *repel* them.

It is not a simple matter to bring someone back from the grave, even if they are not exactly dead. After all, it took the Neptune Salvaging Company over two years to raise the *Wasa*. So I do not think I was being exceptionally lackadaisical in allowing eight months to pass from the moment I recognised Strindberg in the mighty oaken hull until I next saw him in propria persona, laid out in his spruce-wood box. In the meantime, as I said, there was plenty to arrange. For example, there was the problem of accommodation. If only Strindberg could have returned to the Blue Tower, where he would certainly have felt at home; no great achievement in apartments designed to create the illusion that he had never left. But I doubt whether the curators of the so-called Strindberg Museum would have jumped for joy if their hero had stepped in, thanked them for their house-keeping, and courteously shown them the door. Museums depend upon the dead remaining dead.

Instead I looked to Riddarholm quay where, as the son of a shipping agent, Strindberg had watched the schooners come and go. And there I heard of a young widow who, in hopes of maintaining a precarious hold on her privileged mode of existence, was prepared to accept a convalescent gentleman of considerable means as a lodger. Moreover, for reasons of snobbery, she wished to keep the financial basis of their relationship a strict secret, putting it out that she was anticipating a visit from an elderly cousin, Mr August Lagercrantz. What could be more appropriate? Her house was situated on the water-front in a terrace of towering buildings that looked as though they had been constructed hundreds of years previously by wealthy merchants with Hanseatic connections. Gog and Magog held aloft the glass portals which opened upon a colonnaded hall. Marble steps led to the third floor where I knocked upon a heavy wooden door. Mrs Nilsson admitted me and, observing the golden kroner in my purse, led me to the guest room. From its windows I could see both the Mälaren and the Saltsjön and, beyond them, the northern curvature of the globe itself.

It turned out that Mrs Nilsson was also prepared to cook and, in so far as it did not compromise her dignity, clean for her "cousin". Seated upon her leather sofa we negotiated the rent over cups of steaming coffee. Eventually I agreed to pay her 5000 kroner per month, commencing in November.

Throughout Edgar Allan Poe's *The Purloined Letter* the Paris gendarmerie search in vain for a pilfered epistle. Why do they fail so ignominiously? Because they are inflated with arrogance and assume that the criminal, dreading their intelligence, has resorted to the most arcane crannies. It requires Dupin, the master detective, to state a simple truth; the best way to avoid detection is to be excessively obvious. Sure enough Dupin discovers the letter deposited "immediately beneath the nose of the whole world, by way of preventing any portion of that world from perceiving it."

Following the daring example of Poe's ingenious thief (known only as D-) I traversed Norrtullsgatan and entered the North Cemetery on All Souls Eve, when it is customary for the living to visit their dead. Not one of the multitude gave me a second glance, even though I was pushing an empty wheel-chair. They were more concerned with the incessant wind, which made the igniting of memorial candles especially difficult. But eventually they succeeded and the dark November night was enlivened by countless flames dancing in their little jars above the graves.

Finding Strindberg's resting place I saw that he was not forgotten. A dozen candles illuminated his dark marker with its misleading inscription: *O Crux Ave Spes Unica!* Believe me, my dears, it was not the former resident of that unholy relic who knelt on the hard ground above the sleeping corpse but loyal Beelzebub, his unheralded saviour. I breathed upon the sterile soil with hot breath and had the satisfaction of hearing, deep below, the rewarding sound of nails being prised from creaking wood. A pale hand, as blind as an albino in the sunlight, broke surface and groped the night. I grabbed the bony fingers and, with one massive heave, hoisted the remainder of the born-again heathen out of his box and into the al fresco. Needless to say, my exertions went undetected by the passing throng of melancholy silhouettes, who were uniformly preoccupied with the contemplation of mortality. Meanwhile the immortal Strindberg, blinking furiously and wheezing with the pain of inhaling the cold Swedish air, crumpled to the earth whence he had just come. Observed by a handful of approving by-standers, kindly Beelzebub assisted the old gentleman to his feet and into the awaiting chair. And then, having tucked him in beneath tartan blankets, he triumphantly wheeled him out of the bone-yard and back into the land of the living.

Thereafter the clock went rapidly into reverse as we retraced the stations of Strindberg's life from the place of his interment, via the Blue Tower and the Intimate Theatre, to the location of his birth. While we were crossing the bridge to the Riksdagshus, Strindberg began to cough horribly and, once on the other side, I had no choice but to halt our progress. "Take some deep breaths," I said, placing my lips in the vicinity of his ear. He looked up, noticing me for the first time. "Who are you?" he hissed. "Where are you taking me? What has happened to Nurse Kistner?" Like his rôle-model, Rip Van Winkel, he had no idea that many, many years had passed. "You are to have a new chaperone," I said, "Mrs Nilsson of Riddarholm." "Ah, Riddarholm," he whispered, and at once he relaxed and his breathing became easier.

Now that we were in Gamla Sta'n, the Old Town, the streets were narrower, and courting couples, at the outset of their nocturnal adventures, constantly had to step off the pavement to make way for the wheel-chair and its dozy occupant. The buildings were tall, so tall that the sky was barely visible between them. Nonetheless, our way was well-lit by the dazzling shops; book shops, souvenir shops selling reindeer leather and Viking helmets, aromatic coffee shops with twenty different beans and even more blends of tea, antique shops with maritime bric-a-brac and glowing boutiques, outside which fashionable beauties and their arrogant beaux exhibited their temporary charms. I don't know if butterflies live upon the Galapagos, but if they do the islands' hard-topped methuselahs must look at them as I looked upon those Swedish popinjays; with contempt, perfect contempt. On the other hand, they acted as a stimulant upon Strindberg's lethargic senses.

"So I did not die," he observed. "No, my dear, you did not die. You slept deeply, but you did not die. Your sleep, maestro, was it untroubled?" "It was not," he replied. "I dreamed that a photograph was taken of my skull and that I pinned it to the wall beside the mirror in my bathroom. Whenever I looked at my reflection in the

19

latter's silver surface, which revealed wrinkled flesh and a downcast mouth, I became profoundly depressed. The only panacea was to step aside and regard the ever-cheerful image of my skull with its pebble-smooth surface and its wide, permanent smile." This did not surprise me; the undead are generally visited with schizophrenic dreams. Not knowing whether they are dead or alive they tend to idealize the former state, envisioning it as an eternity of bliss, the sunlit country beyond the vale of tears. And yet death, the grinning skull, is not regarded as an essentially different state; merely an improved version of reality. Only the undead could regard it as such; the truly dead would know better.

Turning right off Västerlånggatan we made our bumpy way down steep cobbled alleys until we reached the quayside, upon which stood Mrs Nilsson's handsome residence. A flaming pot of naphthalene flourished like a divine aspidistra on the steps outside the entrance, a sure sign that one of her neighbours was holding a Halloween party within. She had more to celebrate than she knew; namely, another triumph for Beelzebub!

* * *

I did not participate; self-congratulation is not my style. Besides this was only the beginning. Having successfully engineered Strindberg's resurrection I now had the task of plotting his downfall. This was the hardest part of all; how to proceed. The problem was this; Strindberg could still exercise free will. He may have signed a contract but his damnation was not determined. Salvation remained a possible option; either through genuine repentance, remorse and flagellation, or through the commission of good deeds. It was up to me to ensure that he did not take it. I felt like a writer who, having sold an idea to a publisher, must now deliver a novel.

21

Okay, I know what you're thinking, and I cannot disagree; I am certainly a swine. But tell me, my dears, who are you to sit in judgement upon me? I wonder whether your stout hearts would beat so very differently if your lord and master had a cloven hoof. Oh you make me laugh, you armchair moralists with your high and mighty airs. What do you really know of the shameful compromises we denizens of the pit are forced to make simply to stay in one piece? I apologise, but I'm no saint; not one of those types who, expiring on the barbecue, cry out: "Forgive them, Father!"

Nor am I a great thinker, and hesitate to offer any home-truths of my own. However, I have no qualms about borrowing one from Ecclesiastes. "There is no new thing under the sun." Dead right! You, who fancy yourselves modern in word and thought, are nothing but alchemists with academic qualifications. And what is alchemy? Nothing but the astrology of the lower world. And what prompts astrology? Fear of the future; i.e. fear of life itself. To borrow another pearl from the author of Ecclesiastes, "To everything there is a season . . . a time to be born, and a time to die." This is an immutable truth that you find very hard to swallow. Isn't it enough that you have dominion over the animals? No, you want control over the seasons, over the laws of physics – over death itself, luckily for me. *That* is the point at which our fears coincide, our paths cross, our interests become mutual. I am always happy to outwit Azrael on your behalf, my dears, though (to be perfectly frank) I often wonder why you want me to bother. It isn't as though the average *homo sapiens* actually enjoys his life.

There was once a medieval savant named Raymond Lully who was passionately in love with Eleanor of Castello. Or he was until the lady herself cured his obsession by exposing to his longing eyes the ulcer that was eating away her breast. Poor Lully took to his heels and never looked at another woman. Instead he became a missionary who made no secret of his true ambition: martyrdom. At the age of eighty he was granted his heart's desire, being stoned to death after delivering a sermon. Lully's misfortune explains why humanity worships art. Because, unlike Eleanor of Castello, it is safe from decomposition. You live in dread of encountering the Dead Sea Fruit incarnate; that which appears wholesome, but which tastes of ashes. Why the dread? Because you know, for all your wisdom, that you will be unable to resist it, despite your fear of the unpalatable truth. Tell me, my dears, how did I finally catch Strindberg? With what did I persuade that great mind to remain in the material sphere? With the promise of jiggery-pokery, that's what!

You want to control the galaxy? Then first control your nether parts! Let us be fair, some of you do try. This leads to conflict within the body politic, as the intellect accuses the instinct of carnal obsession, and the instinct in turn blames the intellect for the assassination of pleasure. The battle is merciless, as are all civil wars, and the outcome bloody. But however bloody it is, one thing remains certain; the libido will never be defeated. I might just as well try to overpower the devil. What I want to say is this, my dears; we are not so very different, you and I.

Strindberg was no Lully. He may have spent decades with only rotting cadavers for company, but they were no deterrent; he longed to see Mrs Nilsson uncover her breasts from the moment he spied their comely owner (though it is possible, given the circumstances, that any pre-menopausal woman would have appeared desirable in his eyes). Mrs Nilsson, alas, was much less impressed by her new lodger; in fact she was evidently taken aback by his ghastly complexion, his skeletal frame and his helpless state. Although Strindberg made no comment I could see that he was pained by her obvious revulsion. Perhaps I had been unusually cruel in placing him under the same roof as a statuesque woman; but we both needed a challenge, and here it was. How could this semi-articulated death-mask even begin to court such a nubile beauty? Be patient, my dears, and you will see.

First I had to ensure that he was not thrown out on his ear and so, by way of explanation, I informed Mrs Nilsson that the so-called August Lagercrantz had been stricken by narcolepsy in his middle years and that he had slept continuously until his miraculous awakening in the late summer. "Why did you keep this a secret when we made our arrangement?" she demanded. "I am not a nurse." "Nor do you need to be," I assured her. "Mr Lagercrantz's doctors have predicted that their extraordinary patient will be restored to health within weeks. In the meantime, have no fear, you will be well rewarded for any additional services you may be required to perform." Mrs Nilsson looked at me suspiciously. "Such as?" she said. I laughed. "Nothing too dreadful," I said. "As you can see, Mr Lagercrantz has all his faculties, but under-use has atrophied them. In other words, he can feed himself, but the process is painfully slow. His recovery would certainly be accelerated if you could perform that function for him." Mrs Nilsson looked at Strindberg uncertainly. "Is he clean?" she asked. "My dear lady," I exclaimed, "I would not dream of burdening you with an incontinent; I promise you, Mr Lagercrantz has full control of his sphincter muscles, both fore and aft. If you would be good enough to wheel him to the bathroom when he feels the need he will happily take care of the rest himself. The same applies to bathing." I looked her in the eye. "Mr Lagercrantz will not be a burden to you, Mrs Nilsson," I said with great sincerity, "you have my word on that." "I accept it," she said, "he can stay." "One last thing, Mrs Nilsson," I said as I walked to the door, "Mr Lagercrantz loves literature, but unfortunately his hands are still too feeble to hold a book for more than a few minutes. Perhaps you could

24

find the time to read to him, he would appreciate that."

Mrs Nilsson was a good girl; she did as she was told. She fed Strindberg three times a day and then read to him every evening. Actually the benefits were shared. Hitherto unbookish (there were, I observed, only magazines in the apartment) Mrs Nilsson began to respond to the seductiveness of the storyteller, and thereby experienced the pleasure of the text for the first time in her life. She identified with numerous heroines and even began to daydream dangerously whilst reading *Jane Eyre*. Luckily for her Strindberg was not listening. "He sits there for hours," she reported, "just staring at me."

Strindberg was aware that this was an occasion for dalliance, but he was unable to resist the importunate demands of his libido. And so he attempted to possess Mrs Nilsson with his eyes. Sometimes, if he were especially fortunate, Mrs Nilsson would accidentally brush him with an intimate portion of her anatomy whilst delivering a full-fork of cooked flesh. Then he could not help himself; he ate like an animal. Noisily he sucked the juices from the flesh and swallowed the dehydrated remnants whole, whereupon he all but barked for more, salivating and chewing on his tongue. He had to behave in this manner, had to indulge his enormous appetite in some way; otherwise he would have been compelled to snatch his prick there and then and begin to masturbate in front of his hostess.

Begin to masturbate! That was all he could do anyway! Even in the privacy of his own room Strindberg found it impossible to assuage the intolerable greed of his genitals. He gnashed his teeth with frustration and even cursed his benefactor, though he would have done better to strengthen his muscles. As yet normal elasticity had not returned to any of them; even his extremities remained waxen and stiff and so were unable to grip his giraffe-like member with sufficient pressure. In despair he sought to share the necessary functions between his two hands; using the right he closed the fingers of the left around the swollen member, so that the one could do the squeezing while the other supplied the required friction. Alas, Strindberg did not take into account the weakness of his wrists, which gave way after only a few strokes. No, satisfaction only came to Strindberg with sleep, when succubae provided what his hands could not. The resultant blots on the sheets caused him great embarrassment, even though Mrs Nilsson wisely made no complaint, not even to me.

As the season progressed Strindberg seemed to grow younger by the day until, at Winter's end, he resembled a virile man in his fifties. Once again there was an excess of flesh between the skin and the bone. His white hair glowed with the ethereal light of an early-morning mist, his cheeks were ruddy with health. His limbs, formerly stiff, were now flexible thanks to his daily push-ups and rigorous use of the late Mr Nilsson's exercise bicycle. As a consequence his vanity reasserted itself, and he began to chafe at the sartorial perimeters of his new life. He no longer found it acceptable to be seen in pyjamas or a bath-robe during the day, nor did he find the remnants of Mr Nilsson's wardrobe much more pleasing; the man's judgement in women was unimpeachable, but his taste in suits was execrable. Mrs Nilsson, astonished by the transformation, promised to escort him to the best outfitters as soon as the weather became sufficiently clement. In time the ice melted, sap rose, and buds appeared on the trees. Neighbours, left and right, packed away their hats, their boots and their overcoats, and ventured out in colourful jackets. Daily Strindberg nagged Mrs Nilsson to let him do likewise, so that he could begin to furnish his shelves with the latest fashions. At last she concurred and Strindberg's long hibernation drew to its close.

Once outside he was intoxicated by sensation; the smell of blossom, the sun on the water, the light, the birdsong, the chatter of humanity, the downy nape of Mrs Nilsson's neck. The shops were no less tempting. He insisted upon entering every one. Assistants rubbed their hands as he listed his needs, then secretly wept as they went to fetch the fifteenth blazer. In shoe stores, likewise, he was soon surrounded by shoes. Shirt makers fared no better; he fingered every roll of cotton and silk. Tailors unfurled bales of cloth at his behest. Finally he ordered a dozen shirts and two suits; one of tweed, the other of charcoal grey worsted. He also purchased several pairs of corduroy trousers (grey and brown) and, best by far, an array of blazers in all the primary colours. Additionally he bought three pairs of tan boots, floral ties, cotton underwear, nylon socks.

Exhausted he clutched his companion's arm as they shuffled slowly back along the gentle slope to the quayside. For twenty minutes or so they strolled beside the water's edge until it became apparent that Strindberg needed to rest. The sun, being fierce, drove them to seek sanctuary in the shade of an alley. A youth, sporting ill-fitting shorts and a faded sweatshirt that advertised a fizzy drink, squeezed between them. As he passed he stared openly at Mrs Nilsson's face and at her figure. He walked on, then stopped, as though an idea had suddenly occurred to him, whereupon he turned around and retraced his steps. "Good morning," he mumbled. "How are you? What is the time?" He kept repeating the phrases, as though he knew no others. "Good morning. How are you? What is the time?" The boy was clearly an idiot or a foreigner. His eyes did not move from Mrs Nilsson's body. There was a vacant smile upon his lips. As he got closer Strindberg remarked that he was dribbling. He could also see that the boy's left hand was busy inside his shorts. He felt Mrs Nilsson's grip tighten around his arm as she made a similar observation. "Is man no more than this?" thought Strindberg with a shudder. Turning to the boy he said to him, as King Lear had said to Poor Tom: "Thou art the thing itself." Then, dropping his packages, he slapped the boy around the face. The blow was not hard but, being unexpected, it made the recipient howl. Mrs Nilsson relaxed. She did not realize that Strindberg had not intended to strike that unhappy youth's cheek, what he was really aiming at was his own distorted image.

Nevertheless, the incident subtly altered the balance of their relationship. Mrs Nilsson began to see her house-guest as a potential protector, a man on whom she might lean in a time of need. Strindberg, for his part, had been shocked into more cerebral pursuits. Where once his waste-paper basket had been filled with semen-stained tissues, it now overflowed with crumpled sheets of writing paper. Being a curious woman Mrs Nilsson sometimes flattened these discarded pages and attempted to make sense of the contents, but Strindberg's handwriting remained as inde-cipherable as his character and his history.

One evening Strindberg emerged from his room, plucked a battered panama from the hat-stand, and yelled: "Mrs Nilsson, tonight we are going to dine in style!" Mrs Nilsson changed into a short summer frock. A taxi then delivered them to the door of the finest hotel in Stockholm. They entered its famous art deco bar and sat down. A waiter appeared out of nowhere and took their order. The bar remained empty, save for a solitary woman at a nearby table. She was middle-aged, and as plain as the vodka she was drinking.

Strindberg leaned toward Mrs Nilsson and was about to whisper an intimacy when the serenity of the moment was permanently destroyed by the sudden entry of forty Norwegian men in evening dress. Within seconds they were all downing tankards of lager. Strindberg, maddened by their incessant chatter, arose and, still wearing his absurd hat, crossed the room in order to quieten them. Mrs Nilsson watched nervously as her unpredictable beau placed his arm around the shoulder of the nearest Norwegian. Like all Swedes she knew that Norwegians, when inebriated, had violent tendencies (though they were seldom as vicious as the Finns, a notorious people). The conversation lasted for several minutes and ended, not with blows, but with hand-shakes and comradely slaps. Strindberg was beaming when he returned to his escort.

"They are bank managers from all over Norway," he announced, "in Stockholm for their annual jamboree. Why Stockholm and not Oslo? Because they want to be as far away from their wives as possible." Strindberg laughed. "Do you know what he told me?" he asked. In the distance his new friend raised his glass. "He thought that you were my daughter and said, hoping that I wouldn't be offended, that all his mates fancied you."

Shortly thereafter an unsteady bank manager tottered over to their table bearing a potted plant. He bowed, presented it to Mrs Nilsson, kissed her on both cheeks, and declared: "We have just elected you Miss World." Mrs Nilsson blushed and gingerly touched the leaves of the red geranium. Another tipsy Norwegian approached and repeated the entire procedure, at the end of which he announced: "You are also the runner-up." After the third plant had been delivered the lonely woman at the adjacent table arose and quietly disappeared. When Mrs Nilsson stood up, however, there was universal cheering. Feeling like a film star she waved at her fans and, gathering up the three plants, clasped them to her bosom.

Throughout the meal, hitherto sensible bank managers continued to approach their table in order to deposit a tit-bit or to deliver a flattery. The suggestiveness of the latter, which increased in proportion to the amount of alcohol consumed, eventually began to irritate Strindberg; not because he was a prude, but because he saw how much they were titillating his companion. And so when a particularly foolhardy Norwegian bank manager attempted to plant a tulip in the exposed cavity between Mrs Nilsson's breasts Strindberg arose, as if he were the most uxorious of men, and pushed the offender out of the restaurant. It was an unnecessary gesture, but Mrs Nilsson thought it wonderful; it confirmed Strindberg's position as the master of ceremonies, proved beyond doubt that the evening was *his* triumph. Indeed, it was at that moment, in the luxurious dining-room of the Hotel V-, that Mrs Nilsson experienced the first stirrings of desire, realized that it was possible to love such a man as Mr Lagercrantz had turned out to be.

* * *

Somehow Strindberg failed to recognise Mrs Nilsson's new attitude towards him (or, if he did, he did not respond), perhaps because he felt ready to commence work on a new chef-d'oeuvre. How long can a woman wait? Mrs Nilsson decided to give him one last chance, to send him an unmistakeable signal. And so it came to pass, near the end of a quiet day in June, that Strindberg left his study, a room of limitless horizons, and entered the kitchen, where his landlady was preparing the evening meal. She was wearing a loose fitting pullover, which had the colour and texture of an apricot. Light from the afternoon sun fell upon her. She was cutting beef into cubes. "Hello, Mr Lagercrantz," she said, shooing the house-flies away from the bleeding flesh, "today we are going to have a special treat, a mango from Peru."

She knelt beside the refrigerator and delved into the drawer where the fruit was stored. At the same time another kind of ripeness was revealed. Because she was on her knees a gap, the size of a crescent moon, slowly opened between the neck of her jumper and her own. Strindberg, being a polite man, might well have averted his gaze if it hadn't been for a venturesome *musca domestica*

30

that landed, like a winged thought, in the musky heart of that newly exposed valley. The interior landscape glowed dimly, illuminated (like the fruit) by the artificial light that shone from the open fridge. As Strindberg followed the fly's exploration of the late Mr Nilsson's ill-concealed treasures, he remembered his own lost love, Harriet Bosse, and saw once again in his mind's eye her "exceptionally well proportioned figure," as the critics loved to call it. And then he thought, *Where is poor Harriet now?* As I have said, Strindberg was no Lully, but the vision of Harriet in her grave (where, incidentally, she had lain for only a year) tormented him and caused him to turn away from Mrs Nilsson's exposed bosom, only to become aware that he was also the subject of observation. Mrs Nilsson was watching him as he looked at her. She wanted to make sure that he had seen her breasts! And what's more, she wanted him to know that she wanted him to see them. He read the message in her eyes and was flattered. He forgot the fate that awaited her and remembered instead that an attractive woman in her twenties was making sexual overtures toward a man whose flesh resembled gravadlax.

She arose without a word and, having plucked a sharp knife from the wooden block, began to cut into the mango. Strindberg took his seat at the table and watched as she pared and peeled the fruit. Licking the excess juice from her fingers she presented her lodger with the glistening segments. "Thank you, Mrs Nilsson," he said. Then, almost without forethought, he invited her to sit down opposite him. "Do you know, Mrs Nilsson," he said, "that I have been boarding with you for nearly a year and I still do not know your Christian name?" "It is Hinde," she said, "but, alas, it is not Christian." Strindberg was shocked; like every antisemite he thought that he could always spot a Yid, even when she looked like a Greek goddess.

"I am a Polish Jew," admitted Mrs Nilsson, "notwithstanding my married name. I was born in Warsaw at the end of 1938 and would have died there too with all my little cousins if the elders of the Great Synagogue on Wahrendorffsgatan hadn't invited my father to become their *chazan*. My beloved father sang like Chaliapin, and thanks God his fame had spread as far as Stockholm. We followed it and I spent my first birthday in a small apartment on Kungsträdgårdsgatan, within walking distance of the *shul*. Have you ever been inside, Mr Lagercrantz? Forgive the silly question. Of course you haven't. Well, it is dark and exotic, more Moorish than Swedish, and its huge space devours the human voice. Not my father's! It expanded and expanded until the very air the worshippers breathed was replaced by music. God gave him lungs that could have filled Valhalla! But as everyone knows he failed to touch the hearts of our enemies.

"After the war he insisted upon returning to Warsaw. My mother screamed at him, 'You're a lunatic!' But he wouldn't listen, the crazy bastard! God forgive me, but I hated him for dragging us all back to that dingy old house, maliciously preserved, where he lived in the hope that at least some of his family would show up again. You see, Mr Lagercrantz, he just couldn't bring himself to believe the terrible reports from the camps. And there he waits to this day, a broken man.

"Alas, I did not inherit his saintly disposition. Having grown up in a free atmosphere I suffered terribly from claustrophobia in austere Warsaw. I became a teenager and truly thought I would suffocate in that socialist paradise of theirs. And then I met Mr Nilsson, thirty-five years my senior, who was in Poland to purchase timber for his factory on the outskirts of Stockholm. Look, I know I have charms, and I freely confess that I used them on Mr Nilsson. The dear man could hardly believe his luck. Within a week he asked me to be his wife. I didn't love him of course but I said yes anyway because I was terrified that if I didn't I would miss my small chance of happiness for ever. And so my wish was granted, I became a Swede. No longer frightened little Hinde Zelinsky, but Mrs Nilsson, happy and self-confident. I felt reborn, as though I was returning from the dead. And for a few months I was happy."

Mrs Nilsson paused and, leaning forward, placed her hand upon Strindberg's. "The things I am going to tell you next are very intimate," she said. Strindberg was not taken in for a second, he had seen such theatrical gestures used by a hundred mediocre actresses; even so there was some magic about her amateur duplicity that captivated him.

"My kind husband, Mr Nilsson, could see that I was growing restless," she continued, "so he made me a little proposition. Would I like to open a small confectionery shop on Västerlånggatan? He happened to know that the wife of his business partner was looking for a companion of her own to share in just such a venture. Would I? I clapped my hands, screamed, and hugged my poor over-generous husband. Well, between us we turned a dusty old bookseller's hermitage into a beautiful bonbonniere, a veritable Aladin's cave of sparkling sugar-balls, aromatic chocolates, and Turkish delight which we imported from Brussels, Zurich, York, and Istanbul. Children pressed their noses against the window, while confident business-men and diplomats entered to pick out a delicacy for their latest Camille. I was entranced by the sweetness of adultery, unlike my jaded colleague, who soon lost interest in the venture. This led to some unforeseen consequences. First, her husband began to frequent the shop in her stead. Second, after a time a little affair developed between us. It was very nice and it hurt nobody until – I don't really know why – I felt that I had to inform my husband that I was sleeping with his partner. It was a very bad mistake. We had a very dramatic scene. We talked about it for thirty-six hours non-stop until we thought we had said everything there was to say. Then suddenly, a few weeks later, came the third consequence; my husband put an end to his business. For ages afterwards I dreaded meeting his ex-partner. Because of me opening my mouth he had lost his career."

"And what about the workmen?" asked Strindberg. "What became of *them*?" "How should I know?" snapped Mrs Nilsson, taken aback by this irrelevant interruption. "I'm sure that my husband looked after them all. But who is there to protect me now? I still think that I see my erstwhile lover everywhere and that he will stab me – I am sure that he is capable of it. To tell you the truth, Mr Lagercrantz, one of the reasons I accepted you as a lodger was to scare him off, to save myself from the fourth consequence." "My dear Mrs Nilsson," said Strindberg, laughing grimly at the idea of grappling with a blood-thirsty sicarii bent upon the assassination of his former mistress, "your imagination puts mine to shame." Though discomforted by this apparent dismissal of her flattery, Mrs Nilsson, having gone so far, decided to continue with her confession.

"My revelation didn't wreck our marriage," she said, helping herself to a slice of mango, "but I fear that it shortened my dear husband's life, having prompted the flirtation with vodka that, if the doctors are to be believed, actually ended it. I live on in the conviction that my foolish desires have made a widow-woman out of me."

Mrs Nilsson paused, but Strindberg failed to reciprocate with the anticipated pardon. She lifted her fingers, sticky with the juice of the mango, and brushed back the strands of tawny hair that had fallen across her face. It was meant to be an intimate gesture, to match the intimate words, but it failed to elicit any complementary response; no squeeze of the hand, nor even a conspiratorial smile. The silence grew. It gagged her like a malevolent incubus. How much longer would she have to wait before her well-rehearsed

34

words took effect upon her unfathomable lodger? Had she made a terrible miscalculation? Had she shocked him when she meant only to provoke? She need not have worried. Strindberg was provoked, of that there was no question. The only doubt was the direction of that provocation; was it to desire or to anger? Was he reliving the heady beginning of his affair with that wily seductress, Harriet Bosse, or the bitter end of it? Was he remembering their first tête-à-tête, when she had visited his apartment on Banergatan and been so charmed by the flowers and fruit he had arranged in her honour? Was he recalling their first passionate kiss and the subsequent waking reverie, during the course of which he had visited her chambers and possessed her? Or was he regurgitating the sour gall of her betrayal? Surely he had recognised, in Mrs Nilsson's story, a shadow play of his own failed marriage? As the late Mr Nilsson was to Hinde, so was Strindberg to Harriet. Winter wedded to Spring, a pair of old fools who deserved their horns! Hadn't Harriet, like Hinde, been unfaithful? Hadn't she coupled illicitly with her co-star, Gunnar Wingard, who was not – unlike her husband! – thirty years her senior? Mr Nilsson responded to his misfortune by dying, Strindberg developed psychosomatic stomach cramps. Or so the doctors assured him. In fact it was the commencement of the cancer that would have carried him off if I hadn't snatched him from Azrael's embrace. So what will it be, August? Has the imminent redemption of my promise, the unmistakeable whiff of jiggery-pokery, dulled your misogyny? Are you going to take the next step on the primrose path?

"My dear Mrs Nilsson," said Strindberg at length, "what you have just told me comes as no surprise; indeed the only astonishing thing is that you have taken so long to open your heart to me. Are you not aware that we have been enjoying telepathic intercourse for the last two months?" That night Strindberg and his landlady copulated in the conventional manner. It was his first fuck since 1908.

It is true that I had promised Strindberg a new Harriet and here she was, writhing beneath him like a whore in her death throes, a new Harriet *and* a new Frida Uhl, but (satisfaction apart) I am afraid that I did not derive much pleasure from the spectacle. It smelt too much of death.

As far as I am concerned the act of love is an unredeemed suicide pact, a foretaste of eternal amnesia, an unwitting rehearsal for the final heave-ho with Azrael. Beds are death's domain, places wherein to die and to rehearse for dying.

Consider also the indignities Strindberg had to undergo in order to mount his concupiscent mistress. Years before, his sometime friend, Edvard Munch, had seriously injured the vanity of our bare-buttocked hero when he captioned his famous portrait "A. Stindberg," *Stind* being Norwegian for 'stout.' This was a cruel pun, for Strindberg had always been embarrassed by his corpulence. Fifty years under the ground had improved his physique somewhat, but a year of Mrs Nilsson's home-cooking had ruined it anew. Unbuttoned and unlaced, his restored pot-belly expanded like a hot-air balloon. He attempted to hold it in, but Mrs Nilsson was not fooled. "Mr Lagercrantz," she said, "I did not expect you to stand revealed as Adonis. Relax. Be yourself." But he saw that her gaze had already wandered to the valley below the over-hang. Once again he felt the compulsion to defend his physical short-comings. "A small hand is the sign of an aristocrat," he mumbled, "whereas a big one is the sure mark of a plebeian, a masturbator or a cretin." *Hands*, thought Mrs Nilsson, *why is he talking about hands?* She began to wonder about the senility of her elderly lover. "You only have to observe the statues of antiquity to remark that the slaves are better endowed than their masters in this respect," continued Strindberg, warming to his theme. (*Ah ha*! she thought). "It is my considered opinion that the ... er ... hands of elite males will shrink still further as evolution progresses." Mrs Nilsson laughed. "Yours isn't," she said.

*   *   *

They were married in the Spring of 1963. Strindberg was at that time 114 years old, while his bride was just 25. None of Strindberg's relatives was in attendance, nor any of Hinde's. She did not even think to invite her own parents.

Pity poor Mama Zelinsky, with no joy in her life. Pity poor Papa Zelinsky, seated beside his grimy window in a shoddy district of distant Warsaw, waiting for a miracle. He doesn't ask for much, he doesn't require a divine visitation or a grand manifestation, he simply wants a modest miracle fit for the quotidian. He just wants to see the repetition of an unexceptional scene he has witnessed a hundred times before; the familiar sight of his mother or his father, a brother or a sister, an uncle or an aunt, a cousin or an old school-friend turning the corner into their former street. Believe me, my dears, parallel lines will meet before that happens. Even his only daughter, who could have obliged this senile fantasy will never pass that way again, having abandoned Poland as irrevocably as the unburied dead.

In many ways Hinde Nilsson resembled Strindberg's previous three wives, all of them being descended from Diana, goddess of the hunt. Like Siri, Frida and Harriet it was she who did the chasing (Strindberg, a profoundly insecure soul, was too fearful of being rejected by a woman ever to break cover himself). Do you see the irony? As Strindberg was to women, so were the Jews to God. Both were chosen.

Of the trio that preceded Hinde to lawful union, Frida Uhl was probably the most forward. How else to describe a woman who turned up to her first date with our dapper little man of letters looking like a vamp? The leopard-skin coat that crackled with static electricity broadcast her jungle wildness and her nocturnal desires, while the silk scarf that was wrapped around her head like the turban of an odalisque announced her availability.

The ill-matched couple strolled arm-in-arm along Strömgatan, pausing at the locks, where the salt licks of the Baltic mingled with the sweet waters of the local rivers, to watch the city's fishermen in their yellow sou'westers casting long lines in the hope of landing a salmon. At which point Frida, having already hooked her man, began to reel him in. "I too intend to bring sweetness into your storm-tossed life," she whispered as she squeezed Strindberg's arm.

They continued walking through the fragrant April night until they reached the ornate façade of the Opera House, where I sometimes took a seat in the stalls when either *Faust* or *Don Giovanni* was being performed. Behind it, facing a park, was a grand extension containing a bar, a cafe and a restaurant. The proximity offended me; my dears, is it really impossible for you to attend an artistic occasion without becoming hungry? Indeed, I was rather shocked to observe Strindberg entering such an establishment, given his famous fulmination against theatrical boxes with their "tittering diners and supper-parties."

A miniature flunkey in a chocolate uniform welcomed them. How that poor boy was perspiring! And no wonder. This was the tropics, where the discreet scents of the northerly clime were overwhelmed by promiscuous waves of hot and odorous air, in which the distinctive aromas of tobacco smoke from Cuba, coffee from Brazil, and lavender from Provence could be distinguished. To their left was the fin-de-siècle cafe buzzing with bohemian table-talk, ahead of them – up a flight of steps – was the little Operakallaren itself where sweating cooks satisfied the carnal desires of amorous gormandizers and sabre-toothed critics. To tell you the truth, my dears, the whole place reminded me of home.

"In whose name is the table booked?" asked the maître d'hotel, scanning the list of expected diners. Strindberg looked quizzically at Frida, recognising that this was her cue. Silly me, to have cast a doubt upon the iconoclast's sincerity! I should have realized immediately who was responsible for the reservation (even though it had been tactfully made in Strindberg's name). "Allow me to take your coats," said the head-waiter, obviously aware of the playwright's reputation. Standing in the vestibule, in the wings of the restaurant, Frida allowed the feline cloak to slip from her shoulders into his out-stretched arms, revealing a dress that clung to her figure like viridescent skin. "Eros! Now I am lost!" Strindberg muttered to himself, fascinated and repelled in equal measure. He was right. They were married before the end of the month, by which time Strindberg's ambitious new wife was already his literary agent and impresario, thereby setting a precedent that the former Hinde Nilsson was to follow (albeit unwittingly) in 1963.

*   *   *

So far I have said nothing about Strindberg's kultur-kampf, his struggle to resume a career in writing during the opening phase of his new life. I have merely hinted at its existence. My more knowledgable readers, those who yawned at the prospect of Hinde's breasts, might also have recognised a reference to *The Red Room* in

Strindberg's unexpected intervention on behalf of Mr Nilsson's employees. That novel, you'll recall, concerned a strike in a sawmill. We will pass over the fact that its radical author subsequently spent a guilty week as the guest of a timber baron in Sundsvall. Who am I to cast the first stone?

By 1963, however, Strindberg's subject matter had altered considerably. For reasons not unconnected with his temporary sojourn in the nether regions, he became obsessed with ancient Egypt, and began to contemplate an epic play based upon the reign of Rameses II. He re-read Exodus and realized, from bitter experience, that the God of the Israelites sounded exactly like a vengeful wife instructing her lawyer. "Thou shalt speak all that I command thee ... And I will harden Pharaoh's heart ... And the Egyptians shall know that I am the Lord ..." Strindberg had his theme! The moral imperative of divorce.

The Egyptians would stand for the masculine ideal, being potentates, master builders, the guardians of morality; and their sworn enemies would be the Hebrews, the epitome of the feminine principle, all self-interest and sensuality. The conflict would be between the mind and the body, between life and death, between – yes! – Beelzebub and Azrael. Strindberg became fascinated by the famous episode (Exodus VII, viii-xiii) wherein the necromancers of Egypt first encountered the superior skills of Jehovah's messenger. Come on, my dears, turn your minds back to those long-ago Sunday mornings when you learned how Moses (or was it Aaron?) cast down his rod and transformed it into a serpent, whereupon Pharaoh called upon his wise men and his sorcerers to do the same. Now the magicians of Egypt – so the Bible tells us – they also did in like manner with their enchantments. But these were insufficient, for all of their serpents were swallowed by that of the Hebrews. The Bible, with characteristic brevity, omits Pharaoh's response to this singular act of cannibalism. All we are told is that he developed an aortic hard-on, as my

40

crude opponent would doubtless put it. Strindberg decided, equally characteristically, to repair the omission. "People of Chemia, whose soil is black like the pupil of the eye," cried Rameses in one of the earliest drafts, "why has our alchemy failed us?"

Al*chemy*, the art of the ancient Chemi, as the Egyptians were sometimes called, the source of Strindberg's weltanschauung. He saw, in its failure, a prognostication of his own past and future defeats. So Pharaoh's lament should also be understood as meaning: "Why has *my* alchemy failed *me*?" Let us not beat about the bush; Strindberg identified completely with Rameses. Pharaoh knew, in his heart, that it was essential to expel the Hebrews, and he would certainly have done so if God hadn't turned it to stone. He was tricked into acting against his better judgement (not to mention the interests of his country, which would have been well rid of the Jews) by a malicious antagonist whose ultimate aim was *not* the salvation of his chosen people *but* the self-destruction of their enemies.

As Strindberg sat at his desk contemplating the significance of the serpent that destroyed his alter ego's self-esteem, he became more and more convinced that it was a descendant of the sly beast that tempted Eve and thereby ensured Adam's expulsion from Paradise. He noted that both snakes were introduced by their creator for the sole purpose of making mischief, as if he wished to undermine the masculine principle (the hegemony of Adam, the power of Pharaoh, the manliness of Strindberg). Had the latter not, like Adam, accepted fruit from a woman and suffered the consequences? Nor was he moved to revise his harsh verdict upon the Hebrews by the revelation of Hinde's sad history. Quite the reverse, it made him more dogmatic than ever in the defence of his prejudices. He knew that he was vulnerable in the company of his Jewish wife and that she could lead him astray whenever she chose, but in the privacy of his room (from which she was excluded) he was determined to remain king, to be Rameses of Riddarholm. By way of a dramatic experiment he dispensed with all disguises and cast himself as Rameses. And Moses? Can't you guess? You need look no further than a certain semitic seductress. Yes, Moses was a woman! In this updated version of the age-old conflict the snake remained, preserved as a figure of speech, as in: "You snake!" Hinde, shamelessly swaddled in Frida's dazzling green dress, was transformed into a lamia, a destroyer of men. Worse, she was also a deadly rival, one of the many who devoured his works by the score and grew fat upon them, so that the entire literary world sat at their feet.

Poor Hinde, still rejoicing in the termination of her widowhood, was blissfully ignorant of the humiliating insults being heaped upon her behind the closed door of her husband's study (in the very play that she was pledged to proselytize and, if possible, produce). So long as he was able to maintain that portal as a stable borderline between his inner and his outer states she was secure, but if it ever came to pass that the hatreds he was engendering leaked out into the quotidian then she would commence a life of genuine suffering – like Siri, Frida and Harriet. Poor Hinde!

Already she had to endure Strindberg's constant grumbling about the lack of a library in the apartment, as if it were her fault that her first husband had not been a great reader. As a rule Hinde attributed this irascible behaviour to his successor's artistic temperament and made light of it. One morning, however, she chose to do otherwise. Who knows why? Perhaps she was at the commencement of her unclean days, a notoriously volatile period. Anyway, she knocked on his study door just as he – missing a vital fact concerning the reign of Rameses – was cursing her as an ignorant bibliophobe. She ignored that. "Would you like a cup of coffee?" she enquired, as wives of writers sometimes do. Strindberg proceeded as if she had not spoken. "Tell me," he whispered, "tell me all you know about life in Ancient Egypt!" "They mummified their dead, they built pyramids, they were ruled by a Pharaoh," Hinde paused, "they depended upon the River Nile, they worshipped crocodiles and baboons, they thought that the sun was a ball of dung." "Excellent," snapped Strindberg, "now I understand why you don't feel it necessary to own so much as an encyclopaedia!" Whereupon Hinde, who had certainly endured worse, threw down the cup and retreated weeping to the kitchen. Strindberg, wishing to make an equivalent gesture, stormed out into the street.

Summer was over but the air was still warm and he didn't feel the lack of his astrakhan coat. He had made Hinde cry. Later he would probably experience remorse – after all, he did love her – but at the moment he felt triumphant and brave. So much so that he decided to explore his old haunts, to examine the changes that had overtaken the capital during his absence. Why shouldn't he? His legs were strong enough, thanks to his daily stroll around Riddarholm. And so he strode through Gamla Sta'n, which had hardly altered since his heyday, until he lost his way in the New Town and ended up outside the Central Station.

No wonder he hadn't known where he was! Only the churches had remained untouched. All the other familiar landmarks had disappeared – some demolished with hammers, some with dynamite, most with the ball and chain – to be replaced by splendid new edifices of steel and glass, as if man-made structures also had their seasons. Strindberg was not shocked, on the contrary he felt like Rameses overseeing the construction of Thebes. He gloried in the grace and the height of the cranes, in the mindless indifference of the bulldozers, in the brutish power of the mechanical diggers, in the rhythmic swish and thump of the cement mixers, in the pride and dedication of the local workmen. What a pity Rameses didn't have Swedes to help him, thought the old antisemite, instead of the Jews who have belly-ached about manual labour since the year dot. It was certainly no thanks to them that Stockholm would soon have new hotels, new office-blocks, new apartments and new department stores.

Strindberg wandered into the busy station and suddenly experienced a moment of déjà vu. He saw himself as a young man, a leather valise in either hand, standing in the line that shuffled towards the ticket window. Where was he going? And who were those people waving their white handkerchiefs in farewell? Long-dead Dr Lamm! Of course! Dr Lamm and his sons. How could he have forgotten Aron and his brother? He was their tutor and it was in their house on Trädgårdsgatan that he had, in an opium-induced reverie, first discovered his true vocation. But he had also lost something there; nothing less than his essential manliness!

It had happened like this. Dr Lamm, a surgeon, offered to remove three ugly birthmarks from Strindberg's neck. Strindberg accepted gratefully, only to discover when it was too late that their configuration bore an uncanny resemblance to the constellation of Orion. The conclusion was unavoidable; Dr Lamm, a Jew, had plotted to make him one of his own. It was circumcision by other means. Dr Lamm, the Shylock of Stockholm, had robbed him of his birthright; the badge of Orion, the mark of the hunter. From that moment *he* became the prey. And, as such, fell easy victim to those daughters of Diana; Siri, Frida, Harriet and Hinde.

By now Strindberg was at the front of the queue. "Where to?" asked the clerk. "Uppsala," he replied without hesitation, as he must have done all those years ago. Only then did Strindberg remember that the University of Uppsala, where his unhappy alter ego had gone to study a century before, was famed throughout the world for its Institute of Egyptology. He had the questions, they would have the answers. What could be a more appropriate destination? And yet he could not help entertaining the possibility that more mysterious forces were at work, that an unseen hand had been guiding him all morning (even precipitating the unnecessary spat with Hinde) toward the glorious destiny he had unaccountably avoided thus far. First Riddarholm, now Uppsala. Was be being led through the various stages of his previous life to enable him to correct the one vital mistake he must have made? The short answer was: *No.* Our friend was merely following his nose – which ensured that, sooner or later, he was bound to repeat all his former errors rather than redeem the worst of them. It made no difference whether he travelled via Uppsala, Narvik or the North Pole, the final destination would always be the same.

It is generally accepted that Strindberg was not mad in his lifetime, nor had he become so in its posthumous extension, unless you count the continuing symptoms of megalomania. Of these you have been informed already about his identification with Rameses, but you should also be aware that in his previous incarnation he frequently measured himself against Gustavus Vasa (another obsessive builder) who, as Strindberg well knew, was crowned in Uppsala cathedral. In his play about the great monarch's turbulent reign (written in 1899, a lifetime ago) he had managed to combine the thunderous anger of Thor with the single-minded vision of Abraham, characteristics that applied equally well to his rampant version of Rameses, not to mention . . . Is it really necessary to name the original of both portraits? Given this information you probably do not need me to spell out the contents of Strindberg's waiting-room reverie, which brought a regal smile to our dreamer's face. Alas, my dears, just as the Archbishop of Uppsala raised his hands to set the golden crown of Sweden upon Strindberg's leonine head the imminent departure of his train was announced and he was forced to hurry to the appropriate platform.

The locomotive sped through suburbs new to Strindberg and soon entered the region of flat fields and rocky forests that separated the capital from Uppsala. The landscape induced a mood of melancholy in our traveller who, sitting alone, suddenly grew less confident and began to regret his journey. He reluctantly dismissed his former assumption of a grand design in the day's events and saw instead the machinations of a female Machiavelli. Why had his wife responded so piteously to his modest rebuke? Because she was certain that her over-reaction would enrage him and drive him from her sight! And why did she want her husband out of their apartment? There was only one answer to that question! Fornication! He felt a stabbing pain in his groin and knew for certain that, elsewhere, a stranger was penetrating his wife. His lack of proof simply attested to her superior cunning. She was a woman and therefore a born actress. Tonight, when he returned home, she would embrace him and, with tears flowing freely, declare her undying love, but he would harden his heart against her because he knew the value of that declaration, he knew that she was only *pretending*.

As if the old hypocrite wasn't! Every day he lied to his wife about his name, or his date of birth, or his career, or his previous romantic attachments. How could he do otherwise? But he considered these necessary falsehoods to be benign in comparison with the malignancies uttered by his wife. Her apparent innocence and loving-kindness only compounded her crime. And so, while the train sped heedlessly across the peaceful land, he grimly played the cuckold in his Theatre of the Paranoid. This was more like the Strindberg of old! Dreams of imperial splendour were all very well but, being somewhat improbable, would hardly advance his progress to damnation – unlike the venomous fantasies that now tormented him, and continued to plague him all the way to Uppsala. I think it fair to say that, had the train been going in the other direction, he would have been damned within the hour; for all he wanted to do at the moment of disembarkation was to murder his wife.

*　*　*

A few days earlier Azrael had taken a beautiful boy on St Olofsgatan. He had been pedalling an old blue bicycle down the hill when he was hit by a careering automobile which continued on its careless way as though nothing untoward had occurred. The ill-starred youth was flung forward with such velocity that his neck had snapped the instant his unprotected head hit the cobblestones. Even so he did not want to die, but no one arrived to rescue him, and eventually the inevitable came to pass; his strength failed and he succumbed to Azrael's fatal charms. And where was Beelzebub all this time? I'll tell you. I was too busy chasing after Strindberg to be concerned with such a nonentity. The dying boy, however handsome, was of no interest to me. Subsequent enquiries have revealed that he was a brilliant student with a great future in medicine. So what? Let the angels weep over a wasted life, Beelzebub has other fish to fry.

At length the police appeared in their Volvos, confirmed that the victim no longer required medical assistance, gathered tape-measures, note-books and cameras, and – chatting all the while about a forthcoming football match – reduced the accident to a series of impersonal diagrams and photographs. That done, one of their number knelt beside the dead boy and, having dipped a brush into a pot of white paint, traced his outline upon the road. Consequently, when the ambulance men finally took him away, his pale shadow remained, glowing beneath the afternoon sun, just another Icarus. In fact his name was Lars.

A considerable number of mourners attended his funeral at the Kyrkogården which, as it happened, was at the far end of St Olofsgatan. After the service his fellow students returned to their pathology lab where they proceeded to dissect the remains of an unknown woman. They made the usual ribald jokes, but that day their laughter rang hollow. Hitherto they had regarded themselves as god-like at such times, destined to be doctors, not corpses, but since the death of Lars they could no longer sustain that distinction. Though they continued to try, of course. For some days afterward they pretended that Lars was not actually dead and congregated around his penultimate resting place (the cemetery, clearly, was out of bounds) where they engaged him in conversation.

A group of them was standing there in obvious distress when Strindberg trudged past on his way from the station. The sun was hot and he was sweating profusely. This was hardly surprising, given that he had been walking for nearly an hour through streets made unfamiliar by the pocket pharaohs of the locality. Only now, having crossed the River Fyris and found St Olofsgatan, did he feel that he was on familiar territory. He paused for breath in the splashy shade of a sycamore and took in his surroundings. To his left, at opposite ends of a lawn that seemed to have overdosed on chlorophyll, were the Gustavianum (the erstwhile heart of the university financed, like the *Wasa*, by Gustavus Adolphus) and its nineteenth-century replacement, the Universitetshus. Beside the Gustavianum was the great red-brick Cathedral with its twin black spires; testifying to the essential link between religion and scholarship. To his right, ornate offices in the art nouveau style, all occupied by university functionaries, had replaced many of the marmalade-coloured houses where the professors used to live, and there was even a small

48

cinema (showing, of all things, Ingmar Bergman's *The Seventh Seal*), but the atmosphere of the street remained essentially unaltered.

Having surveyed the architecture Strindberg examined the people and saw, immediately, the young men and women crowding around the white figure on the road. At first Strindberg thought about the chalky giants carved into the green hills of England, but those were erect and this was prone, its head contorted, its arms outstretched, its legs bent. Thus he realized, with a shock, that it was the record of a fall, of a death. Make no mistake, he was genuinely upset. Despite the heat, his face turned white. He thought: Actors die every night in the theatre. Sometimes, if the scene is sufficiently moving, the audience weeps. But always the corpses arise to take their curtain calls and the illusion is destroyed. Then the house-lights come on and all trace of the tragedy is wiped from the stage and the memory of the erstwhile mourners as they hurry elsewhere, to catch a bus or to fill the tables at the Operakallaren. Not so here. See how the spectators linger long after the body has disappeared. See how they weep over an empty space, the mere outline of a man. How can this be? How can such a crude representation of human frailty sustain more powerful emotions than the full-blooded death of Cordelia, Hamlet and Miss Julie? Is it because of the figure's very emptiness, which allows each of the onlookers to superimpose their own body upon it? C'est bien ça, a memento mori!

Maybe I'm wrong, maybe Strindberg was thinking about something else entirely, like the weather; maybe he approached the students because he wanted to ask the way to the Department of Egyptology (which, as he well knew, was located in the Gustavianum) or to learn the time of day. In which case why did he make the following enquiry: "What are you all doing here?" "We are mourning the death of a friend," he was told, "a medical student named

Lars who was knocked off his bicycle and killed by a hit-and-run driver." This unexpected information, this sudden personalization, evidently gave Strindberg cause for further meditation. He possessed one of the most famous faces in the country and yet not a single student had given him a second look, a glance that said, "Hey, haven't I seen you somewhere before?" Why? Was he invisible like their dead comrade, nothing but the animated circumference of a man? If so, did he also lack the inner characteristics of humanity, in addition to its outward manifestations? At last he fully appreciated the enormity of his isolation. He was trapped; locked in solitary confinement. The melancholy truth was this: there was not a person in the wide world to whom he could reveal his real identity. Is this why he had bartered his soul? To be a human being in form only, lacking all necessary content; in short, to be a zombie?

Strindberg a zombie? The suggestion was little short of slanderous. As if my working methods had anything in common with those of a voodoo priest! Oh Strindberg, where is your gratitude? Would you rather be a cadaver on the slab in Olof Rudbeck's Anatomical Theatre (its windows glittering like gold braid around the greenish dome of the Gustavianum), or would you rather be like Lars? The thought of Lars shook him, as I knew it would.

Strindberg, the nineteenth-century scholar, never felt at home in Uppsala. He was popular with his fellow students, but not with the professors. Typical of them was the Professor of Greek, a sarcastic aristocrat of the old school. When he died unexpectedly a postmortem was performed, as was the custom. The cause of death was established in the late afternoon and the remains were left overnight in the laboratory. During the early hours a group of boisterous students sneaked in and gleefully deposited a Greek lexicon in the dictatorial didact's empty cranium. Strindberg stalked the corridor, keeping watch.

He approved of the deed, but could not participate fully in the execution of another's idea. A few years later he exacted his own revenge; he published a book of stories about the University. The best of these begins with the funeral of a medical student, not unlike the recently deceased. The coincidence disconcerted Strindberg. He felt somehow responsible for the death of Lars, as though his fictional characters were being brought to life simply to be sacrificed in their creator's stead. Tell me, Strindberg, are these the sort of worries that plague the typical zombie? And what of your jealousy? I suspect that we will have many future opportunities to observe that all-too human emotion.

* * *

Professor Terenius, of the Department of Egyptology, had a tendency to walk sideways like a crab. His colleagues joked that he was under the influence, by which they meant the influence of the archaic wall-paintings he studied every day. Lest the point of this erudite jocularity is lost on you, my dears, it is necessary for me to reveal one of the characteristic secrets of ancient Egyptian art. Next time you visit a museum take a good look at the pictures on display in the Egyptian galleries and you will notice that (in accordance with traditional perspective) all the figures have two left feet (or vice versa if they are facing the other way). It is undoubtedly true that such a peculiarity could lead to an eccentric form of perambulation, but the real cause of the Professor's unique step was the innumerable hours he had spent in the Victoria Museum, shuffling from exhibit to exhibit. Indeed, that is where he makes his debut in our story; to be precise, he was standing before the coffin of Tauher, the temple singer, idly observing the entrance of a rare visitor.

The fellow's round face was disturbingly familiar with its crown of white hair, its deep-set eyes, and its bristling grey moustache. The Professor pinched himself, hardly daring to put a name to the person. He looked again, more carefully; he stared, almost rudely. *There was no mistake.* This was definitely the same man he had seen when, half a century before, he had been taken by his father, a passionate autodidact, to join the torchlight procession that stretched the entire length of Drottninggatan. The colourful parade with its banners and its bands and the awesome sight of the ubermensch upon his balcony, from where he waved like a mythical king, made an indelible impression upon the youngster's imagination. So much so that the furious boy refused to believe his weeping father when he announced, a few months later, that their hero was dead.

At about the same time he was introduced to the arcane world of the ancient Egyptians, for whom he developed a precocious passion. Their religion, far more than the simple Christianity of his parents, provided him with a satisfactory explanation of Strindberg's eternal fate. The phrase *after-life* was to be taken literally. Strindberg would be reincarnated, not as another creature, but as himself. To this end his body would have been embalmed, as if he were a pharaoh, in anticipation of the return of his exiled spirit. The boy, exhibiting all the morbid curiosity of a seven-year-old, began to speculate upon the precise method of preservation.

He discovered that mummification was available to the ancient Egyptians in a variety of prices. The regal version (the most expensive) involved the removal of the brain and the viscera and the transplantation of the same to canopic jars (save the heart which was returned to the body after the completion of a fragrant dehydration process). Unfortunately the priests developed the habit of placing the wrong organs in the wrong jars, which must have occasioned the most unpleasant complications when the time for reassembly came around. Artificial eyes were also inserted as required, a detail which did not appeal to the apprentice necromancer, who wondered if prospective purchasers were informed that they would wake up blind with a pair of glassy orbs in place of eyes. Moreover, the whole procedure took seventy days, cost a small fortune, and on reflection seemed far too unreliable. He also dismissed the cut-price alternative, favoured by paupers, which treated the corpse as if it were a kipper.

No, Master Terenius became convinced that the mid-range package, which offered immortality at reasonable rates, was the one that would have appeared most congenial to Strindberg's executors. Its methodology was far simpler and considerably less destructive than its high-price competitor; all that was needed was an injection of unidentified oil, potent enough to dissolve the internal organs. How the young researcher loved the word, *unidentified*; it spoke to him of unsolved mysteries, of an ancient wisdom that surpassed modern learning. He did not doubt the efficacy (in theory at least) of these procedures. Nor did he lack proof of their success. The books which the young scholar consulted made frequent reference to empty sepulchres, a vacancy invariably ascribed to "tomb robbers and other plunderers." It did not seem to have occurred to the authors (as it did to their unprejudiced reader) that the body, once revived, would have quit the tomb of its own volition, and returned to the outside world as quickly as possible.

There was a third contingency, which did not bear thinking about. For centuries it was firmly believed that the resin found upon the integuments was bitumen. This is no idle speculation, my dears, *mummy* means bitumen in Arabic. Alas, bitumen was regarded by those children of the desert as a useful panacea for toothache and the colic. Consequently the banks of the Nile resounded to the thump of mortar and pestle as bootleg pharmacies pulverized mummies into saleable powder. Gradually the belief in the curative properties of such a bizarre remedy spread across Europe, so much so that the budding Egyptologist never reported tummy aches to his parents lest he be force-fed upon the dust of his hero.

Of course he eventually outgrew such nightmarish fantasies, but the intervening years did nothing to diminish his fundamental convictions. On the contrary, the longer he studied the ancient Egyptians the more he came to respect their beliefs. Therefore what he found most amazing on that fateful day in the Victoria Museum was not the resurrection of the great man of letters, but that he should have the extreme good fortune to witness it. This was surely the culmination of his academic career, the ultimate confirmation of his eccentric theories, the chance to be world-famous rather than an object of universal derision.

He felt an enormous urge to embrace Strindberg, but was equally conscious that such a gesture would be socially unacceptable. This was Sweden, not France or Italy. In the great academic institutions of Scandinavia it was simply not the custom to greet strangers, however welcome, in such an enthusiastic manner. As an alternative he considered a variation upon the most famous salutation he knew, i.e. "August Strindberg, I presume?", but came to the conclusion that the playwright would probably not welcome such a sudden breach of his anonymity. And so Terenius remained in front of Tauher's mummy, desperately trying to contrive a means of approaching the dramatist's doppelgänger without scaring him away when, with characteristic flair for the unexpected, Strindberg suddenly turned the tables and addressed the Professor.

"Excuse me," he said, "am I correct in believing that you are connected with this establishment?" The Professor, open mouthed, could only nod. "Excellent," said Strindberg, "I came here hoping to examine your relics of Rameses, the biblical pharaoh. Could you direct me towards them?"

Professor Terenius, hardly able to believe his luck, led Strindberg to a bright little cabinet which contained nothing but a nondescript limestone relief. As it turned out, Strindberg was less interested in the carving – of a libation offered to a priest of Osiris, among others – than in the rock itself, which was pitted with lumps of flint. He became particularly excited when his guide, anxious to impress, pointed out the stone-mason's vain efforts – still plainly visible – to remove them all with his copper chisel.

"This presents us with a wonderful image," said Strind berg. "It speaks primarily of the natural human impulse for purity, of course. But it has a further, specifically local, significance. The rock is Egypt and the impurities represent the tribes of Israel. They were a contamination, as our ancient craftsman was only too well aware. Had he removed them when the world was young and the rock was soft there would have been no problem. But he was forced to wait, until it was too late. Likewise did the heart of Rameses harden against the Hebrews, so that their inevitable expulsion left scars as deep as chisel cuts. Do you know what a priceless treasure you have here, my friend?" Professor Terenius, who had hitherto dismissed the artefact as a mediocrity, could only shake his head. "Rameses was the greatest of the pharaohs," continued Strindberg, "even the most disputatious scholars agree upon that. I am no scholar. Perhaps that is why I dare venture further. In my opinion Rameses was more than a pharaoh, he was Egypt personified. My friend, what you have shown me is nothing less than the bedrock of Egypt, which is also the heart of Rameses – his very heart! I thank you from the bottom of my own."

He finished speaking and tears filled his dark eyes. For a moment Professor Terenius fully expected his unconventional new acquaintance to kiss him, but all he finally received was another question: "Do you have anything else to show me?" Professor Terenius, still wondering how to broach the subject of his companion's identity, slyly took him to a second cabinet which contained a stela inscribed with hieroglyphics. "Can you read this?" he asked. It was Strindberg's turn to shake his head, disturbing a few of his thick locks as he did so. "Alas, no," he said. "Allow me," said the Professor. "It is what we call an 'ideal biography', which means that the deceased – before they became the deceased, of course – were able to write their own epitaphs which, in the manner of such things, tended to be shameless recitations of self-glorification. For example, the gentleman whom this stone commemorates boasts how he gave bread to the hungry and was of much use to the pharaoh. You can still see how the unlucky stone-cutter, obviously embarrassed by his client's self-regard, kept incising the wrong word. If the mistake was bad enough the poor devil had to cover the error with stucco and start all over again." "He must have been a very bad writer in some earlier existence to have earned such a severe punishment," remarked Strindberg, considerately providing Professor Terenius with the opening he had been awaiting. "Are you a writer, by any chance?" he asked. "Are we Swedes?" replied Strindberg. "I was born a writer, as I was born a Swede. I firmly believe that on the day of my birth the soul of a great writer reawakened and smouldered down through hosts of spirits to enter my body. Yes, my friend, I am a writer. In fact I am the reincarnation of Edgar Poe."

This was not exactly the answer that Professor Terenius had been hoping for; to tell the truth it was downright confusing. What possible connection was there between the American occultist and the Swedish misogynist? Nevertheless, he decided to pursue the matter to its conclusion. "Is it possible that I may be acquainted with your work?"

he enquired. "It is not impossible," replied Strindberg, "though I have not written anything new for many, many years. But no more of that! I prefer to think about my work-in-progress. As you may have guessed, I am composing a drama about Rameses, about his regrettable defeat at the hands of Moses." This was more promising! Who else but Strindberg would be so contrary as to turn a hated biblical villain into a tragic hero?

Anxious to keep his enigmatic visitor under surveillance for as long as possible Professor Terenius offered him the run of the library. "Last year was an annus mirabilis for books about Egypt," he explained, "with excellent volumes from Alfred, Edwards, Emery, Fakhry, Gardiner and our own Säve-Söderbergh. We have them all. Come." Alas, my dears, this manly list did not fill our hero's head with the joyous anticipation of scholarly insights; instead he began to speculate upon the actual name of the gigolo who was, at that very moment, nailing a pair of horns to his head. Was he an Englishman – Alfred or Edward – or a man of mixed blood, say Henry Säve-Söderbergh? Was the human limpet, now obtaining him a seat in this book-lined annex, the seducer's accomplice (why else had he stuck to him all afternoon)? Out of spite he barely looked at the publications that this hypocrite, this pandar who called himself Professor Terenius, placed so unctuously on the table before him.

Strindberg, growing fiercer by the moment, uncivilly dismissed his two-faced attendant, picked up a pencil, and made a few ferocious markings upon a scrap of note-paper. This, as it turned out, was the beginning of an elaborate cartoon. The original curlicues became a mane of hair, below which he rapidly sketched in a self-portrait, emphasising his eyes, moustache and pointed little chin. At that moment one of the book-jackets caught his attention and, inspired by the example, he gave himself the body of a lion. Strindberg the Sphinx! Sans riddles. This Sphinx had other ideas. His pencil danced upon the page. With a few strokes he raised the beast's hind leg and added prominent genitalia out of which gushed a torrent of piss. It fell upon his enemies – his rivals, his wife, her lovers – mongrels and curs every one. Satisfied, at least for the moment, Strindberg arose from his chair, walked out of the library and, having descended the wide stone staircase, quit the Gustavianum too.

Professor Terenius, returning on tip-toe, was distraught to find an empty place. He ran from reader to reader asking if any of them knew what had happened to the gentleman with the white hair. They all shook their heads. Nor had the librarian seen him go. Sadly Professor Terenius placed the unopened books in a pile. He was about to hug them to his chest when he noticed the unsigned doodle, crumpled and consigned to an ashtray by its creator. Here I must confess to inexcusable ignorance, ignorance worthy of Azrael. Believe me, my dears, had I been aware of the significance of that silly little scribble it would have been consumed by hell-fire in an instant. Professor Terenius knew, though, he knew as soon as he saw the thing, which he had retrieved and flattened. Having done so he was compelled to sit down, his heart was beating so fast.

That night, in the privacy of his bachelor apartments, he removed a leather-bound volume of Strindberg's correspondence from his shelves. Flicking through the pages with less than steady fingers he quickly found what he sought. There, in a letter to the painter, Carl Larsson, was a line-for-line replica of this afternoon's masterpiece, complete with an impolite caption in the artist's own hand which commenced: "Egyptisk Sphinx pissause . . ."

This was more than coincidence. As was the fact, ascertained shortly thereafter, that the year of Strindberg's birth – 1849 – was also the year of Edgar Allan Poe's death (shame on me, I should have known that too). He may have lost his man, but by way of consolation he had his confirmation. Of this he was certain: Strindberg did not die in 1912. On the morrow he began the first of his daily vigils in the Victoria Museum, optimistically awaiting the immortal playwright's return.

* * *

What shall we do in the meantime? Shall we mooch around for an indeterminate number of days in a dusty museum with a potty scholar who's got embalming fluid dripping through his veins? Or shall we follow our hot-blooded hero back to Stockholm? Quickly! We must fly if we mean to catch him!

Strindberg's blood may have been boiling but he still felt the chill when he emerged from the capital's over-crowded terminus into the lengthening shadows of evening. Then, for the first time that day, he missed his warm coat. He was ready to go home, to return to the scene of the crime. How he hurried, hoping to catch Hinde in flagrante delicto. Even so it was six o'clock before he finally reached Riddarholm.

He had been away for nearly nine hours, during which time his wife had grown increasingly frantic. In order to take her mind off the possibilities of a divorce or, God forbid, a second widowhood, she set about sprucing-up the apartment. She scrubbed the floors, vacuum-cleaned the carpets, emptied the ash-trays, washed all the windows, wiped down the wallpaper, dusted the shelves, stripped the bed of its soiled sheets and, gathering up the rest of the dirty washing, descended to the laundry room in the basement of the building.

It resembled a catacomb, dark and labyrinthine, the diurnal haunt of living nightmares, not a place wherein to linger. Quickly she stuffed the lingerie into the machine's port-hole and started the cycle. Immediately her undies began to rotate like white rodents in a wheel. While the cat's away the mice will play, she thought. But such jocularity completely failed to lighten the burden of her anxiety. She felt anything but free. She was just like a caged animal trapped in the laboratory of a merciless scientist, her actions being as predetermined as the movements of her panties.

Hinde began to resent her absent husband for subjecting her to such a day of misery, then felt instantly guilty lest he were unavoidably detained in a hospital bed. Suddenly, standing beneath the dimly glowing light-bulb, she had a brain-wave. She would perform an unpremeditated and unpredicted act; she would go out and spontaneously buy her unsuspecting spouse a present. As soon as the idea came to her she knew exactly what it must be, as though the knowledge had been awaiting its cue.

Although unaccustomed to buying books, she recalled seeing a likely shop on Västerlånggatan. Unfortunately she could not remember its exact location, and so decided to start her search at the higher end, near the German Church, an area she visited with reluctance since the demise of her business. To her consternation she discovered that her erstwhile sweet-shop remained deserted, as though it were still in mourning for its sugar-daddy, the late Mr Nilsson. Hinde would have been more comfortable if it had been transformed into a gaudy retailer of pornography, anything except this permanent landmark, this unwanted aide-memoire. She was extremely fond of the phrase, To Move With the Times, which she took literally. As far as Hinde was concerned "time" and "motion" were synonymous. The possibility that time might stand still horrified her, conjured up the irrepressible image of her pathetic father, frozen at his soot-stained window in

Warsaw. Goodness only knew what pictures from the past he saw in that grubby glass (if only someone would wipe it clean and restore its transparency!). Why couldn't her father wave goodbye to his dead as she had said goodbye (with regret, of course) to Mr Nilsson?

Hinde strolled down Västerlånggatan with such a confident air that a passing stranger would never have guessed at the unease in her heart. In fact she was anxious to put as much distance as possible between herself and her guilty past, until Hinde Nilsson had receded beyond recall. This was her way. She preferred to deal with her conscience as if it were so much dirty linen, to be cleansed only in a secluded basement. On the day that she married Mr Lagercrantz she gladly flushed away the former years, so that she was able to begin her new life in an immaculate condition, as a brain-washed virgin.

Almost imperceptibly, during her slow descent of the ancient street, her previous persona slipped quietly back to oblivion and her present identity reasserted itself so that, by the time she reached the book-shop at the far end, she was well and truly Mrs Lagercrantz again. It was a cheerful store, with countless colourful volumes laid out upon wooden tables in no discernible order. The assistant, a man, wore his hair in a pony-tail. He was sitting cross-legged on a wooden chair beside the till, reading a paperback and sipping black coffee from a chipped cup. "Excuse me," said Hinde, "I'm looking for a special book about Ancient Egypt. Do you have such a thing?" The man gazed up at her and smiled. All at once Hinde understood what was meant by the phrase, "a warm smile." It was as though heat flowed from his white teeth. Transgressing the seventh commandment, she wondered what it would be like to kiss that mouth. "You're in luck," he said cheerfully, "we've just received a few copies of *Everyday Life in Egypt in the Days of Rameses the Great* by Pierre Montet. It's supposed to be the last word on the subject.

61

Shall I fetch one?"

And so Hinde went home with her peace-offering, half hoping to find her husband already there to receive it. But the only response to her optimistic greeting was the faint echo of her own voice. Needing something to do, she placed clean sheets upon the bed, collected the laundry from the basement, ironed it, folded it and then, having completed all the household chores, had nothing to do but wait for the sound of the key in the lock. As she did so, time itself appeared to slow until the rhythm of its march – tick, tock; tick, tock – seemed nothing more than a sluggish crawl. Close to despair, desperate to do *something*, Hinde walked over to the window and looked down into the busy street below. Tears came to her eyes when she realized that, in so doing, she had adopted her father's hopeless pose.

And then, as the ebbing day erased the last of her hopes, the ormolu clock on the marble mantelpiece miraculously lifted the curse; it chimed six times and, as if there were some unknown mechanical connection, the front door opened and Strindberg reappeared.

Happy Hinde hugged her husband as though to say, "Forgive me, I accept total responsibility for our tiff." If this was insufficient she felt sure that the handsome book would expiate her minor sin of omission. Poor girl! She had absolutely no idea of the depravities that had branded themselves upon Strindberg's tortured mind, was innocent of his Torquemada-like need to obtain a full confession to a more carnal crime. To her dismay she felt his body stiffen, as though he found her affection repulsive. Worse was to come. He actually pushed her away, and then examined her as if she were an unfamiliar object.

Strindberg was no greenhorn, he did not really expect to observe a scarlet letter branded upon her forehead, but he looked there nonetheless. Finding an unmarked youthful brow he sought tell-tale signs elsewhere; an unnaturally flushed cheek, an amorous bruise upon the neck, smudged lipstick or dishevelled hair. The fact that none of these give-aways was apparent only served to increase his suspicions, made him realize that his wife would not be caught out so easily. Of course she wouldn't! (Had this been a theatrical drama the stage direction would have read: He hits himself.) What a fool he was! She already knew all the tricks of the trade. Had she not been unfaithful to the unfortunate Mr Nilsson? Why should he be spared the same fate? Perhaps she had already resumed the relationship with her former boy-friend, that city-slicker, that kike, that Max the Knife.

"Have you had a good day?" he asked coldly (as if he didn't know the answer in advance!). "No," she replied, "I cried for a bit, after you walked out, then I spent the remaining hours worrying that I would never see you again." God, he thought, she's very good. In the same class as Siri, Frida and Harriet. She *almost* had me convinced. Strindberg sniffed. The atmosphere in the apartment had altered unmistakeably during his absence, as though some fragrance had been wantonly sprinkled to disguise – what? – obviously the cigar her lover smoked after he had finished his business with her. "It smells like a French brothel in here," he said. Hinde giggled like a schoolgirl. "I won't ask how you know," she replied. This answer caused Strindberg a few moments of remorse. What right had he to complain if his wife merely followed his example and occasionally sought her pleasure with others? Then he recalled that he was only servicing a physical need, simply indulging in a straight-forward transaction; whereas a woman, being naturally devious, would always have an ulterior motive – in this case, the humiliation of her husband. He may have idly contemplated uxoricide, but this woman – his mortal opponent – was already an accomplished patricide. He could not afford to show her

63

any mercy. "I'm still waiting for an explanation," he said. Hinde turned, walked towards the kitchen, and returned with a bottle of furniture polish – the sort that has a beaming housewife on its label. She unscrewed the top and held the glistening cavity beneath her husband's nose. "I was going crazy with worry," she said, "so I gave the apartment an unseasonal spring-clean. What else can a woman do when she is left alone?"

Strindberg had picked up a few Yiddish expressions from his wife. One of them came unbidden to his mind. He had to admire her . . . her *chutzpa*! "What else can a woman do?" Let her lover rather than her husband answer that one! He was also compelled to applaud her feline cunning. How she had turned an incriminating necessity – the removal of clues – into a positive advantage, an act intended to inspire sympathy! Strindberg, not without an internal struggle, managed to withhold it. He convinced himself that she was simply following the example of an experienced cat burglar who, having completed the robbery, carefully wipes the room lest any identifiable fingerprints remain. Besides, if she were really so concerned about his absence, why had she still not enquired where he had been all day?

Hinde, by now somewhat disconcerted by her husband's accusatory behaviour, decided it was the proper moment to unveil her secret weapon. She invited Strindberg to sit upon the newly plumped-up cushions of the most comfortable sofa and, kneeling at his feet, handed him the gift-wrapped consequence of her inspiration. Looking up at her husband, the golden flecks in her large sea-green eyes shone with the pleasure of giving. Strindberg, taken by surprise, tore open the paper and examined the substantial volume with its perfectly appropriate title. He consulted the index and fanned through the pages. It was exactly what he required. He was actually on the point of expressing his gratitude when he realized that what he was clutching was not evidence of his wife's devotion, but the precise opposite – proof of her betrayal. This pseudo-gift, this mock tribute, was the rotten fruit of a guilty conscience. Moreover, she had almost certainly acquired it in the company of her self-satisfied paramour.

"Where did you get this?" he demanded, as though he were a lawyer determined to expose the lies of the accused. "In the big book-shop at the bottom of Västerlånggatan," replied his crestfallen wife. Ah! He knew the place well. It was always full of students, handsome youths in the prime of their potency who, being sexual novices, would have reluctantly deferred to the rampant male and his submissive mate, both of whom must have been reeking of their recent activity. He could picture the pair of them, as they browsed among the shelves, making merry at his expense. "How about getting the dotard a book about trolls?" laughed the snappily-dressed lounge-lizard. "No," replied his false-hearted mistress, "it has to be something he'll appreciate." "You mean something like this?" asked the slick exile from the Levant. He was holding aloft a veritable encyclopaedia entitled *Everyday Life in Egypt* etcetera (which signified a further traitorous breach of confidence). "Eureka!" cried Hinde. Her excitement vanished, however, when she discovered its price. "Put the thing back," she said, "I can't afford it." With a disgusting spiv-like grin upon his face the Jewboy dipped his hand into his checkered blazer and pulled out a wad of kroner from the inside pocket. "Here," he said, passing her the bank-notes, "let me pay. It's the least I can do to recompense the old *schlemiel* for the use of his wife." A *schlemiel*! They couldn't fool him by speaking in that sub-German jargon. Thanks to his faithless spouse he understood the insult only too well. Unable to strike the speaker, Strindberg uttered a curse: May he die like a dog! What he saw next made the words wither on his lips and the book burn like hot coals in his hands. The whore took the money! Strindberg felt sick, evil-tasting bile flooded his mouth. She had paid for her purchase with shekels from the snake. He spat upon it.

"How have I offended you?" cried Hinde. "Tell me what crime I have committed to deserve that?" Her tears looked genuine. Saliva trickled across the face of Rameses and began to roll down the spine of Montet's masterpiece. Ignoring it, Strindberg laid the book down and placed his palms upon the shoulders of his wife. Looking straight into her eyes he said: "You tell me." "What do you want me to say?" she whispered helplessly. "That I rented my body out for the duration of the day? That I forgot thee? Just dictate the charge and I will sign the confession. Even though it won't be true. The truth is that I was longing for your return from the moment you departed. When you finally reappeared my heart overflowed with joy. But yours was filled with a strange poison. And now mine is broken." Huge unselfconscious sobs shook her body.

What is this? Has Strindberg become senile? Has his heart turned to putty? Is he really leaning forward, with the intention of embracing his wronged wife? We shall never know, because Hinde instantly recoiled from his touch. It was an understandable reaction, but it was an error. As was her next announcement. "I need to calm down," she said, "if you'll excuse me I'm going to take a bath." Strindberg consulted his watch. It was seven o'clock. His wife had never before taken a bath at such an early hour; hitherto bathing was exclusively nocturnal, a soporific prelude to sleep. There could only be one reason for such a break with tradition; she needed to wash away the olfactory consequences of that other man's intimate trespass. Strindberg could have kicked himself. If only he had prolonged the hug his calculating wife had proffered when he returned he would have had the opportunity to fill his nostrils with the alien's amatory spoor. He rushed to the bathroom, intending to make good the omission, but he was too late, Hinde had already locked the door, nor would she unbolt it. His demands were drowned by the water within, powerfully descending.

So Strindberg turned his attention instead to the bedroom where, at last, he found proof positive; the sheets had been changed, gone were the afternoon's semen stains and the tangy juices of his wife's ruptured orifices, in their place was the virgin white of untainted cotton. This was eloquent testimony indeed! All doubt of their previous existence was removed by the incontrovertible fact of their present absence. Weary Strindberg impressed his pinched buttocks upon the mattress and basked in his pyrrhic victory.

Eventually Hinde emerged from the bathroom wrapped in an oriental robe. The silky material clung to her skin and made it obvious that she was naked beneath, which signified that Strindberg's next accessory to the fact was available for examination. Now it was his turn to secrete himself in the bathroom, which was so steamy that even the mirrors seemed to be sweating. Upon one of them, a small oval looking-glass before which she applied and removed her make-up, Hinde had written with her finger: *I love you.* The letters wept. Strindberg wondered if the message was intended for him, but concluded that its composition probably predated the previous occupation by some hours.

Having secured the door he unceremoniously upended the laundry basket, and was surprised to find that it was almost empty. No soiled bed-linen, only the clothes Hinde had just removed. He picked out her sweater and pressed it to his nose; no trace of cigar smoke or of masculine perfume, only the faintest hint of her pungent under-arm odour. At the bottom of the small pile he found the true objective of his search; a pair of black knickers.

The material, though dark as night, became transparent when stretched. Off duty they were tiny, in situ they barely covered her crotch let alone her buttocks. They never failed to arouse Strindberg, so much so that their appearance began to serve as a private signal that Hinde would respond to a sexual advance. She must have had this semiotic property in mind when she first pulled them on that morning, though he would have thought that the mere act of stripping in her lover's company would have sufficed. He turned them inside-out. The first thing he saw was a little label covered with strange hieroglyphs; an iron, a basin containing the number 60, the letter P within a circle, and a triangle. Strindberg was outraged! So loose were the morals of women nowadays that even the manufacturers of underwear felt it necessary to advise their perfidious customers – through a secret code known only to women – how best to remove the evidence of their sins. Luckily he had been too quick for Hinde.

Strindberg raised the pants to his face and examined the gusset, which had absorbed various unsavoury discharges from Hinde's crotch. A prominent white smudge looked especially promising. It was dry and chalky, and smelled of fish. Alas, he was an alchemist, not a pathologist, and so lacked the necessary equipment to isolate its constituent parts. This did not prevent him from making an educated guess, however.

The half-concealed presence of the panties in the bathroom was suggestive in itself. As a rule Hinde never undressed there. Even on those occasions when she bathed she always disrobed in the bedroom beforehand, invariably leaving her underwear on the floor. Why had she not done so this evening? There could only be one answer. All the same, Strindberg did not feel ready to confront her directly with his knowledge. He would rather be patient and wait for her to give herself away.

By the time he had finished his analysis and returned to the bedroom his cold-hearted wife was either asleep or pretending to be so. This infuriated him, but he decided that it would be tactically unwise to wake her. For one thing it would demonstrate that he (rather than she) was the more concerned about their estrangement. He stared at her like a mesmerist, trying to enter her mind, trying to understand her careless indifference to fidelity. But she was inscrutable. Her unlined face seemed so innocent, so peaceful, so unlike his own.

Strindberg caught sight of the unoccupied pillow beside her unconscious head and felt tempted to . . . well, even the Angel of Death, unlettered Azrael, would have known what was in that hyperactive mind. He reached down and his fingers, gripping the pillow, sank deeply into its feathery substance. As he did so he thought he heard a cricket chirrup, a phenomenon that did not strike him as extraordinary. He reasoned that the insect had once vibrated with joie de vivre in a field full of cotton and that the sensitive fibres had become a sort of phonograph, now replaying the pastorale to his inner ear, that unusually receptive instrument. He squeezed the pillow harder, by way of an experiment, and bird-song arose as if from an accordion. The message was obvious; nature was on his side, was eager to smother the life out of his unfaithful wife. It would be a very gentle death, and so easy, so easy . . . *Do it*! *Do it, Strindberg*! But my entreaties vanished like summer snow when his vanity arose. He simply could not follow a plot-line dreamed up by that bumpkin-actor, the so-called Bard of Avon.

Maybe Strindberg was right. Maybe *Othello* is crap. What do I know? All I can tell you for certain is that instead of murdering his wife he went to bed with her, meaning to take advantage of her indifferent slumber and browse through *Everyday Life in Egypt*. As he lowered himself into the nuptial bower dressed in his flannel finery, Hinde sighed and rolled over sluggishly. Strindberg remained very still and waited, hoping that she would dreamily reveal the name of her seducer, but all he heard was the slow rhythm of her steady breathing. He turned to his book. This is not intended as a slight upon that monumental text, but within the half-hour Strindberg had also nodded off. Being one of the living-dead he had become unaccustomed to dreaming, and so was caught unawares by the vehemence of the vision that awaited him.

Black crows descended from the heavens and circled his head like satanic halos. The dreamer, having abandoned the stage and become a film director, was holding an old-fashioned movie camera. He was accompanied by his three previous wives. "These crows don't like to be photographed," they warned him. Disregarding this advice, Strindberg turned his camera upon the flock as they performed their aerial ballet above him. The clock-work motor whirred. Some crows, obviously infuriated, dropped out of the circular formation and dive-bombed the elongated lens like kamikaze planes. Others glided to the ground, folded their ragged wings, and began to jab at his feet with their vicious beaks. More came out of the sky and landed, squawking, upon his hands. They secured their perches by digging their wiry claws, sharp as scimitars, into his wrists and then began to peck lumps of flesh from his fingers. Siri, Frida and Harriet watched impassively. They did not even scream when one of the birds, more bloodthirsty than the rest, began to spiral upwards into the endless sky, higher and higher until the spring suddenly uncoiled and it hurtled beak-first into the fleshy part of Strindberg's back, enbedding itself up to the eyeballs. Strindberg screamed, dropped the camera, and staggered backwards until he reached a high stone wall. In desperation he pressed himself against it, harder and harder, intending to crush the life out of the winged assassin.

Blood and black feathers! You don't have to be Sigmund Freud to recognise in those the negative image of his murderous fantasy. The more dirty-minded among you (i.e. the psychoanalysts) will probably go further and claim that the dream bubbled up from even murkier depths, was born out of a profound and unacknowledged fear of homosexuality.

"Before you contemptuously dismiss our suggestion as absurd," the shrinks will argue, "consider the denouement; which is, after all, a bloody attempt at penetration from the rear. What else can this be but a reference to love as practised in Sodom and Gomorrah? If we are so wrong can you explain to us why Strindberg didn't simply pluck the bird's beak (its *pecker*) out of his back, why he chose to squeeze it blindly against a wall? No need to scratch your head, Beelzebub, we'll answer that ourselves. It was because he could not bear to face the reality of the situation, because he could not admit (least of all to himself) that *this was what he actually wanted*. And that brings us to the real reason why he was so jealous of Hinde; not because she had made love with another man, but because she had done what he secretly desired but dared not do. And now, with all eternity at his disposal, his unconscious has finally recognised the impossibility of suppressing his true nature. In our opinion, this man is a faggot."

Wow! It pains me to admit this, my dears, but there are those among you whose low opinion of humanity rivals that of my master. Indeed, I sometimes fear that you will eventually put me out of business. I mean, all I read in Strindberg's nightmare was a replay of the day. When he walked out of the Gustavianum it was already late in the afternoon and thousands of screeching jackdaws from the nearby woods were beginning to congregate around the Cathedral's twin spires, so that it seemed – like a souvenir in a ball of glass – to be surrounded by black snowflakes. This, I have no doubt, explains the presence of the crows in Strindberg's unconscious mind. Equally I am convinced that the homicidal bird was Hinde herself.

71

Had she not, in Strindberg's fevered imagination, *stabbed him in the back*? And did he not plan to take his revenge by suffocating her? This is why she was not present alongside Siri, Frida and Harriet, all of whom were trying to protect her – unsuccessfully as it turned out – from her husband's prying eyes and suspicious mind. What could be more straightforward? Only a person with the most depraved mentality would claim to have uncovered sexual perversion in such a guileless dream. Nonetheless, I do not wish to altogether deny a deeper significance. It is my opinion that the three former wives were not his enemies but his muses, who (far from conspiring against him) were actually warning him against squandering his creative energies upon the crows, dark representations of the insane forces that sometimes threatened to overwhelm his reason. "Stick to writing," they seemed to be saying, "forget about sex." (That tumescent camera was a phallus, of course.) Fortunately for Beelzebub and his plots, Strindberg was constitutionally unable to act upon their excellent advice.

To give Strindberg credit, he made an effort. He awoke in a lather, and rapidly became aware that his vertebrae were still aching. A cursory investigation quickly exposed the source of that pain: Hinde's bony elbow. It was also, presumably, the immediate inspiration for his nightmare. Believe it or not, my dears, but Strindberg considered himself a rationalist. He was of the firm opinion that every phenomenon, however incredible, could be properly explained. For example he attributed each of my infrequent appearances to an excess of alcohol. I will happily describe his reasoning, even though it is less than flattering: all phantasmagoria have a symbolic meaning, he stated. Thus the projections of alcoholic delirium are *always* the same; rats and flies. Why? Because they are the direct progeny of filth. Upon catching sight of me he would invariably say, "Welcome, Lord of the Flies," as though I were an invited guest. This is not to suggest that he doubted my solidity; Strindberg was no solipsist. He was ... well, this is the point at which our hero's rationalism becomes typically eccentric.

Strindberg habitually compared his imagination to a conjurer's top hat, out of which he pulled tangible creations that immediately achieved independence. As far as he was concerned I was a figment of that imagination, but also real. Likewise he regarded dreams as both self-induced hallucinations and substantial experiences of frightening proportions. The only way to deal with them, he had long ago concluded, was to lie quietly in bed and tick off the various torments against the bad deeds that had occasioned them. He even had a formula to serve the purpose; understanding equals liberation. He saw at once that his dream (not to mention Hinde's elbow!) was an apt punishment for the feather-brained scheme to asphyxiate his erring mate. "That's what you get for that, then," he chided himself. "Take care and don't do it again!" Having resolved the problem of his guilty conscience he arose from the bed and performed his morning exercises.

Alas, while it was easy enough to abstain from murdering his wife, it proved considerably harder to control the jealousy that gave rise to the vengeful mania in the first place. In earlier years (during his gilded youth!) Strindberg had succeeded in utilising the traumas of his social existence as raw material for his writing. Even when he had raged like a tempest he generally remained in control of his emotions, carefully recording his own responses and the reactions of the loved ones around him. In those long-ago days it had been an effortless thing to shake off the borrowed cloak of the unbending paterfamilias and bare his soul for the real act of creation. It was as if a magic beam had played upon the threshold of his study, transforming all his problems, so that by the time he sat down at his desk with its neat pile of paper and row of sharpened pencils they had

74

simply ceased to be *personal* and had become exclusively *artistic*.

In the same way he planned to use his continuing feud with Hinde to fuel his new work-in-progress, but (as I had anticipated) he found it increasingly difficult to keep the outside world at bay. He just could not concentrate upon the raw text, could only wonder what his wife was plotting at that precise moment. Instead of losing himself in the dialogue of imaginary beings he found himself listening intently to his wife's movements as she wandered aimlessly from room to room. What was going through her mind?

Unable to read that, he quickly found another way of decoding her desires. It involved the invention of a complete vocabulary for her wardrobe. Casting aside the draft of a great speech by Rameses he began with what he already knew – the translation of her transparent briefs into *fuck me* – and progressed from there. Those pants were brazen, boldly provoking examination by lascivious eyes, whereas the white panties with the lace trim and the pink bows were more coy; they almost blushed as they whispered *seduce me*. The pair with the red and black hoops that shamelessly entered the crannies of her crotch and buttocks were clearly also exhibitionists; all but screaming *bull's eye* at the blessed observer. Even the tight school-girly knickers which seemed genuinely surprised by the presence of another were prick-teasers whose protestations of *virginity* fooled no one. Her skirts and dresses all offered subtle variations – according to colour, length, style and material – upon the same basic meaning; *see me, feel me*. She never wore a brassiere, a significant absence that announced *I'm free*. Her exact availability was made manifest by the tightness of her pullover or the number of buttons she left undone on her blouse. Those buttons were the small change of infidelity. With two or more disengaged she only had to lean a few feet out of true and her breasts, nipples included, would be visible to anyone who cared to look. Strindberg knew, from experience, the significance of their display. When he pointed out this negligence to her she laughed and usually buttoned up one of the offenders, obviously meaning to undo it again as soon as she was out of her husband's sight. Only when she wore corduroy trousers or denim jeans did Strindberg feel truly comfortable; these masculine garments repeated one gruff word, *chastity*.

On most days Hinde went out to purchase their daily necessities at the local market. Strindberg's subsequent mood depended upon what she was wearing and how long she was gone. If she was absent for any length of time *and* was wearing clothes that pronounced her sexuality he assumed the worst and received her accordingly when she reappeared, even if she returned with an enticing goodie calculated to win back his affections – especially then! (Hinde could well afford such trifles. Being an essentially honest girl she had reported her new marital status to me. However, I continued to pay the agreed maintenance regardless.)

On the occasion I am about to describe, Hinde, very womanly in a loose-fitting lace blouse and a short white skirt, kissed her husband on the lips and went out into the world. She naturally assumed that while she was willingly fulfilling her connubial chores that strange husband of hers was at home hard at work. Alas, how wrong she was! It is true that Strindberg was stationed at his desk, fully intending to write, but he found that his hyperactive mind, tormented by that day's mock trousseau, too easily wandered from the subject at hand; instead of transporting him to the banks of the Nile it took him to the adjacent alleys of Gamla Sta'n. That's right, my dears, he followed his wife *without moving from his chair*! He tip-toed behind her as she slowly filled the shopping basket, and then walked somewhat faster as she darted out of sight, having taken an inexplicable detour down a dark little street. He glided through the shadows until he was suddenly arrested by a head-splitting hammering. For a dreadful moment he feared that it was the sound of his heart about to burst, but he quickly reassured himself that the disturbance was external. Some comfort! Hinde was obviously knocking at her lover's door. How did he know? There was a *mezuzah* on the jamb. And within was a hirsute man – Jacob's cunning brain in Esau's powerful body – who greeted a stranger's wife with revolting intimacy.

Unnoticed by the passionate couple, Strindberg sneaked inside and crept up the creaking stairs. The bedroom was vulgar. A zebra skin covered the floor. Hinde carelessly dropped her shopping bag, cracking the eggs, and began to unbutton her blouse. Each delivered its own little message. The third button said, *my defences are down*, the fourth button said, *my responsibilities are at an end*, and the fifth said, *behold, the portals are open*. Her breasts, now fully exposed, cried: *we belong to you, kiss us, bite us*! Hinde removed her skirt and knelt upon all fours. Her pants said nothing; she was not wearing any. Her flesh parted eloquently, as did the Red Sea for the Israelites. Her lover, that bastard, lit a cigar. The tip glowed like the end of a circumcised penis. What a cool customer! As yet he had not even untied his shoelaces. He patted Hinde on the backside and she, as if responding to a signal, rolled over and assumed the position a woman takes when awaiting a gynaecological examination. But her lover was no medical man; he was, in effect, a rival magician.

Bowing towards his invisible audience this latter-day Moses placed the smouldering cigar between Hinde's moustaches and she, with exemplary muscular control, sucked in the aromatic fumes and exhaled perfect smoke rings. These feathery quoits floated around the room until they dropped over Strindberg's clenched fists, coming to

77

rest upon his wrists like handcuffs. Others shackled his ankles. Unable to move, Strindberg was compelled to witness various trespasses that made a mockery of the seventh commandment.

Poor Strindberg. Behind his closed eyes the offending images continued to dance upon his lids, and to prey upon his mind. Thanks to the perfidy of a woman – another Cressida, another Delilah; another Siri, another Harriet – he had fallen into the hands of philistines. They would put out his eyes and bring him down to Gaza, they would bind him with fetters of brass. They would mock him, their prisoner of love. Steaming tears streamed down his cheeks. His strength was gone. Self-pity and paranoia overwhelmed him. He rained ineffectual curses upon his wife and her gigolo.

Bastard. Adulterer. Yid! Strindberg incised them all on the top page of his pad, pressing down so hard that the lead point of his pencil broke upon the final exclamation mark. True, it was not art, but at least it was activity. Hitherto he had found it well-nigh impossible to flesh-out a character until he or she was formally christened; likewise he now urgently required to know his enemy's real name, so that he could have a definite target for his vituperative energy.

Accordingly he arose from the desk and, entering their besmirched bedroom, began to search through her papers. What did he hope to find? (Yes, *hope*. When Hinde returned, having completed her errands, she was bound to eventually ask: "Why are you so angry with me?" Lacking proof he could not, of course, admit the real reason, any more than she could explain why all the eggs in her basket were broken. Instead he would have to accuse her of a stupid domestic crime; the butter was hard, his toast was cold, her cooking had given him indigestion, his shirt was creased. He was well-aware of the childishness of these accusations, but he also knew that he could not prevent them, his outrage at Hinde's behaviour was too strong. If only it weren't based exclusively upon intuition. What he required was substantiation. On that happy day he would devour her with his fury.)

He pulled out all the drawers which contained her letters, meaning to read through every one until he came upon the package from her lover (or lovers). In addition there were numerous diaries, doubtless full of incriminating entries. Writers often claim that their lives are passed in the pursuit of high-minded purposes, but in my opinion this is the true image of their calling; on their knees rummaging through the inconsequential effects of a loved one in a mad effort to smell a rat. Their natural habitat is not the study but the sewer. Give me an honest devil any day; at least you know where you stand with us.

Unfortunately most of Hinde's archive was written in Polish or (even worse) Yiddish, which meant that Strindberg had to call upon his imagination to provide the translation. The bulk of the Swedish items came from the pen of his predecessor, the late Mr Nilsson. These were, in the main, lustful reminders of what they had already done together, coupled with passionate assurances of eternal love and promises of eventual matrimony. Although the letters contained vivid descriptions of Hinde's willing flesh Strindberg experienced no jealousy as a consequence of reading them, rather he felt sympathy for the elderly businessman whose crudely expressed sentiments were destined to be so casually destroyed.

More insidious was a postcard he found, incongruously stacked amongst the matrimonial sequence. On the face was a portrait of Queen Christina. On the reverse, crossed out but easily legible, was the following message in Hinde's hand: "Still thinking of you. I'd like to write you a letter, if that's okay." There was neither date, nor destination.

Even so, Strindberg had no doubts as to the addressee. Why else the attempt at erasure? Why else the phrase, "if that's okay"? Why shouldn't it be "okay", unless the intended recipient was also married? What were those dozen or so words when measured against the thousands in Mr Nilsson's correspondence? An ant compared to an elephant. And yet that insignificant speck had ruined them all, as surely as a single woodworm will eventually turn a timber house to sawdust.

Just such a worm, a poisonous thing, was now gnawing into Strindberg's brain. Why oh why hadn't that parsimonious girl thrown the postcard away and, if still in need of a heroine, purchased a clean picture of Queen Christina? He looked at the back again. "Still thinking of you . . ." Why *still*? It surely meant *in spite of what has happened*. In other words the message was written *after* everything had come to light, when the affair was supposedly over. The two-faced whore! It was a miracle that she never mistakenly murmured her lover's name when squashed beneath her foolish husband's late-flowering passion. Of course Mr Nilsson already knew it, but in another context. Of that other context – Mr Nilsson's business affairs – there was no sign. Why hadn't he paid closer attention when Hinde narrated the sordid history of her infidelity? Had she called her lover anything other than "my husband's partner"? He couldn't remember. The fact that she had so shamelessly deployed the tale of her unfaithfulness to ensnare her second husband now filled him with disgust. It meant that he could never again recall their courting with nostalgia, for he would ever-after see the smirking face of her fancy-man, about whom his wife – on some unspecified day in the recent past – was illicitly thinking.

He tore the postcard in half, and then he tore the halves in half. Strindberg's patience was running out. He was no longer prepared to wait for his wife to incriminate herself. He decided to confront the adulteress in the kitchen and expose her crimson sins as soon as she returned.

Hinde's face lit up on first seeing her husband so keenly anticipating her reappearance. It certainly made a pleasant change from the grouchy hermit whose normal greeting was a sour face. Nor was she disappointed when he rose up and embraced her passionately. She felt Strindberg's hand caress her thigh and, in response, slid her tongue between his lips. How could she possibly guess the real reason for his manual exploration of the hidden area beneath her skirt? Therefore when he prodded her crotch she groaned with pleasure (and to encourage him to proceed further). Strindberg, for his part, was surprised to feel the springy dampness of cotton. The discovery that she was now wearing pants altered nothing, however; merely confirmed her tactical skill. The strumpet must keep a whole drawer of underwear in that other place, he decided. He slipped his finger beneath the tight elastic (*virginity*, ha!) and touched the palpable evidence of desire, which Strindberg misinterpreted as his rival's semen. Innocent Hinde, by now certain that sexual intercourse was imminent, carefully placed her shopping basket on the table (though she would have done better to drop it), and began to undo her husband's shirt. The collar stud positively screamed *take your hands off me*. Of course Hinde didn't hear that. What she did hear was her husband's voice triumphantly exclaim, "Would you mind explaining why all the eggs are cracked?" Hinde, taken aback by the incongruous demand, promptly showed him that he was mistaken. All the eggs were in perfect condition. Strindberg could hardly believe his eyes. Then he realized what must have happened. The crafty bitch had replaced the damaged goods, had purchased another six!

"Please tell me," whispered Hinde, as he knew she would, "please tell me what I have done to make you so angry with me." Once again Strindberg found himself unable to deliver the coup de grace, which meant that he was forced to invent yet another trivial misdemeanour to justify his performance. How could he say, "Because you've been out whoring with X," when X obstinately remained such a complete blank? Gratification was therefore denied to both parties.

*   *   *

Dozing in Mr Nilsson's favourite armchair (now relocated in his study) Strindberg was awakened by water gushing from the tap in the bathroom. The significance was not lost upon that perceptive listener. Hinde was evidently preparing to wash off the last intimate traces of the afternoon's effusive encounter. Leaping from his resting place Strindberg moved with astonishing agility and trapped his wife, half-undressed, in their bedroom. Her knickers, for once, looked positively startled to be observed. *Why, Mr Strindberg*! they protested, provoking him immeasurably. Hinde's hands moved indifferently to dispose of them. "Wait," said Strindberg gently, "I'd like the pleasure of uncovering your private parts." Hinde looked at him in amazement. "Why the volte-face?" she asked. "Why have you suddenly decided to be nice to me?" "I'm just a temperamental old artist who's had a very bad day," he replied, "I beg you to let me end it with an act of love." Hinde, basically a good-natured girl with a first-class degree in eudemonism, bowed down before her husband's superior will. To be more precise she knelt upon the eiderdown, like the she-wolf who suckled Romulus and Remus, and permitted him to unpeel her panties from behind. I naturally assumed that Strindberg was preparing to perform a bestial act, but it soon became apparent that he had deliberately placed his wife in this undignified position so that he could conduct his examination unhindered by her quizzical gaze. His observations were as follows.

The slowly descending material first revealed the empty eye-socket of her anus (undamaged), and then the hairy folds between her legs (brownish without, as pink and shiny as a conch within). The interior of the garment, he noted, was copiously stained. This was promising, but inconclusive.

There remained but one way to confirm the veracity of his waking vision. Repeating a gesture favoured by the male protagonist of that unsalubrious fantasy, he playfully slapped his wife's white buttocks and, sure enough, the foolish woman immediately flipped over onto her back. She's like a circus animal, thought Strindberg, trained to respond whoever gives the signal. Nevertheless, he knew that certain protocols still had to be observed before he would be permitted the liberties he required.

And so he removed his jacket, his shoes and his socks; his waistcoat, his shirt and his trousers. That done he approached his wife's supine figure and began to slobber over her breasts and her belly in the approved manner. Between her navel (or *pupik*, as she called it) and her pubic hair was a convexity of flesh that was as smooth as the side of an egg. His lips ski'd down this little Mount Venus. Now his tongue was in her thicket, within centimetres of its destination. I'm ready to believe that Hinde was enjoying herself, but as she stretched out in tense anticipation of the deep plunge of his tongue into her genitals she reminded me of a naked prisoner about to receive the obsidian blade of the Aztec priest. Can you honestly maintain, my dears, that Strindberg's ultimate purpose was so very different? Didn't he also want to tear out her living heart? Finally he thrust his whole face into her odiferous pouch, penetrating her with his tongue and sniffing the resultant stinks for any trace of cigar smoke. To Strindberg's astonishment there was none. He simply could not understand, after what he had seen, why her vagina did not smell like a Cuban's ashtray.

Instead of reaffirming his love this absence caused Strindberg to sulk. Why? Because he had been unable to prove that his wife was a courtesan! In a reasonable man this would surely have been cause for celebration, but for Strindberg it was nothing less than an intolerable defeat. Without bothering to offer an explanation he abruptly ceased his ministrations and retreated, wearing nothing but his yellow singlet and long-johns, to the sanctuary of his study.

Hinde, humiliated, embraced her pillow and fell asleep sobbing. Strindberg, for his part, ended up slumped in his chair, head in his hands, completely deaf to this world and the next. Come, my friends, come see how quickly your prize specimen has reverted to the simian condition. I'm not exaggerating; with his wrinkled and sagging underwear, his angry jowls, his pot-belly and his spindly legs he looked like an alopecic orang-outang. Yes, ladies and gentlemen, here is proof positive of a curious paradox; which is that excessive dependence upon the intellect turns *homo sapiens* into a monkey. Believe me, if Strindberg had stopped brooding and followed the natural inclination of his instincts he would presently be slumbering in the arms of his wife, a self-satisfied smile upon his face, instead of undergoing such an embarrassing metamorphosis.

"Give strong drink to him that is ready to perish," quoth Lemuel the King. Strindberg, it seemed, had taken that biblical monarch's suggestion to heart and was attempting suicide with an over-dose of Absolut. He was mumbling under his breath, no doubt rehearsing his final message to the world. It probably went something like this: "Surely I am more brutish than any man, and have not the understanding of a man. I neither learned wisdom, nor have the knowledge of the holy. Who hath ascended up into heaven, or descended?" An excellent question! It certainly prompted me to intervene personally on behalf of his downward journey.

Some have complained about the brimstone I exhale, but I trust that my breath has never been as offensive as Strindberg's, which positively reeked of vodka. "I've had enough," announced the latter. "That's indisputable," I agreed. "I mean of life," added Strindberg. "Why?" I asked, as if I didn't know. "My wife is a whore," said Strindberg, "she sleeps with my enemies." "How can you be sure?" I asked. Strindberg pounded his heart. "This never lies," he replied, filling his tumbler to the meniscus for the umpteenth time.

No, my friend (I thought), it is the merciless looking-glass that never lies. Have you studied your reflection of late? Do so forthwith and you will behold a silly old man who has just cut off his nose to spite his face. At which point I must tell you frankly, ladies and gentlemen, that I have no sympathy for this jealousy of yours. Knowing the pre-ordained conclusion of all passions I am unable to comprehend why you (no less aware) are incapable of appreciating each instant for its own sake. Why is it necessary to constantly torture yourselves with the before and after, the pre and the post? What does it matter, Mr Strindberg, where your wife was a few hours ago if she is prepared to be with you now? Instead of making false accusations you should go on your knees and thank that beautiful woman for every moment she grants you.

This is what I thought, but it is not what I advised. For I am the Voice of Doubt, that insidious Iago, whose raison d'etre is to undermine your certainties. "In that case," I pronounced after some consideration, "you must divorce her." "Divorce?" exclaimed Strindberg. "Of course," I replied. "Marriage to Hinde has made you lame and barren. You can't write, and you won't fuck. If you want to do either again you'll have to *dispose* of the fourth Mrs Strindberg." Her intoxicated spouse shook his head. Not because he found the recommendation distasteful, but because he was vainly attempting to dispel the illusion that

85

his visitor was disintegrating.

He awoke suddenly, like King Priap, with his prick on fire. It was no less than he deserved. In addition his head throbbed, his spine creaked, and his addled brain was in a vertiginous spin. For a few seconds he was absolutely lost. Then his bloodshot eyes became accustomed to the moonlight and, with relief, he recognised his surroundings. Having established his location he quickly became aware of new discomforts; for example, his feet were chilled to the bone. Looking down, he immediately discerned the cause; they were bare. Glowing in the eerie light of early morning they looked as if they had been hewn from blocks of blue-vein stilton. Where were his shoes and, for that matter, his trousers? Unable to account for their absence, Strindberg slowly arose and staggered back to the bedroom where he crawled beneath the quilt. The drowsy incumbent, interpreting this as a gesture of rec-onciliation, murmured softly: "I love you, August." The recipient of this endearment feebly raised his hand as if he fully intended to reward this unmerited declaration with a slap, but fortunately his strength failed before the blow could fall.

On every other morning Hinde brought her husband croissant and coffee in bed. On that morning she didn't. Who can blame her? Personally I wouldn't have blamed her if she had kicked the old bugger down the stairs, but apparently she was not a vindictive woman. She merely left him to marinate in his night-sweats until nearly midday when she at last raised the venetian blinds. Sunlight poured into the room. Strindberg opened an eye. He did not immediately recognise the woman who stood over him, but assumed that she was one of his wives. "*God morgon*," he said cheerfully. He received a frosty reply. In fact Hinde told him to fuck off. This made him sit up and, as he did so, an uncomfortable spasm zig-zagged through his intestines, reanimating (in this order) his hypochondria and his memory (excepting events irretrievably erased by alcohol). Although Strindberg knew that the cancer which had officially killed him could not recur he nevertheless worried about the consequences of mistreating his digestive system. In effect he liked to eat well. Therefore, having diagnosed the stomach cramps as pangs of hunger, he attempted to butter up his wife in the hope that she would forgive the previous night's bad behaviour and, having done so, prepare lunch.

Writing off breakfast (in bed or elsewhere) he retired to his study in more suitable attire and, lost for words, walked restlessly from window to window, from the Mälaren to the Saltsjön, as though he were a monarch with a world of troubles upon his back. His island kingdom with its urban coastlines and manifold waterways was spread out beneath him. Looking westwards he could see a flotilla of wind-blown yachts criss-crossing the inland sea and, to the east, larger vessels sailing towards Helsinki and Leningrad (which he continued to think of as St Petersburg). Would that he could really be the pharaoh, the sultan or the emperor of the whole archipelago. Then the masculine principle would truly prevail. His present consort would be lodged in a harem where the only alternative males would be eunuchs. His plays would be performed nightly in every theatre. Critics would be chained to gateposts. His subjects would love him. He would dine off golden bowls. He wondered, more prosaically, about their contents. (He was, by now, ravenous.) The appetizing smell of hot olive oil crept reassuringly in from the kitchen and he imagined his wife, her cheeks flushed by the heat of the stove, dropping thin slices of beaten veal into the frying pan. He began to salivate in anticipation of her schnitzels, sadly demonstrating her *mastery* over his appetites. Alas, concluded poor Augustus Rex, far from being a potentate I am a supplicant, entirely dependent upon Hinde for my emotional and financial needs. In place of a subservient wife and an overflowing exchequer I have an unclean bed and empty pockets. This well-appointed study, from where I look down upon Stockholm, is nothing but a gilded cage in which real work is impossible.

Strindberg had long felt a manly need to establish his independence. So what did he do? Did he fuck his wife into submission like a real cock of the walk? Not him (don't forget that we're dealing with an intellectual)! You guessed it! He did precisely the opposite. He trimmed off the end of his penis (like a Jew!) and was left holding a pen. Yes, ladies and gentlemen, the man who had already made Harry Houdini look like an amateur was planning to write his way to freedom. But, alas and alack, the play was impossible to complete so long as its author remained in Hinde's clutches. In other words, his only exit was blocked by his obsession with the very thing he wished to escape. Even an amphisbaena wouldn't envy that conundrum. The sole satisfaction this sorry state of affairs afforded was the ironic fact that, in volunteering to act as his agent, his wife was busily promoting their divorce – except that she had nothing to sell so long as the play remained unfinished. There was no other conceivable source of income, no other way of redemption. Royalties continued to accumulate from his established oeuvre of course, but their originator was unable to claim authorship let alone the monies.

He padded around his eyrie, the epitome of frustration. It was as though Blaise Pascal had penned his famous dictum with Strindberg in mind: "All the misfortunes of men derive from one single thing: which is their inability to be at ease in a room." It has been the goal of innumerable regimes since time immemorial to calm this dis-ease, to quell the unbearable itch of boredom; in short, to create quiescent specks of humanity happy to be imprisoned within their own four walls. Many generalissimos have made the effort, a multitude of isms and ions have been tested and tried, from fascism to television, but to no lasting effect; all have been found wanting. All save my master who, true to his perverse genius, has turned humanity's restless spirit upon itself, has invented a fate ... but I must not anticipate. Strindberg was still his own man, still wracked with melancholia, egomania, bitterness, jealousy, big-headedness and emerods; not to mention a wretched hangover.

Wandering back to his vacant desk in the forlorn hope of resuming his work, he eventually brushed aside his neglected manuscript and, awaiting his wife's summons to the table, began to draw triangles upon an otherwise empty note-pad. Being something of a fogey when it comes to art, I naturally sought a figurative basis for the shapes and quickly found it in the view from his window. If pressed further I would have described the work-in-progress as a seascape with sail-boats. However, I must concede the possibility that Strindberg thought he was creating something rather more earth-shattering, for he suddenly looked at the paper and cried *Eureka!*

It serves me right for traducing Pascal. Had I not been so contemptuous of his scientific abilities I would surely have recognised, more quickly than I did, that Strindberg had sketched, almost unconsciously, crystals of alum or, more significantly, *ammonium alum*. (I'm sure I don't need to tell *you* that.) But perhaps I do need to explain why the unexpected appearance of such a modest substance had prompted so great an outburst. Let us begin with its name, which derives from the place where salty deposits of ammonia were first discovered; namely the sands in the vicinity of the temple of Ammon. Follow me to that sun-baked wilderness and you'll find, just below the intolerable surface, a sample of smooth-sided crystals. Please, scatter some upon the palm of your hand and you'll see immediately that they are actually miniature versions of the Great Pyramid itself. That miraculous edifice which Strindberg, like Strabo before him, believed to have been lowered from heaven. Whatever its origins the Great Pyramid undoubtedly possessed mysterious powers, as did the various salts of ammonia (known to the alchemists, among other things, as *anima sensibilis* and *lapis angeli conjungentis*). These became the source of many fantastic dreams, the most persistent of which was the conviction that, with some such catalyst, base metals could be transmuted into gold. Yes, my dears, our immodest hero had actually convinced himself that the same divine hand which had designed the Great Pyramid was now instructing him to go forth and make his fortune. No wonder he yelled *Eureka!*

* * *

And so August Strindberg put aside his writing altogether and began to concentrate upon the creation of artificial gold. This was a pity, for otherwise he would surely have remembered the fate that befell those Israelites who abandoned their invisible deity in favour of Aaron's false god. Moses, you'll recall, was sceptical from the very beginning. He warned his divine instructor (disguised as an inflammable bush) that the philosophy most commonly connected with slavery was materialism. "Behold," he stammered, "when I come unto the Children of Israel, and shall say unto them: The God of your fathers hath sent me unto you; and they shall say to me: What is his name?" To which God (anticipating Popeye the Sailorman) replied: "I AM THAT I AM." Moses knew that this would not do; he could not go to the people with a manifesto (a land "flowing with milk and honey") but no manifestation. "They will not believe me," he said, "nor hearken unto my voice; for they will say: The Lord hath not appeared unto thee." Whereupon God taught Moses the trick that subsequently caused Strindberg's Pharaoh to exclaim: "People of Chemia . . . why has our alchemy failed us?" Even so, Moses made a final effort to evade his destiny, claiming to be as dumb as Harpo Marx. "Oh Lord," he said, "I am not a man of words, neither heretofore, nor since Thou hast spoken unto Thy servant; for I am slow of speech, and of slow tongue." God was not impressed. "Now therefore go," he thundered, like an angry playwright at a bad rehearsal, "and I will be thy mouth, and teach thee what thou shalt speak." Are you listening, August?

Popular materialism had its day in the wilderness at the foot of Mount Sinai. Moses had been gone too long, collecting the twin tables of the testimony "written with the finger of God." An invisible God was bad enough, now the Children of Israel had an invisible leader as well. In panic they approached Aaron, who obligingly provided them with an artistic realization of the promised land. Milk was transformed into a teatless calf, honey became gold. Needless to say, it was the Golden Calf itself, rather than the values it represented, that the Children of Israel proceeded to worship in their famously unruly fashion. Returning to find an orgy in progress, Moses waxed hot with anger and ground the offending idol into powder. Having done so he mixed the gold-dust with water and forced the sinners to swallow the fatal concoction. Perhaps I have done Strindberg a disservice. Perhaps he never forgot that episode. After all his plan was to pee until he produced *goldwasser*.

To this end he imbibed only boiled liquids and pissed into glass jars which he stored, unstoppered, in his study. Within days of his revelation the room was filled with the piquant stench of evaporating urine. He was of the opinion that the ammonia, thus obtained, would display the superior qualities required to ensure the successful conclusion of his experiment. At first Hinde, already careless of her husband's eccentricities, tried to live with the strange smell that slithered under the study door. It was generally unpleasant, but it also possessed an underlying warmth that mysteriously reminded her of the lost happiness of her brief childhood. Every time her pretty nose was tickled

by the alien odour she shrugged her shoulders and thought: why disturb him? They never had any visitors to impress with domestic cleanliness.

But then, one day, the entire apartment was suffused with a dangerously mordant gas that choked her and filled her eyes with tears. She had no idea what it was, but there was no doubting the source. Without knocking she angrily penetrated Strindberg's inner sanctum, dimly conscious that in so doing she was violating a patriarchal taboo. He was not at his desk. Instead he was standing in the middle of the room, ankle-deep in swirling vapour, pouring vitriol upon the white deposits left in one of his portable latrines. In order to protect his lungs from the consequent reaction he held a spotted handkerchief over the lower part of his face. His eyes were uncovered. He turned them upon the intruder. Their blood-vessels were as prominent as the canals on Mars. "This is an unexpected pleasure," he said quietly. Poor Hinde, anticipating abuse, was transfixed. She had no strategy against kindness. "Have you burst in to whet your husband's jaded appetite," he asked, "to offer him a little love in the afternoon?" Hinde was nonplussed. However, her failure to respond had a more pathological cause. She couldn't stop coughing. Strindberg, in mock concern, hopped around the room opening all the windows. "Is that better?" he enquired. Hinde was no longer angry. Now she was frightened, frightened of the red-eyed stranger clutching a bottle of acid. Always conscious of his blood-shot stare she fought to control her breathing, assisted by the autumnal air that sweetened the poisonous atmosphere.

"Perhaps you would like to tell me what you want?" said Strindberg, his fury beginning to show. "I was worried about you," she lied. "There was no need," said Strindberg, "I'm a big boy now." "It won't happen again," said Hinde. Strindberg didn't reply. He walked meditatively to the chaise longue that stood against the room's only blind wall and, having sat down, patted the space beside him. Hinde approached tentatively. Although it was late October she was wearing the white mini-skirt she had sported during the summer. This was unfortunate, it reminded Strindberg of that season's infidelities. He remembered how willingly she had performed for her anonymous puppet-master. He remembered everything. And just as tin or lead may be transmuted into precious metal, so were those putrid imaginings transformed into art, as yesterday's whore became today's muse. Strindberg raised his hand. Hinde stopped and, like a good actress, listened to the maestro's stage directions.

"Pretend that you have just entered your father's study where an old friend awaits him," he said. "You have loved him ever since you were a little girl. But you are no longer a child. Now is your opportunity. You must seduce him." Hinde couldn't decide whether it was safer to appease him, or to refuse. She chose the former course and lowered herself upon his lap, where she remained like a ventriloquist's dummy awaiting her master's voice. It never came.

Unable to endure the chilly silence for another moment Hinde (doing her best to ignore the cold jar of vitriol which, still held, was pressed against her coccyx like a weapon) put one arm around Strindberg's shoulder and began to tease his white hair with the other. For some reason ice had formed over his soul and Hinde, being a woman, could conceive of only one way to break it; she would *really* have to seduce him. And so intimate exhalations began to warm his cheek. "Just because there is snow upon the summit," she whispered coquettishly, "does not mean that the volcano is extinct." Strindberg was astounded. Where did she learn such a phrase? With a horrible shock he realized that she was no longer following his script but was uttering lines that had previously been practised upon the unfortunate Mr Nilsson.

Hinde, unwisely, began to unbutton her blouse. The fresh air flowed through the open windows and over her breasts, causing her nipples to pucker. Strindberg of course mistook the involuntary reflex for sexual desire, desire not for him but for an imaginary other. At this point Hinde arose and stepped out of her skirt as if it were a hole in the ground, from which she rose like Aphrodite. All that remained were her flimsy bikini-bottoms, the ones which spoke an unambiguous lingua franca. So tightly did they fit that, after their removal, deep marks remained around her belly and the tops of her thighs, as though boundaries had been marked upon her flesh. It was obvious, given the proximity, that she was surrendering all her territories to her prospective sugar-daddy.

Strindberg, outraged, repulsed her so suddenly that she tumbled heavily onto the floor. "Trollop," he screamed, "slut! Compared to you Messalina was a virgin." He arose, roaring like a tormented bull, determined to regain control of the drama that he had initiated. Towering above his naked wife he began to agitate the sulphuric acid until it rocked from side to side like transparent quicksilver. He imagined splashing the carnivorous liquid upon her unprotected breasts and watching, like a voyeur in a sarcophagus, as it ate through her delicate flesh, ceasing only when it reached her unpalatable heart. Perhaps then, when he finally saw that tell-tale organ beating in her open chest, he would understand her treacherous nature. All the colour drained from Hinde's face as she, in turn, recognised that her husband was capable of murder. Her limbs became petrified, making it seem that she was trying to protect her body from a falling mountain. Indeed, her recumbent pose brought to mind the plaster casts that Fiorelli made in the ashes of Pompeii. The tableau vivant lasted for some minutes, until Hinde suddenly recovered her voice. "August," she cried, "what have I done to deserve this?" She covered her face with her hands and rolled herself into a ball, accidentally exposing her genitals. Strindberg was not moved. He spat upon them and his spittle dribbled between her buttocks like an overflow of semen. It was, as it were, miraculous proof of her guilt, analogous to the stigmata. Punishment was inevitable and inexorable. He ignored her pleas for mercy and, very deliberately, tipped the bottle so that a thin stream of the corrupting fluid dropped – dropped not upon her body (damnation!) but upon her abandoned clothes. It was her pants that fizzled and dissolved, leaving a bubbling stain upon the floor. Smoke curled up from the remains of her white skirt. Hinde fled, naked as she was. *Finis*.

Much later, when Strindberg had calmed down, he observed a second puddle where Hinde, in her terror, had passed water. He knew then that his production had been good; well satisfied, he slept upon the chaise longue, covered by a Persian rug. Strindberg may have been happy with the night's work, but I wasn't; I had been expecting a real death, not a soft-core phantasmagoria. In retaliation I disturbed his slumber with a nightmare, of such magnitude that when he awoke he immediately left the apartment and haunted the streets of Stockholm for many hours. Meanwhile Hinde, who had been too frightened to sleep, took an appropriate revenge. Commuting between the study and the bathroom she disposed of all his accumulated waste products in the proper place.

* * *

I decided to take a vacation from August and his claustrophobic art. Who needs a dismal night in a dimly-lit theatre when they can sit in a deciduous wood or a public park and enjoy a display of natural alchemy? As with all spectacles, menials must be employed to attend to the obsequies. And so – at the end of every October in the northern latitudes – men on mobile vacuum cleaners may be observed approaching mounds of golden leaves in order to suck up the desiccated remnants of autumn. Allow me to present two of these honest fellows who, after a hard morning's work, were chewing their tuna and lettuce sandwiches on the granite pedestal that supports the statue of Erik Gustaf Geijer, beloved chronicler of the Swedish race.

The memorial is situated in the middle of the little arboretum that shades the grassy slope between the Gustavianum and the Universitetshus. "Time for the Crab," said Worker A to Worker B, as the clock in the nearby Cathedral struck the hour. He was not referring to his next course but to Professor Terenius, whose nickname had obviously spread to the hoi polloi. Every day for the last few weeks he had shuffled past the park-keepers as they ate their lunch, acknowledging them with a nod, en route to his apartments on Kyrkogårdsgatan where he prepared his own frugal meal. Early in November the first frosts appeared and the gardeners looked for work elsewhere. Nevertheless Professor Terenius persevered with his daily visits to the Victoria Museum in the obstinate hope that August Strindberg would one day reappear.

On a bitterly cold afternoon towards the middle of that month his patience was at last rewarded with a sighting. It had begun to snow in the morning. By mid-afternoon it was falling heavily. Looking out of the window the Professor decided to follow the example of the sun and abandon the remainder of the day. Outside it was as dark as night. Within seconds all the bright buildings, including the one he had just left, seemed impossibly distant. He began to walk up the slope in the direction of home. Half a century had not acclimatised him; he still found it hard to cope with the violence of a Scandinavian winter. Already his ears had almost succumbed to frost-bite. The snow was descending in horizontal lines. It buzzed. It stung his eyes.

It all but blinded him. In order to cross St Olofsgatan, however, it was necessary to look up. When he did he could hardly believe his eyes.

There, striding majestically through the blizzard, was the unmistakeable figure of Strindberg. He was wearing a tall hat and a long astrakhan coat with its collar turned up against the wind. Snow was beginning to settle on his shoulders, on his woolly collar and on the rim of his matt-black topper. His hands were in his pockets. Professor Terenius waved and shouted, but Strindberg did not even pause. Grinding his teeth with frustration, the Professor changed direction and slithered after him. He threaded his way between the illuminated shapes that crept slowly up and down the road, like lumbering beasts with whiskers of light, but got tangled in the crowd at the busy junction with Sysslomansgatan. By the time he reached the other side Strindberg was nowhere to be seen. The Professor crossed the River Fyris. Looking down he saw that it was frozen. In despair he hailed a predatory taxi. "To the station," he ordered the driver. The journey through the commercial district, though of no great distance, was agonisingly slow. Commuters filled the forecourt, where Terenius paid his fare, but Strindberg was not among them. The Professor picked up a damp copy of *Upsala Nya Tidning* and read it from end to end. The fools, he thought, they have missed the day's biggest story. But then, so had he.

That night the temperature unexpectedly rose above freezing and continued to rise, causing the snow to melt with great rapidity. All over Uppsala fitful sleepers were aroused as avalanches of snow and ice crashed down from roofs, gutters and window sills. Having been awakened in such a manner Professor Terenius was thereafter condemned to insomnia by continuous dripping. Until, in the early morning, an uncanny stillness intervened. An inspection of the barometer explained the cause; the temperature had dipped below zero. As the sun slowly rose it revealed a wondrous sight. The whole city sparkled as though the Snow Queen (Strindberg's true consort) had commissioned Fabergé to gild it with ice. All the trees looked silver-plated, the streets resembled mirrors. Aesthetics are not always compatible with convenience, however. The pavements, as the Professor discovered, were almost impossible to walk upon. Indeed, many of his fellow citizens couldn't keep their feet at all and ended up in one of the local hospitals, providing the doctors and nurses with a record number of broken wrists, sprained ankles and concussions.

Returning, as usual, for lunch the Professor witnessed a typical accident at the foot of Erik Gustaf Geijer's statue. A pedestrian lost his balance and flopped heavily upon his back, losing his hat in the process. He did not arise. Anxious to assist, the Professor (his eccentric gait being well suited to the conditions) hurried to where the black figure was splayed upon the glittering surface. Only then did he realize that fate had finally delivered Strindberg to him.

He was hurling abuse at the statue as though the late Erik Gustaf Geijer had just floored him with a knock-out blow. "People wanted to stone me to death for knocking you off your pedestal," he cried, "but it now seems that you have been restored and I am on the ground." Hearing these words the Professor's remaining doubts vanished, this was certainly the same August Strindberg who had (at the commencement of his notorious career) accused the famous historian of being nothing but a sycophantic apologist for Sweden's kings and their lackeys. He coughed diplomatically, thereby attracting Strindberg's attention. "And who are you?" he demanded imperiously. "My name is Terenius," replied the Professor, "we met briefly in the Victoria Museum." "Of course," said Strindberg, "you are the scheming procurer who beguiled me, thus allowing your young protegé plenty of time in which to enjoy my wife. Have I hit the nail on the head?" The Professor was not unduly distressed by this response. It was, after all, in character. "I am deeply sorry that your wife has let you down," he replied, "but I do not see how you can blame me. I did not even know that you had remarried. Besides, what else could you expect from a woman? You should be like me and confine your interests to those who have been dead for two millenia."

Strindberg had banged the back of his head on the hard ground but he was not concussed; far from it, he had heard the word *remarried* and was aware of its implications immediately. This ubiquitous meddler had guessed his identity! He decided not to prevaricate. "You know who I am, don't you?" he said. Professor Terenius, who had merely hoped to establish a certain masculine camaraderie with his misogynistic banter, was astounded by the sudden frankness. He opened his mouth but no words emerged. In the end he silently nodded his assent. It was many hours later, as that extraordinary day was drawing to a close, when he finally worked out that a simple prefix had inadvertently betrayed his knowledge. And by then he was very glad that it had done so.

Sometimes even the most predatory of spiders becomes trapped in the bath-tub. It gets so far but, in the end, always slides back. Strindberg found himself in a similar situation, unable to arise without external aid. The Professor watched his efforts and was about to respond to the inevitable call for assistance when it occurred to him to make his help conditional. Strindberg had no choice but acquiescence. Whereupon the Professor slipped his hands beneath Strindberg's arms (as though he were taking his temperature) and confidently raised him. I have no doubt that Strindberg, restored to his feet, shamelessly intended to break his word. In fact he nearly broke his neck as he attempted to flee. "Shall I take you to the hospital?" asked the Professor, lifting him again. "No," snorted Strindberg, accepting defeat, "I'll settle for your hospitality."

Ladies and gentlemen, if you but knew how fragile was your foothold upon this earth you would also walk as cautiously as did those two elderly gentlemen on that icy afternoon. The sky was still blue and the light was sharp. A transparent moon was slowly turning silver in the heavens. They proceeded cautiously over the frozen cobblestones in Slottsgatan, past the low orange and ochre houses with the red-tile roofs and the cafe that smelled distinctly of mocha and cream. An enormous cloud of white smoke drifted over from an unknown source and swirled above their heads casting giddy shapes on the ice, apparently the consequence of divine shadow-play. Professor Terenius felt he was being offered a privileged glimpse into the origins of the universe. Worlds were made and destroyed in moments, civilizations rose and fell in seconds. But there was a greater imperative than the secret of the universe; it was Strindberg tugging at his sleeve.

They entered Kyrkogårdsgatan, whereupon the Professor was astonished to see two fire-engines, an ambulance and a police-car outside his building, now revealed as the origin of the smoke. Tongues of fire tasted the air as if a nest of dragons had hatched, incongruously, in the first-floor apartment whence they came. As the Professor and Strindberg drew nearer, a fireman, wearing yellow boots and a matching helmet, bellowed into a megaphone: "Don't come any closer!"

They watched as other firemen, upon ladders, turned their hoses upon the incandescent window-frame. Another, with a shining axe but a sooty face, appeared at the conventional entrance, having returned victorious from his expedition into the dragons' lair. Leaning on his arm, in a nightdress and carpet slippers, was the elderly resident of the devastated apartments. Two medics led her towards the

101

awaiting ambulance while a concerned neighbour tossed a tartan rug over her unprotected shoulders. All the other occupants, having been evacuated, were standing in a group. Professor Terenius, proprietorially curious, joined them.

What had happened was this. A workman who was renewing the asphalt on the building's back balconies (an annual chore) had carelessly directed his torch in the direction of the unfortunate woman's curtains. These, in turn, ignited the woodwork. Sparks flew into the room — her personal library — which was filled with manuscripts and printed books, each of which passed on the flames as if participating in a relay race, until the front windows burst and the conflagration that greeted our comrades poured forth. When Professor Terenius saw that the blaze was likely to spread to the upper stories he became agitated and began to fear for his own papers. It was his lucky day, however, and they were spared. The fire burned but, in the end, the structure was not consumed.

Finally a weary fireman picked up the megaphone and announced that the last spark had been extinguished. "You may return to your homes in safety," he declared. The residents applauded and obeyed.

Their mutual home, 27 Kyrkogårdsgatan, had four floors. Professor Terenius lived on the second. Because the lift was still out of bounds (on account of the emergency) Terenius and his guest were compelled to ascend under their own locomotion. In normal circumstances this would have been no hardship, but on this exceptional occasion the entire stairwell stank of smoke, and they were both coughing like terminal patients in a TB clinic by the time they reached the Professor's front door.

The interior was filled with golden fog, like some private chapel, as the intense light of the setting sun fell upon the smoke. "I think we need some fresh air," remarked the Professor, opening the lounge windows and revealing a winter landscape that could have been painted by Peter Bruegel; a snow-covered park, lines of bare trees, ochre houses. There was but one anachronism; an elegant nineteenth-century Observatory which, being a white cylinder with a hat-band of red stars, resembled an ocean liner's funnel.

The room exhaled the smog, enabling Strindberg to examine its contents. There were numerous alcoves in the white walls, all stacked with fragmentary frescos, faience hippopotami or other stylized statuary. The furniture was sturdy, the carpet thick. Professor Terenius might have his eyes fixed upon the ancient past, but he did not neglect his present comforts. He would obviously be a cunning adversary, though something of a relief after the domestic histrionics that were a daily occurrence since Hinde's declaration of war. At least he would be able to confront the Professor with a clear mind, a mind not occluded by unbidden passions. His only doubt concerned the Professor's motive; what did he want of him? Money? Did he intend to blackmail him, to demand substantial payments in return for silence? In which case he was in for a big disappointment. What else could he be after? At least Strindberg knew what *he* required.

The other rooms, through which Strindberg followed this strange scholar, all smelled like the antechambers of hell. The Professor, apologising profusely, ventilated each of them. In the last room, the kitchen, the duties were divided. Strindberg opened the windows and breathlessly beheld the twin spires of the city's medieval Cathedral, around which the familiar crows were already flocking, while the Professor raided the refrigerator and discovered an unopened bottle of Wyborowa. "We must also flush the smoke from our throats," he said. As a matter of fact Professor Terenius rarely touched alcohol but was well aware of the volatile writer's predilection for hard liquor, which (he hoped) would loosen his tongue. "Come, Mr Strindberg," he said (using his visitor's name for the first time), "let us become acquainted."

The sun had long since disappeared and the lounge was illuminated by a single candle, which created an intimate cavern of light. They were seated opposite one another on leather couches, a mode of discourse pioneered by Dr Freud. The bottle was on a low table between them. It was nearly empty. Maybe it was the fiery Polish vodka, maybe it was the unexpected release of being able to share his dreadful secret with a credulous listener; either way Strindberg apparently poured out his heart (to the delight of his host).

"Of late I have been plagued by nightmares," he confessed. "They are so upsetting that I hardly dare to shut my eyes. Last night, for example, I dreamed that I found an embryo on the floor of my study. The flesh of its body was grey, that of its face was yellow. It made a sound like this . . ." He tapped his glass against the bottle. "Instead of arms it had two stumps with which it flailed the air. It was trying to fly! Whereupon I realized that this was no deformed baby but a fledgling." He shook his head, as though wishing to dislodge the grotesque image. "I picked up the featherless thing and, tossing it skywards, tried to return it to its nest," he continued. "Somehow I had forgotten that I was indoors, and so the unfortunate creature kept hitting the ceiling and plummeting back to the ground. I grew very angry. It seemed spitefully ungrateful to die as a consequence of my assistance. The unexpected denoue-ment was manufactured by a deus ex machina in the shape of a hen, which descended from the nest and picked up the ailing offspring with her beak. Placing it in her womb for safe-keeping she took off with its denuded head showing beneath her tail feathers. Whereupon I awoke and was overcome with nausea. What do you make of that?"

Professor Terenius quickly realized that, if he wished to retain Strindberg's interest, he would have to assume the mantle of Joseph (or Daniel) and read his drinking companion's dream. "The fact that the bird had a womb is clearly of the utmost significance," he announced. "It suggests that her plumage was merely a disguise and that what we really have is a woman of flesh and blood. In which case your initial assumption was actually correct; the fledgling was indeed a child." Professor Terenius, an experienced lecturer, paused on the brink of an amazing revelation. "Mr Strindberg," he said, "excuse me for being blunt, but I think that the child was you and that the bird-woman with the well-developed maternal instinct was actually Mrs Strindberg." "Do you mean my wife," enquired the writer, "or my mother?" "The ambiguity was deliberate," replied the Professor (thanking his lucky stars that he had, despite misgivings, read the Viennese doctor's analysis of Moses). "For all your bravado you seem strangely reluctant to leave the security of your parental home. Consider the facts. You now reside in an apartment close to where you lived as a child. It was purchased by a father-figure who then, with exquisite tact, bowed out. You moved in and gradually assumed his role, bedding his former wife in the process. I put it to you that this nubile woman was, in your mind, none other than your own mother. This, surely, explains your overpowering jealousy; the crippling certainty that your wife had slept with another man. *Of course she did if she's your mother!*"

There was silence. The outraged rebuttal, fearfully anticipated, never materialized. The Professor, sensing that the resolve of his opponent was weakening, decided to risk a bolder touch. "I hope I am not the first to inform you," he continued, "that some of your biographers have seen a similar pattern in your first marriage to Siri. No doubt you recall that when you made her acquaintance she was living with her husband in the *very* apartment on Norrtullsgatan your own family had once rented. I'm afraid that several commentators have seen your subsequent flirtation with Siri as a rather blatant attempt to return as a brigand to the scene of your adolescence, in order to do away with your father and possess your mother. They have also used as evidence a simultaneous entry in your biological father's diary: 'Attacked in my own rooms by my son-in-law H. v. Philp and my son August with the coarsest insults. End to my knowing these fellows.' Since your assumed death such diagnoses have become commonplace. Indeed, many believe that the so-called Oedipus Complex is a universal condition."

It was not the possibility that he had covertly done away with his father the better to enjoy incestuous relations with his mother that upset him, not Strindberg; no, he was chastened by the probability that everyone else did it too. "Hence your dream," cried the Professor, triumphantly driving his point home, "it was warning you to get out of Riddarholm before you suffocate there!" "Do you think I enjoy staying in that place?" shouted Strindberg so loudly that the candle flickered. "Do you think I take any pride in living off the immoral earnings of a Jewish prostitute? Why do you think I have returned to Uppsala? I'll tell you. Because I know that somewhere in the Victoria Museum is alchemy's lost secret; the art of making gold. Only when I have found it will I be wealthy enough to leave my wife. And, of course, to reward you for your discretion."

Professor Terenius was shocked. "I don't know where you got that idea, Mr Strindberg," he protested. "Personal gain is of no consequence to a true scholar." He moistened his lips. "You can leave your wife tomorrow, if that's what you really want," he said. "You can move in with me." This is what Strindberg had been waiting to hear. "Can you imagine a more ideal situation?" continued the Professor, trying to sweeten the bait. "Up here you are poised midway between two celestial transmitters: to the west is the Observatory, the Voice of Rationality; to the east is the Cathedral, the Voice of Inspiration. No less important is the fact that this building is *earthed*. You probably missed it in all the excitement but on the ground floor is a little shop owned by a monumental mason which provides memorials and headstones for the cemetery that gives our street its name." He paused. "What do you say?" he asked, offering his hand. "Why not?" replied Strindberg, shaking it. Terenius had his man, Strindberg had his apartment. They had, as it were, achieved mutual satisfaction. "This could be the beginning of a most fruitful partnership," concluded the Professor.

* * *

And so Strindberg left Riddarholm and established a laboratory in the Professor's spare bedroom (which overlooked the Observatory). On the floor were numerous piss-pots; some filled with urine, others with a crystalline patina. Every morning Strindberg would harvest the ripe crystals, which he ground to a fine powder with a mortar and pestle. This would subsequently suffer the same fate as Hinde's pantics. The resulting concoction, bubbling and gaseous, would then be transported to his work-bench where it would be carefully added to the interconnecting network of alembic, ambix, bain-marie, kerotakis and athanor, which burbled and steamed like the internal organs and intestines of an alien god. In this rare and varied apparatus several experiments were being conducted simultaneously. For example, a liquid of vivid turquoise was undergoing distillation in the alembic, while a crystal of ammonium alum, a perfect octohedron, was glowing in the athanor.

As in Riddarholm the relationship between tenant and landlord was unequal; Strindberg naturally took upon himself the role of magus, while Professor Terenius assumed the lesser position of researcher, translator and amanuensis. This was not employment undertaken lightly. Although not forced to sign any documents with his own blood, Professor Terenius was compelled to take a vow of secrecy "under pain of the peach tree."

Alas, for all the Professor's delving into arcane papyri, for all Strindberg's practical efforts, progress in the new laboratory was discouragingly slow; indeed, the only positive achievement to date was the transformation of some silver kroner into featureless discs that were gangrenously green. Nevertheless, Strindberg remained in good heart. After all, the omens were excellent.

One morning, in great excitement, he summoned Professor Terenius back from the Victoria Museum. "Look!" he cried, pointing to the almemor or furnace. Within the glass dome the transparent octohedron had split and the two halves stood like tiny pyramids on the broiling sand. They pulsated with heat as if trying to dictate a message in an unknown cipher. "Do you not see?" cried Strindberg. "Do you not see that what we have here, encapsulated beneath this cupola, is the entire history of Egypt? The almemor is like the mosque of the Moslems which has swallowed the ancient religion; but look, deep in the hidden recesses of the land, beneath the ancient pyramids, the old magic thrives!" The two men leaned over the gleaming lid of the little oven so that their flushed faces were reflected in the curved glass; these were not a pretty sight, their jowls were elongated, their eyes were bulging and obsessive tics (as represented by the red-hot crystals) gnawed at their brains. "All we have to do," said Strindberg, "is to discover the secrets of the old magicians, those wise men who confronted Moses. Having witnessed this miracle I have no doubt that we shall succeed. Now return to the museum with a good heart."

Professor Terenius obeyed diligently, even though he had already obtained all he required from the Egyptians; for had he not, securely lodged in his apartments, his very own El Dorado? True, he had sworn not to reveal the identity of his mysterious lodger to an astonished nation, but the consequences of so-doing did not strike him as frightful. What harm could there be in the sweet fruit of the peach tree?

Lest the punishment is as much a mystery to you as it was to the Professor, allow me to describe the sad end of a promising poet whose final agonies I recently attended. He had returned from a walking holiday in Portugal with a bag of bitter almonds, kernels obtained from the broken pits of peaches and apricots. He ate the lot and thereby discovered, empirically as it were, that they derive their bitter flavour from the cyanide they contain. Let us therefore hope that the Professor had the good sense to put aside his longing for worldly honour and hold his tongue.

However, the good sense of an over-ambitious academic was not something I cared to stake my reputation upon. To tell you the truth, my dears, this Professor Terenius was something of an intrusion. He was only meant to be an eccentric diversion on Strindberg's path to damnation, not a way-station. To be frank, he was a bloody nuisance. Without his interference I would certainly have engineered a mortal sin at Riddarholm. Now, thanks to Terenius, I would have to invent a new scenario. This time I resolved to take no chances; I would intervene decisively in Strindberg's affairs, and lead him to damnation down a different road.

* * *

The wild-eyed alchemist was in his laboratory unbuttoning his flies. His intention was to piss down the neck of a brandy bottle, an absurd ambition given that he had personally consumed its entire contents. As urine squirted indiscriminately over his shoes and the floor, he looked unsteadily down and observed that his trouser-buttons were undergoing a shocking metamorphosis. The shiny black surfaces quickly became carapaces, the edges or rims turned into wings, and the broken threads that hung limply from the holes suddenly became articulated and blessed with movement. Within moments his flaccid member was crawling with fat bluebottles. "Ugh!" he grunted with disgust, and tried to brush them off. This produced the opposite effect; more and more insects landed, exerting such pressure that he felt the unmistakeable onset of tumescence. "I'm flattered that you're so glad to see me," I said, appearing from nowhere. Strindberg, unspeakably embarrassed by his indecency, covered himself up as quickly as he could. Having humiliated the great egoist, I proceeded to my true purpose. "Do you remember that I once blithely assured you that the alchemists were horribly wrong when they maintained that posthumous putrefaction was a beginning and not an end?" I asked. Strindberg, still bothered by his spontaneous erection, did not know what I was talking about and simply shook his head. "It doesn't matter," I replied, "I was lying anyway." I couldn't resist a tactless cackle of self-satisfaction. "This is the theory," I said. "Just as the human soul is perfected by the passage through death and the subsequent resurrection in heaven, so do metals develop in the earth from the baseness of tin or lead to the perfection of gold. It is my business to interrupt the former process and deliver superhumanity to my initiates, it can be yours to hasten the natural procedures of the latter and create gold in the laboratory." "Are you going to tell me how?" gasped Strindberg, miraculously clear-headed. "By careful nurture and long heating," I replied breezily, "by killing the metal, as it were, and then reviving it in a more perfect form; by repeating this modus operandi until the final purity of gold is achieved." "With what do I revive it?" asked Strindberg. "With the philosopher's stone, naturally," I replied, "the fabled elixir of life that quickens the dead and, by analogy, heals sick metals." "So there is such a thing?" said Strindberg. "Of course," I replied, "and you were remarkably close to finding it. As you correctly surmised, it is deposited in the Victoria Museum. Not lost among dusty shelves but on show, obvious to all. So obvious that it remains, like Poe's purloined letter, unnoticed to this day."

On the following forenoon Professor Terenius was despatched to the precise location. He returned, before lunch, with the thing itself, a nondescript object. Strindberg, clutching it, walked to the window of his lab and looked out upon the snow-bound cemetery and the Observatory, respective domains of his good and bad angels; of Azrael and Beelzebub. Beyond that was the university, seat of all earthly knowledge, and beyond that the uniform dwellings of the multitude. Further still were the dark woods, the subconscious of the city, home of atavistic terrors that still howled in the night and shook the civilized world to its foundations.

It was as though Strindberg had a second heart beating in his hand. Waves of divine energy passed from the stone into his body; he felt all-powerful, omnipotent. He was Vasa, he was Rameses; he was Alexander, he was Moses on Mount Nebo. Only he intended to enter the Promised Land, unlike Moses; to enter it and to conquer it. He whispered two words: *Augustus Rex*.

* * *

Beelzebub, you are a genius! Soon Strindberg will truly be yours, body and soul. Power will corrupt him even more surely than the acid in his heart.

He knew that kingship was no dream, that anything was possible with the secret now in his possession. He had watched the miraculous transformation of base metal as it passed through the gaseous entrails of the athanor and the alembic. He had held out his hand and caught the gold as it dropped from the glassy ovipositor.

However, the word *secret* continued to trouble him. Strindberg was not stupid, he was well aware that the route to the throne was never direct (unless you happen to be a crown prince), that his machinations to that end would best be clandestine. At the same time he found it almost impossible to curb his craving for immediate recognition from his peers in the scientific community. Without the applause of a wider audience his great discovery seemed nothing but a still-birth (just as a script was not considered fully alive until it had been performed in public). In short, the crazy bastard wanted the Nobel Prize as badly as the crown. This desire for universal admiration is a weakness common to all artists. And Strindberg, although he had ceased to write plays, remained a man of the theatre. It was in his blood. He therefore began to bombard likely departments of the university with letters that, because of their extravagant claims, were dismissed as the ravings of a crackpot. Alas, Strindberg did not receive a single reply, let alone the offer of an honorary doctorate or better.

After a month of waiting for a positive response his patience was finally exhausted. He summoned loyal Terenius to his newly furnished study (the latter's former library). "I want the name of the university's top chemist," he demanded, "in order to complain about the unpardonable rudeness of his half-witted colleagues." Professor Terenius did not hesitate. "Bonnier's your man," he replied. "Not yet thirty-five and already in charge of the Kemikum Institut. There's nothing he doesn't know on the subject of chemistry." "Except how to make gold," said Strindberg. "Except how to make gold," echoed Terenius.

112

"Please repeat his name," said Strindberg, attempting to suppress a falsetto (suggestive of an interest in something more than accuracy). "Bonnier," said Terenius, "Professor Max Bonnier." So his ears had not deceived him! "Is he, by any chance, a relative of Albert Bonnier, my erstwhile publisher?" he asked. "So it is said," replied Terenius. Strindberg clapped his hands with excitement. Here was an omen, an unambiguous omen! The wheel of fortune had turned another circle. Albert (that prince among publishers!) had helped establish his fame as a writer, and now it seemed that another Bonnier was destined to do the same for his reputation as a scientist.

"Dear Professor Bonnier," he began, "I feel the force of destiny guiding my hand as I compose this letter." He held a fat fountain pen, filled with black ink, from which words flowed fluently. He wrote directly onto expensive stationery. He made no drafts, nor did he cross out a single word. "I have already communicated with your underlings," he continued, "but they, being petty-minded individuals, have chosen to ignore my momentous revelation. What I have done, my dear sir, is easily told; I have transformed base metal into gold. 'What *chutzpa*!' you cry (you have, I assume, a passing familiarity with Yiddish). You call to your wife (forgive this presumption if you are unmarried or homosexual). 'Darling,' you ask, 'what would you say to a scientist, an *amateur* scientist, who claims he has solved alchemy's oldest problem?' 'Stuff and nonsense,' replies your admirable wife. Yet you choose to ignore this sound advice. For you are – despite your better judgement – strangely impressed by the incontrovertible *proof* that the object of your mockery has thoughtfully provided. Feel it, weigh it; you are welcome to analyse it in any way you wish (or, if you prefer, you may simply take my word that it is one hundred per cent kosher). Let us now assume that the gold has been authenticated and that your professional curiosity is aroused. These are the questions that you must be asking yourself. Who is the unknown genius who has finally resolved one of nature's greatest mysteries? And how did he do it? You will, of course, have observed that this correspondence is unsigned, deliberately lacks the appendage of a name. You must believe me, my dear professor, when I assure you that I have withheld my appelation simply because my identity is of no consequence. All credit for this unprecedented achievement *must* go to the late August Strindberg (the same Strindberg who, even now, lines the pockets of the Bonniers with his hard-earned ducats). You are certainly too young to recall the sensation that resulted when he first announced that he had manufactured gold in the laboratory. Was this great breakthrough greeted with joy? Was Strindberg hailed as a hero? No! He was called mad. His enemies did their best to crucify him. They circulated fanciful tales about his sanity and urged his relatives to have him certified and confined to a lunatic asylum. Well, my dear sir, they were wrong and Strindberg was right. His methods have been vindicated, triumphantly so. I therefore invite you to join me in trumpeting his name and his marvellous achievement, so that people will hereafter honour August Strindberg, writer *and alchemist.*"

I did not approve of such communications, but was comforted by the fact that Strindberg had been content to adopt the role of a third party. On the other hand he was very pleased with his work. He folded the letter (without re-reading it), and posted the envelope in the yellow box at the corner of the street.

* * *

Professor Max Bonnier, it turned out, was a practising philanderer. He showed up at Kyrkogårdsgatan on a bright morning in February with a young lady who was wearing nothing (beneath her camel-hair coat) but a turquoise blouse (through which bare breasts were clearly visible) and a tiny skirt. It was obvious even to unworldly Terenius, who admitted them, that such women were not generally in the forefront of scientific research. He decided to ignore her presence. "Our distinguished guest has arrived," he announced, addressing the locked door of the laboratory.

White-coated Strindberg emerged from within fully expecting to behold a typical Bonnier, a delicate red-head with semitic features and dapper outfits, only to find himself facing a muscular man with blond hair, sporting jeans and a check shirt. This was a bigger surprise than the presence of the floozie (what else could she be?). It seemed that the Jews had not only succeeded in aping the behaviour of Swedes, they actually looked like them now. Perhaps, after all, he had nothing to teach young Max about changing base metal into gold!

His attention wandered to the half-naked savage who was Bonnier's companion. Like his estranged wife she had the body of a whore and the face of a saint. Should he give his visitor the benefit of his wisdom (painfully earned) in this matter also; warn him that such women exist for the sole purpose of wasting man's creative power? He shook his head (as it were). It was going to be hard enough persuading a gung-ho chemist that what he was about to witness was something more than a theatrical special-effect. He would spare him his anti-feminist diatribe. Let him discover the dangerous characteristics of women for himself!

Strindberg extended a welcoming hand. Bonnier shook it. "Your face is strangely familiar," he said, "do I know you?" "That is very unlikely," replied Strindberg, "since it is only recently that I returned to my native soil — which I left before your birth — after a very long and lonely journey."

Everything came easily to Max Bonnier. His beautiful wife adored him and turned a blind eye to his multiple infidelities. His colleagues shook their heads in wonder at his precocious talent and spoke of him as the new Arne Tiselius. "It's about time the department won another Nobel Prize," they said without a trace of malice or envy. Moreover Bonnier was, thanks to the family business, exceedingly wealthy. Yet he remained an unfulfilled man, depressed by the fact that there was nothing under the sun that he could not explain away, be it lipstick on his collar or the molecular structure of albuminous substances. Take the advice of Beelzebub, my dears; if you want to be happy abandon all hope of the miraculous, shun the irrational like poison. Turn your backs upon God. Forget ecstasy, be grateful for contentment. Strindberg wasn't; and neither was Bonnier. That was why the latter so readily agreed to visit the former; in hope of rapture and astonishment.

The conventional purveyor of such suspect emotions was left in the charge of a goggle-eyed but tongue-tied Terenius while Strindberg led his visitor towards the laboratory. "What I am about to show you is secret," he said. "I must therefore insist upon a vow of silence." He put his finger to his lips, then said enigmatically. "Swear, or else suffer the pain of the peach tree." Bonnier, a sucker for mysteries, happily complied. "In that case," said Strindberg, "you may follow me." He opened the door.

At first the anachronistic equipment made Bonnier laugh, as did the mad passion of the eccentric alchemist whose unruly white hair rivalled that of Albert Einstein. But gradually the powerful commentary, not to mention the persuasive evidence of his own eyes, convinced him that he was in the presence of a remarkable phenomenon. "Would it be permissible to attempt a repetition of this experiment in my own laboratory?" he enquired. Strindberg had anticipated the request. He agreed on the condition that

116

the catalyst (that is, the philosopher's stone) was not the subject of any specific analysis. Again Bonnier complied. He was no slouch. Within three days he had reproduced Strindberg's result.

* * *

Strindberg and Professor Terenius were retracing the route of their first journey together, from Kyrkogårdsgatan to the Universitetshus. On this occasion, however, Summer was in the air. Uppsala was prematurely efflorescent. Even the bone-yard across the road looked like a botanical garden. It was noon on the first Friday in June and our heroes were dressed in white ties and tails. I know what you are thinking, my dirty-minded friends; that Strindberg, unable to find satisfaction with a woman, had turned to a man for comfort, a man notorious throughout the community for his mincing step. *He fancies himself as Augustus Rex*, you say with a smirk, *but in our opinion it would be more accurate to call him Augusta Regina*! Read on, you cynics, and prepare to eat your words.

As the church clock around the corner struck the quarter hour the long procession of academics (to which they had attached themselves) began to file into the Universitetshus. A grim visaged doorman with a walrus moustache admitted those who had not forgotten their invitations. (Why are these bastions of good intentions all so inhospitable? My dears, we practise no such prohibition, we'll welcome you all with open arms at the gateway to hell.) The lucky ones entered the vestibule and passed into a world of petrifaction.

The floor which, at first sight, appeared to be covered with a layer of autumn leaves revealed, upon closer inspection, tiles laid to form a dazzling geometric pattern, an abstract representation of universal order. In the forests of northern California, where the giant redwoods grow, there are copses which are known as tree cathedrals; these are very like the huge arches that soared towards the ceiling of the great entrance hall, where they supported no fewer than three ornate domes. The smaller columns were as numerous as trees in a wood; trees that had been stripped, bleached, smoothed and scalloped.

And who were the indigenous inhabitants of this shrine to the triumph of intellect over instinct? They stood in every alcove; alabaster replicas of Greek beauties, happy souls who possessed my brain and Azrael's physique. When I compared the perfectly proportioned torsos of those demi-gods with the stick-insects in frock-coats who called themselves the Swedish intelligensia I thought: *Progress? Evolution? Bah!* I felt as though I had accidentally glanced in a mirror and grew ashamed of my own bloodless face, of my shrivelled limbs, of my atrophied muscles, of my whole puny existence. Let me be frank, I was jealous of Azrael.

Despite its fossilized interior and antiseptic atmosphere the Universitetshus was rank with the stench of mortal diseases. An examination of the audience, nearly two thousand in number, quickly revealed numerous irregular heartbeats and wheezing lungs. Of course the majority of the infirmities were resolutely concealed, except by those whose last defences were down and – most especially – by an elderly exhibitionist who leapt on to the stage and began to parody the symptoms of various nervous ailments; he started with shaking arms, the unmistakeable sign of Parkinson's disease, but soon his movements became more violent and rhythmic, which suggested epilepsy; however, the anticipated fit never materialized. Instead he began to hop as though in the throes of St Vitus's Dance. It was only then, when I heard the accompanying music and associated it with the baton in the man's hand, that I realized I was not witnessing a sick comedian's response to some of life's horrid conclusions, but rather the prelude to a performance by the Royal Academic Orchestra. It certainly explained the lack of accompanying laughter.

Bach's dainty rhythms poured forth like liquid geometry while the academics smoothed down their capes and their hair (if any remained) and prepared to receive their higher degrees; doctorates, be they common or garden, jubilee or honorary. The Rector, fiddling with his chain of office, opened the proceedings from the summit of Mount Parnassus (i.e. a lectern on the stage) with a few well-chosen introductory remarks, (e.g., "not only must we think freely, we must also think rightly"). He then summoned the *promoters*, the local equivalent of the actors who open the envelopes and say, "Ladies and gentlemen, the winner is . . ." on Oscar night in Hollywood. Each faculty had its own *promoter*; literature being represented by Professor Foolscap, music by Professor Glockenspiel, religion by Professor Pulpit, and chemistry by Professor Bonnier.

Once summoned, the successful or worthy candidates had to approach the podium and climb the steps to the stage, no simple task if a zimmer frame is normally required to maintain a vertical stance. I observed each ascent with increasing impatience, until I began to hope that a few of the elderly scholars would slip and fall, thereby breaking both their necks and the monotony. But scores came and went, without a single accident. As in life most passed unremarked, except by their colleagues. In fact, only one person attracted the attention of the entire auditorium.

To the astonishment of all, Professor Bonnier announced that his department had decided to take the unusual step of awarding an honorary doctorate to a former student of the university, the late August Strindberg, in recognition of his pioneering work – much derided at the time, but recently justified – concerning the mutability of certain precious metals. The above is a rough translation from the Latin, the lost lingua franca of academia. The Professor then called for Mr Lagercrantz to come forward and receive the insignia on Strindberg's behalf. Elderly men in their aisle seats slapped him on the back as he progressed through the aula, en route to the podium. More distant spectators arose and threw their hats into the air. The ovation was such that even the orchestra was silenced. It continued unabated while Professor Bonnier presented Strindberg with the tokens that confirmed his new status; the ring and the diploma. As for the laurel wreath . . . Professor Bonnier, intoxicated by the atmosphere, placed it upon Strindberg's head as though it were a crown, as though the new doctor were the rightful King of Parnassus. It was more than Professor Terenius could bear. After all, what was Strindberg's achievement compared to his? What was gold when measured against eternal life? "Are all you blind," he screamed, "do you not recognise August Strindberg when you see him?" I began to lick my lips, anticipating the final exit of that troublesome Egyptologist, but the cheering was such that no one heard him, and he was spared to live another day. Lagercrantz (*né* Strindberg) returned to his seat, still sporting his leafy tiara. It was, I concede, a glorious triumph.

* * *

But it didn't suffice. Our hero required more than the plaudits of a few academics, however eminent. He wanted to be loved by the people.

Now it so happened that Strindberg had never forgotten how the manual workers of Sweden (at least forty thousand of them!) had rallied to his support after the terrible disappointment of 1909, when Selma Lagerlöf was awarded the Nobel Prize that should have been his. Determined to raise the spirits of their wounded champion, they dreamed-up and presented the inaugural *Anti*-Nobel Prize (no less than 45,000 crowns, all raised by public subscription) to August. The money was donated in the fond belief that he would purchase a green oasis of peace, where he would grow old, dream, and die – without financial worries. They should have saved their ore and their kroner; Strindberg was not born to enjoy a rural dotage, nor to experience eternal rest.

As the days of his immortality grew in number that ancient debt began to trouble his conscience, especially when he noticed, concealed within the pages of the *Upsala Nya Tidning*, sad and sordid tales of urban deprivation. Now Strindberg was no politician (though he did have the politician's eye for the significant gesture), so it would be wrong to see premeditation in the subsequent chain of events. It pains me to say it, but all he wanted to do was to perform *mitzvot*, good deeds. Therefore his subsequent claim, that his only intention was to repay the unfortunate descendants of his anonymous benefactors *in as dramatic a manner as possible*, should be taken at face value. In other words, he sought recognition not for his generosity but for the skilful way in which he bestowed it.

For example . . .
It is night. The streets of Fålhagen, an unsalubrious district on the wrong side of the railway tracks, are dark. Strindberg enters a newly built tower, already showing signs of decay. The corridors smell of cabbage and garlic (the area, teeming with refugees, is privately known as Garlic Hill). None of the doors are locked, for there is nothing worth stealing. Behind one a woman sits, rocking back and forth in a state of catatonic misery, her hands full of crumpled paper, the final demands of her insatiable

121

creditors; all hope gone, she is in mourning for her life, helplessly awaiting the beast that will terminate it. Oh yes, the omnivorous creature that haunted her peasant ancestors has also migrated to the city, where it lords it over the urban jungle; yes, even in Uppsala the wolf may still howl at the door. And so, when that door suddenly swings open she gasps in horror, half expecting to see a gimlet eye, gaping jaws, a dripping tongue and ivory fangs. Instead she beholds a mysterious stranger; neither lycanthrope nor woodman. In his black coat and tall hat he looks like a stage magician or a confidence trickster. Though, to tell the truth, Strindberg is not at all confident. He is wary of the melancholy woman, does not trust Red Riding Hood (even in her midnight disguise). With characteristic perversity he perceives that fairytale as the tragedy of an unfettered creature, lured by a nubile girl into transvestism, emasculation and decapitation; the Fall of Man as retold for northern latitudes. Nevertheless, he bows politely in the direction of the sweet enemy he has come to save and commences his act. As you know, the Israelites were compelled to make bricks without straw; well, Strindberg goes one better – he plucks gold from the empty air, as though the very darkness were a repository of sunbeams. The nuggets glow like electric lights in the palm of his hand. At first the woman refuses to accept the gift, believing that this strange man – who asks for nothing in return – is either a criminal or an undiagnosed madman. She holds up her hands and shakes her head; whereupon he displays the testimonials and credentials he has received from the Kemikum Institut; impressed by the official letter-head and the distinguished signatures, she at last accepts the offering, even though she has nothing to give in return. Elsewhere a baby cries. "I must go to him," she says. As Strindberg flees from the temptress she asks his name, but as always he brushes the question aside. Even so his identity emerged, his *new* identity. Soon it was common knowledge that the city's anonymous benefactor was August Lagercrantz, the Midas of Uppsala.

122

Throughout the clement Spring of 1965 ever-increasing crowds congregated in Kyrkogårdsgatan chanting his name. "Long live August the First!" they cried. "Long live August the Confessor!" Sweden already had a perfectly adequate constitutional monarch, Gustav VI Adolf, but it seemed that the common folk were eager to elect their own king. Strindberg was enchanted, though he was sensible enough not to acknowledge the demonstrations (which the local press, encouraged by the police, interpreted as a symptom of gold-fever).

On a mild afternoon towards the end of April (by coincidence, the fourth anniversary of the raising of the *Wasa*) Strindberg unwisely entered the street, intending to post a letter to Professor Bonnier, whereupon he was seized by his over-enthusiastic supporters and marched shoulder-high down the road to Hammarby. I could hardly believe my luck. The common people, meaning to honour their champion, were about to deliver him to me.

The ecstatic cavalcade danced for ten kilometers or more along the straight highway until all that could be seen of the receding city were the slender spires of its Cathedral and the bulbous projection of its Castle. Strindberg, slightly sea-sick, couldn't decide whether he was enjoying the triumph to end all triumphs, or had merely been adopted as the figurehead of an insane gold-rush. That was certainly how he felt, raised aloft, at the prow of the swaying mob. On either side of the seemingly endless road were flat fields seething with new life, but beyond this narrow band of cultivation stretched the dark anarchy of the conifers. Could I bring order to such a place? wondered Strindberg doubtfully. It required a physical struggle to husband his own tangled emotions. How could he possibly take on a whole forest – the disorderly secret lives of an entire population – single-handed?

He was deep in such speculation when the column

123

suddenly came to a standstill beside what looked like a royal bus-shelter, adorned with the crown of Gustav III, tragic hero of *The Masked Ball* (a work that once held me spellbound at Stockholm's Opera House). Behind it was an unploughed field which, within seconds, was temporary home to the multitude. The sky above them was as blue as the Swedish flag. It looked warm and comforting and seemed never-ending, like the history of a blessed nation. Only in the western quadrant of the heavens, where the descending sun was bleeding upon the saw teeth of the pine forest, was there any hint of drama, any suggestion that an old king was about to be sacrificed and a new one elected. Thin clouds burned with desire. Flocks of long-necked fowl flew overhead, their A-formation seeming to give divine sanction to the subsequent coronation.

Strindberg, still shoulder-high, could do nothing but passively watch as a small man with a neat white beard emerged from the crowd, which he proceeded to address with considerable vigour from the advantageous position of a protuberant rock. "My friends," he began in true oratorical fashion, "our free-born ancestors once gathered in this very field to choose their king. The actual stones – the Mora Stones – upon which those ancient monarchs took their oath of office are preserved to this day in the building behind me. What say you that we add the name of August Lagercrantz to the illustrious list already carved upon them?" The vox populi was unanimous. A makeshift coronet of tinsel and tin was produced and passed from hand to hand until it reached the gent with the white goatee. He was no archbishop and this was no cathedral, but there was solemnity in his step as he approached his sovereign. Thus it happened that on the 24 April 1965 August Strindberg was crowned Augustus Rex in a muddy field beneath the infinite vaults of a Spring sky.

After the ceremony the joyful marchers returned to the city along narrow country lanes in order to display the new king to his rural subjects. They basked in his reflected glory, in the power *they* had bestowed upon him. It was a slow journey but at its end it was agreed – as it was in former days – that Augustus Rex had "ridden the right progress."

Of course the frontiers of his kingdom remained, like the equator and the tropics, imaginary lines. But within those boundaries his potency, though clandestine, was tremendous. Above all he possessed a bottomless exchequer and a loyal army, whose war-cry was *Viva Augustus Rex*!

PART TWO : 1967–1968

While Strindberg dispensed largesse in the pleasant city of Uppsala his father-in-law slowly fell to pieces in Warsaw. So complete was his disintegration that, by the time of his wife's death in 1967, he had lost all interest in the world beyond the sight-lines of his window.

The wretched woman had expired unexpectedly one bleak mid-winter morning. It was a Wednesday, the day reserved for the procurement of meat. She had swaddled herself in her fox-furs, ancient victims of alopecia, kissed her unresponsive husband on the forehead, and set off breathing like a steam-engine down the road in the direction of the butcher's shop. It was there, some three hours later, that she had collapsed in the snow. The butcher did not have a telephone. Nor did his neighbours. By the time the ambulance arrived Azrael had already ravished the moribund woman. The indifferent medics felt for Mrs Zelinsky's pulse. There was none. Her face was blue and her heart stationary. The ambulance, which had rushed to the scene, lazily returned to the hospital with its inanimate cargo.

Papa Zelinksy was informed of his wife's death, but the news meant nothing to him. As far as he was concerned she was merely out of sight, like the rest of his family and friends, all of whom would one day reappear, cheerfully walking along the street in the direction of the family home – if not at this minute, then the next. Papa Zelinsky would almost certainly have starved to death in the meantime if Hinde had not somehow arranged for a woman to cook for him. This was Mrs Bauman, who still remembered (and wept at the memory) how beautifully Cantor Zelinsky had sung in the days before he was lured to Stockholm, in the days before the war, in the good days when ... Mrs Bauman did not like to dwell upon those times, to do so (she reasoned) would lead to the madness that had overtaken her employer (or, rather, her employer's father), who had no concept of the present, who had to be reminded to eat and even (God help him) to defecate.

Mrs Bauman, though sentimental, was a sophisticated woman; she knew that there must be more to life than was presently on offer in Poland. Therefore she tried to concentrate all her ambitions upon the future. She saw none in Poland, not for the Jews, so she looked elsewhere; to Israel, which retained the allure of a promised land. Like many Poles she did not believe a word that was written in the party newspapers. The more they slandered Israel the more attractive it became in her eyes, until she rhapsodized that unseen country almost as well as Ibn Gabirol.

Imagine her horror when she read that Nasser, as belli-cose as any pharaoh of old, had determined to do what Rameses could not; to destroy the Israelites. Even King Hussein, hitherto peaceable, was smacking his chops at the prospect of victory. Then there were the Syrians, the Iraqis, and the Saudis, not to mention the Algerians and the Palestinians. Millions and millions of bloodthirsty enemies. The newspapers naturally took the side of the Arabs, almost gloating over Israel's probable fate. For once Mrs Bauman believed them.

*　*　*

Nor did the proceedings escape the attention of a ruler in a distant land. One night he dreamed that he was a bird. What sort of bird? A house sparrow? Strindberg a *sparrow*? No, this bird was an aristocrat of the avian world. He wore a black crown, a slate-grey cloak, and sported a fine black moustache (made more conspicuous by his white cheeks). His claws (scimitars in miniature) were as merciless as a *fatwa*. His toes, elongated and delicate, were the extremities of an artist, an artist whose medium was death. His limbs were protected by fluffy leggings, as dark as the pantaloons of a Cossack. His underparts were barred, and his wings were the colour of smoke, save for the tips of the primaries which were black. He glided effortlessly around the infinite acres of heaven, as he used to pace around the restricted space of his study, until he spotted a flock of migrating doves, no bigger than dots on a radar screen, at the periphery of his domain. His eyes missed nothing; one was made of silver, the other was made of gold. He rose upon a thermal. The doves, flying towards the rising sun, saw no danger. Strindberg hovered, fanning the air with his outspread wings, awaiting the propitious moment. Then, when the unsuspecting doves were directly below him, he dropped upon them, diving out of the sun like a fighter pilot. He tore into them with his claws, ripping through their yielding flesh, creating a whirlwind of feathers and blood. He circled the scene of his triumph and watched as the insensate lumps of flesh, so artistically despatched, entered the nether world, where death is nothing but a cold-hearted butcher.

"What do you make of that?" he asked Professor Terenius at the breakfast table. Terenius thought for a moment, picked up his cup of coffee, and laughed. "What did we have for dinner last night?" he enquired. Strindberg flushed, realizing that his inevitable answer would be the cause of much merriment. "Pigeon pie," he replied. "My dear colleague," said Professor Terenius, buttering his toast, "you are to be congratulated, you have managed to turn indigestion into an aesthetic experience." "My bowels function perfectly," snapped Strindberg, banging down his hand and making the condiments jump, "they deliver a perfect stool every morning. Obviously the source of my dream lies elsewhere. I would be grateful if you could devote a few moments of your precious time to finding it. Let's start with the bird. Can you identify *that*?" "Obviously a falcon of some description," replied Terenius, "perhaps a *falco peregrinus*." "Doesn't that have some significance?" asked Strindberg. "Didn't your friends, the Egyptians, often represent Horus as a falcon?" "Of course they did," replied Terenius, concentrating at last. "Its eyes," he said, "repeat your description of them." "One was gold and the other was silver," said Strindberg. "The sun and the moon," exclaimed Terenius. "He was lord of them both." The Professor looked serious. "Shall I tell you what I think?" he asked. Strindberg nodded. "First I must beg forgiveness for my levity," he said. "Granted," said Strindberg. "As you know," continued the Professor, "the falcon-god was generally associated with the idea of kingship, which probably explains the crown that you described. It is my belief that Augustus Rex was last night possessed – and blessed – by the spirit of Horus."

Strindberg was beginning to enjoy his breakfast. "Tell me some more about Horus," he said. "Well," said Terenius, searching for flattering attributes, "he was considered a great leader and protector, especially in times of war." At that moment Strindberg caught sight of the headline in that morning's *Upsala Nya Tidning*. "My dear friend," he said, "these *are* times of war – or they will be. The doves that I destroyed were, among other things, symbols of peace, a peace that is about to end. Yes, my friend, I have seen the commencement of war and I have seen its conclusion. For my dream was nothing less than a prophecy, a prophecy of victory. The falcon was certainly Egypt and the migrating doves were clearly the wandering

129

Jews, the children of Israel. In the war that is to come their nation will be defeated by the Egyptians, destruction being visited upon them from the skies. This is the true meaning of my dream." Consequently Strindberg took it as a personal affront when, on the first day of the Six Day War, the Israelis wiped out the Egyptian air-force before it had even left the ground.

*　*　*

"It's a miracle!" screamed Mrs Bauman, bursting into the house. "A proper miracle!" Papa Zelinsky responded by looking out of the window, fully expecting to see his loved ones parading down the street. They were late, as usual. "*Am yisroel chai!*" cried Mrs Bauman, shaking the bewildered man by his shoulders. "The people of Israel live! They have risen from the dead and smitten their foes!" Without further ceremony she plucked Papa Zelinsky from his chair and propelled him through the open door into the summer sunshine. He was like a mole who, having just broken surface, was blinded by the light. *Where am I?* he thought. He wondered if it were the blessed day of judgement. "God be praised," cried Mrs Bauman, "at last the Jews have something to celebrate." Papa Zelinsky did not hear. "I must go home," he mumbled, "someone may come." "At your age you can expect but one visitor," she replied, "the Angel of Death. It will hardly be a tragedy if you miss that *momzer's* call." There was no response; compared to her companion, a somnambulist was a man of action. Undeterred, Mrs Bauman continued to prod him along the city streets. They rested in an over-crowded cafeteria, where Papa Zelinsky sat like a golem while his lemon tea grew cold. Afterwards they entered a store that specialized in woman's clothing. An argument was in progress between the manager and one of his assistants, a young girl. I couldn't swear to it, but I think she was a Jewess. Anyway, her boss hit her. When his open hand made contact with her cheek it was as though a branch had snapped in a quiet forest. The unexpected sound galvanized Papa Zelinsky. Without a word he strode across the store and smote the girl's task-master. "She looked like Hinde," was all he said by way of explanation. "It is a second miracle," said Mrs Bauman in amazement. And she was right; the light of understanding had returned to the old man's eyes.

However, the following morning Papa Zelinsky stared at Mrs Bauman as though she were a complete stranger. Who was she? Of one thing he was certain, she was not his wife. "Where is Mrs Zelinsky?" he demanded. First the good news, thought Mrs Bauman, now the bad news. She gently touched the poor man's skeletal hand, noticing (without revulsion) the long finger-nails and the proliferating liver spots. "Your wife died nearly six months ago," she explained, "and I have been looking after you ever since. My name is Mrs Bauman." Papa Zelinsky arose from his chair. "*Boruch ata adonai*," he mumbled, "Blessed art Thou, Lord our God, King of the Universe, the true Judge." Then he began to chant the traditional lament for the dead: "*Yisgadol viyiskodosh shi'my rabbo ...*" His voice, though long neglected, remained as powerful as a Polish onion. So freely did Mrs Bauman's tears flow in response that a stranger would be forgiven for assuming that it was her spouse who was being mourned. And in a sense the stranger would have been right, for Papa Zelinsky was commemorating not only his wife but all the victims of those unspeakable times. Gradually, however, the melody shook off its infinite melancholy and began to imply that a light had just been spotted at the end of the tunnel. "*Ousay shalom bimromov hoo ...*," sang Cantor Zelinsky, almost jauntily, "May the most high, source of perfect peace, grant peace to us, to all Israel, and to all mankind, and let us say: Amen." "Amen," echoed Mrs Bauman.

131

At which point, my dears, I'm afraid that I sniggered. What else do you expect? I am a devil, after all, and those pious sentiments tickled me. Just look at the history of the Jews! If you can find any real evidence that God means well by his chosen people, I'll take holy orders. Even then, even after Israel's miraculous victory, I did not anticipate a season of perfect peace. No, the only place the Jews will find that is in the grave. Unless they decide to throw in their lot with Beelzebub, of course. It is true that I cannot promise perfect peace, but at least I can guarantee longevity.

Although it was only mid-morning Mrs Bauman opened an ancient bottle of slivowitz. "I think we both need this," she said, pouring the plum brandy into a couple of tumblers she had plucked from the baroque cocktail cabinet, undisturbed for two decades. She turned around Papa Zelinsky's heavy armchair, so that it no longer faced the window, and patted the cushion. "Sit down," she said. They sipped their drinks in silence. Papa Zelinsky looked around the room that had, for years, been nothing more than his watch-tower. The room was constant, it was its erstwhile occupants who had abandoned it or changed beyond recognition. There was the same oblong table with the bow legs where, once upon a time, the whole family had dined. There was the scallop-backed sofa where his parents had rested after the evening meal. It was, incidentally, also the site of his first stolen kiss, stolen from a girl whose face he no longer recalled. There were the photographs, in ornate frames, of his brothers and sisters; some wild, others pious, all dead. There were no flowers in vases nor any potted plants. The only signs of life were his own asthmatic wheezing, Mrs Bauman's quieter more regular breathing, and a rap at the door.

The postman, a man of routine, was unpleasantly surprised that morning not to see the familiar waxwork in the window. Although not fond of Jews in general, he liked to greet the old dummy as he passed. Papa Zelinsky's plight reassured him; representing, as it did, the comatose state of Polish Jewry. Imagine his horror, then, when his knock at the door was answered by Papa Zelinsky himself, as large as life! True, a look of fear crossed the old man's face, a pavlovian response to the sight of a uniform, but it quickly vanished when he realized that he was not dealing with a Nazi. He giggled tipsily. "Mr Postman," he said, "today ish an awe-full day." The postman, for his part, recollected his childhood, and recalled a game he used to play with his cousin; cops 'n' robbers. It always ended in tears, for his cousin was a cheat. However many times the postman cried — "Bang! You're dead!" — his cousin would always refuse to stay down. The Jews were just the same. "Are you Papa Zelinsky?" he snapped (as if he didn't know the answer!).

Papa Zelinsky nodded, and opened his hands to receive the proffered parcel. Alas, he had forgotten that he was still holding the glass of slivowitz. Fortunately its fall was broken by one of the postman's shoes. Unfortunately the postman was rather proud of those shoes. They were genuine Irish brogues, a precious gift from an expatriate Catholic. From above they now looked like Finland, the land of a million lakes. Each hole was a pool of alcohol.

"I know what you've been up to," the postman rasped, so unpleasantly that his bristling moustache looked like an offensive weapon. "What do you mean *up to*?" Papa Zelinsky asked. His tone was somewhat jocular, appropriate to banter between old friends (or even adversaries). This was a serious miscalculation. "You have been toasting the Zionists," said the postman, "drinking to their victory." Papa Zelinsky did not immediately deny the accusation, another mistake. "What if I have?" he asked, genuinely surprised. "Are they your enemies? Has someone discovered that the Poles are actually Arabs?" The postman was not amused. "The military adventurism of the Zionists is a threat to world peace," he explained, trying to remember the editorial he had read in yesterday's paper. "Any threat to world peace is, by definition, a threat to Poland. Therefore anyone who supports Israel is a traitor." The postman felt justifiably proud. It is not every worker, he reasoned, who can commit such a complicated argument to memory.

He touched his moustache with his tongue and eyed the Yid. He felt a strong urge to punch his face. Instead it was his duty to deliver contraband from Scandinavia. He felt utterly humiliated by this. But what choice did he have? If he struck the Jew he would lose his job and his family would starve. This realization made him even angrier, because it was the Zelinskys of this world who had caused the failure of the latest five-year plan. General Moczar was right; the Jews were crucifying the country. Like all his fellow countrymen he was merely an unwelcome spectator at their blasphemous feast. Zlotys were their wafers, and Polish blood was their wine.

"Take your parcel," he snapped, handing it over with a violent thrust. Papa Zelinsky should have taken it and shut the door. He took it, but he didn't shut the door. Before he had the chance, an infectious mosquito flew straight into his eye, greatly discomforting him. He returned the parcel to the postman and, with the corner of a handkerchief, tried to fish out the fly. "It is true that I am a Jew," he admitted, unwisely continuing his self-defence (as I hoped he would), "but I am not an Israeli, I am a Pole." "Is that so?" mocked the postman, maliciously accepting his cue. "I repeat," said Papa Zelinsky, rubbing his eye, "I am a Pole." "Where were you born?" asked the postman. "In Warsaw," replied Papa Zelinsky, "as were my parents and their parents. Their grandparents came from a *shtetl* near Cracow, where their ancestors had lived for hundreds of years. So how can you question my Polishness?" The postman was not fooled for a moment.

"What language did your parents speak at home?" he demanded. "Yiddish," said Papa Zelinsky, "but I have not spoken it since before the War." "Not so!" shouted the postman. "It is still your mother tongue. How do I know? Because you do not speak Polish like a native. You could be a German or a Jew, but you are definitely *not* a Pole. When you claim otherwise you are – a liar!" He licked the spittle off his moustache, resumed his cheerful whistling and, having dumped the parcel on the doorstep, continued on his round. Papa Zelinsky returned to the lounge. "I see that nothing has changed," he remarked.

His unexpected confrontation with the postman continued to trouble him during the night, as did the detritus that lingered in his right eye. With the coming of dawn he arose befuddled by insomnia and saw, to his horror, that the eyeball was bleeding and that he was weeping ruddy tears. Was this God's punishment for relinquishing his post after all those years of singular dedication? Eventually his mind cleared and he recollected the cause of his injury. However, this rational explanation only served to make him more frightened. He could accept blindness if it were God's will, but not if it were the consequence of an accident. Panic-stricken he returned to his old armchair and awaited assistance, not daring to shut the eye for fear that the blood would coagulate behind the lid and form a crusty membrane. And that was how Mrs Bauman found him, mopping up the ceaseless tears with an increasingly spotty handkerchief. Aghast she insisted upon escorting him without delay to the nearest hospital; there a young intern calmly bathed the wound and advised him to wear an eye patch until it had properly healed. They purchased one at a nearby pharmacist. Papa Zelinsky regarded the black cup with some embarrassment. "It will make me look like a pirate," he remarked. Nevertheless he allowed Mrs Bauman to tie it in place. They returned to find the postman hammering on the door with yet another parcel from Sweden. He stared at Papa Zelinsky as though the latter had just insulted his mother, but did not linger to explain the slight. "What have I done?" asked Papa Zelinsky. Mrs Bauman shrugged.

In fact the postman had taken exception to Papa Zelinsky's eye patch. He too ignored the cause (which he had witnessed) in favour of a simpler explanation. "Have any of you seen what the Yids are up to now?" he asked his cronies in the sorting office. None of them had. "They are all strutting around like little Moshe Dayans!" he announced triumphantly.

* * *

Strindberg, having toyed with his cousin's camera at an impressionable age, subsequently became one of the pioneers of photography in Scandinavia (although his most famous pictures were taken at Gersau, a spa in Switzerland). It was from Gersau that he wrote to his publishers with the proposal for a new book. Inspired by the photographic essays that were being printed by *Le Journal Illustré* (not to mention the availability of a new-fangled shutter release that enabled him to be, simultaneously, both subject and photographer) he offered old Albert Bonnier the dernier cri in autobiography; a sequence of self-portraits, both photographic and verbal. Alas, Bonniers turned it down, and thereby failed to anticipate the coming of the television documentary.

Their more visionary author looked upon the craftsmen of television – the script-writers, directors and cameramen – as his heirs. He adored watching the programmes they produced and was horrified to discover that Professor Terenius did not possess a set. My dears, will you be shocked if I inform you that the first object he acquired, having established residency in Uppsala, was the latest model from Bang & Olufsen? That very night, after a fruitless day in the laboratory, he slumped in the chair opposite the television and established a routine that he thereafter adhered to religiously. He watched and, while watching, hurled abuse at the screen. His favourite programme was the news.

One night, as the third anniversary of Strindberg's coronation was approaching (i.e. March 1968), the main item concerned a protest in Warsaw occasioned by the recent closure of a popular play at the National Theatre. The play was *Dziady* by Adam Mickiewicz. "In normal countries when the theatre is full the run is extended," explained one of the demonstrators, one among thousands, "but here that is considered a reason for the authorities to take it off." "Why would they do that?" asked the Swedish reporter. The protestor (identified only as a student of philosophy) laughed. "Why?" he said. "I'll tell you why! Because *Dziady* is a call for liberty and independence, because the audience responded to that call and enthusiastically applauded every anti-Tsarist speech. Our Soviet friends became uncomfortable. They did not want Warsaw to be another Prague. They became determined to stop the arrival of Spring. So be it! Let them have a winter of discontent!" Those around him cheered. Many were holding floral tributes which they intended to lay at the nearby monument to Mickiewicz. Their way was barred by the steel-helmeted *milicja*, who looked ready for trouble. Behind them were armoured vehicles mounted with tear-gas launchers. The barrels were aimed at the demonstrators. Without warning they opened fire. Clouds of gas obscured the view as masked police began to crack heads. Some said it was a riot, others called it a rout.

Strindberg bristled with fury. "Who is this Adam Mickiewicz?" he demanded. It was a rhetorical question. He knew the answer. Let us be blunt, my dears; Strindberg

137

was green with envy. He too wanted to provoke riots in the street, wanted to be the idol of the young, wanted to be adored by all as the voice of the nation. He wanted his works to be the inspiration of new generations, he wanted children to die fighting their oppressors clutching *his* plays in their hands. Since this had never happened he found it impossible to accept that another playwright could incite such spontaneous combustion. He preferred to believe that the students had been stirred up not by Mickiewicz but by anti-patriotic agitators, by rootless cosmopolitans and Zionists. In this (if in nothing else) he was of one mind with Papa Zelinsky's postman.

* * *

President Gomulka had informed his people that three types of Jews dwelt among them: the first, Poles who openly admitted their Jewish origins, were tolerable though permanently liable to schizophrenia when it came to the question of ultimate loyalty; the second, rootless cosmopolitans, smart-aleck intellectuals and other such flotsam and jetsam, were also acceptable *so long as they did not impersonate real Poles*; but the third, Zionists, were completely beyond the pale.

Since Papa Zelinsky was undoubtedly numbered among the Zionists, the postman decided that it was his patriotic duty to personally persecute him. He began his campaign by writing and then delivering poison pen letters which accused the recipient of using the blood of murdered gentile children for ritual purposes. "Dear Moshe Dayan," began another, "I wish to inform you that your mistress, Golda Meir, has other lovers. I know for a fact that she shares her bed with Martin Bormann. She agreed to prostitute herself in return for 1,500 Nazi officers. How else could a nation of ghetto-dwellers achieve such an improbable victory? We will not permit the same evil alliance to poison Poland. You have been warned."

At first the postman merely wished to frighten Papa Zelinsky out of his wits. In this he succeeded. Then he became more ambitious; he decided to drive him out of the country altogether. And so, late one night, towards the end of March, he plastered the walls of the neighbourhood with advertisements which informed interested parties that Mr Zelinsky, having elected to abandon the fatherland in favour of Israel, would be holding a sale of his belongings on April Fools Day. This proved to be a self-fulfilling prophecy.

Mrs Bauman, distressed by Papa Zelinsky's consequent retreat from the world he had only recently rediscovered, took the liberty of hinting at his condition to Hinde. Hinde did not reply. Mrs Bauman, giving her the benefit of the doubt, wrote again. This time she received a grudging response, which implicitly accused Mrs Bauman of exaggerating the situation for her own purposes. To add insult to injury Hinde offered Mrs Bauman a small increase in her salary. Mrs Bauman who had, in reality, been trying to spare Hinde's feelings, lost her temper and, putting pen to paper, described the true nature of Papa Zelinsky's plight. This time even Hinde had to admit that she was asking too much of Mrs Bauman, that she could no longer evade her daughterly duties.

There remained a simple choice; either she returned to Poland, or her father came to Sweden. Hinde chose the lesser of the evils. Who knows, she thought, maybe I'll persuade the old boy to assimilate? "If you think it will help, you should inform the authorities of the threats that are unbalancing my poor father," she wrote. "You could also register a complaint about the abusive postman with his superiors. However, I fear that it will be to no avail and could even be detrimental. So what is to be done? As you may know I begged my father not to leave Sweden after the War. Events have justified my pleas. Now it is time for his return. You must convince him by example. If you come he will have no option but to follow. *Money is no object.* I am prepared to take full responsibility for all expenses. My first husband left me some property and my second, who has caused me untold misery, seems to have an inexhaustible supply of ready cash. It will give me some satisfaction to make the bastard – who is something of an antisemite himself – fork out for my father's rescue. I am counting upon you, Mrs Bauman."

Mrs Bauman did not hesitate. Compared to Poland, Sweden was Utopia. She began to dream of its sparkling lakes, its dense forests, its clean cities. She signed a document that was, in effect, a renunciation of her Polish citizenship. After some persuasion Papa Zelinsky did likewise, thereby proving his disloyalty and providing the government with an excuse to expel him – not because he was a Jew (perish the thought), but because he was an ingratiate. Although Papa Zelinsky's fragile spirit had been broken by his postman's ferocious onslaught, he remained alert enough to pick out the situation's little irony. "At least they were forced to give the lie to that *momzer's* assertion that I was not a Pole," he remarked to Mrs Bauman as he leaned upon her arm in labyrinthine corridors of the Council of State, while she stuffed the freshly stamped papers that attested to their stateless condition into her handbag. "How could I renounce my Polish citizenship otherwise?"

In order to leave the country to which they no longer belonged they were compelled to apply for Israeli visas. The fact that their ultimate destination was Sweden cut no ice. The government simply wanted to demonstrate that the three categories of Jews were (like the Father, the Son and the Holy Ghost) really one; to make public the information that, in their hearts, they were all Zionists. As

Poland had broken off diplomatic relations with Israel in a fit of pique following the latter's outrageous triumphs, Mrs Bauman and Papa Zelinsky had to deliver their applications to the Dutch Embassy. These were accepted, and the visas were issued. But what use are visas without a passport? And where, pray tell, can a stateless person go to obtain such a thing? Anticipating this impasse, the Ministry of the Interior produced a four-page travel document in soft blue covers which informed immigration officials that the bearer (in-between countries, as it were) was no longer a citizen of the issuing state.

Thus it came to pass, as the postman had predicted, that strangers came to the house of Papa Zelinsky and carried away the goods which he no longer required, including the comfortable armchair in which he had spent so many years. The treasured remnants − family photographs, Hebrew books, records by respected pre-War cantors, a pair of silver candlesticks, a menorah, and a spice box that smelled overwhelmingly of cloves − were packed into an ancient trunk and examined in situ by bored customs officials who, being bribed by Mrs Bauman with vodka and sausage, turned a blind eye to any illicit items.

Mrs Bauman made a bonfire of the left-overs. Broken furniture, old boxes, unused cheque books, bank statements, out-dated insurance policies and unwanted letters all burned merrily in Papa Zelinsky's back-garden. He stood at a safe distance, in dressing-gown and carpet slippers, watching the flaming sheets of paper ascend like incandescent angels. He felt that he was making a final sacrifice, returning his unused Polish years to the Almighty. He half-heard his bad-tempered neighbour (who had purchased his dining-room table for a song) scream at her little boy, "Take off those muddy boots immediately! It's about time you learned some respect for this house." The words registered at some deep level in his psyche and (as if the image had long been awaiting the pre-ordained trigger) he remembered how Moses, suddenly confronted with the burning bush, had also been ordered to remove his footwear. For the first time he thought actively about his imminent flight and realized that his true destination – his true *destiny* – was nowhere but Israel. God had sent him a sign (in his own garden!) which he dare not disobey. There and then all the love he had reserved for his relatives, those invisible figments, was transferred to the promised land.

Mrs Bauman was horrified when he re-entered the house, his face smeared with ashes, and informed her that he would, after all, be using his Israeli visa. "Your only daughter lives in Stockholm!" she cried, continuing to fold his shirts and pack his underwear. "She is expecting you. You don't know a soul in Israel. You have no money. Who will look after you there?" "God will provide," said Papa Zelinsky. Mrs Bauman wanted to hit him. "God will provide! God will provide!" she mimicked. "He didn't in Poland. Why should he bother elsewhere?" "Because Israel is the Promised Land," said Papa Zelinsky. "He has provided his people with a great victory. He will provide me with bread." "What shall I tell Hinde?" asked Mrs Bauman, slamming down the lid of the suitcase. "Tell her that my mind is made up," he said. "Tell her that I am a cantor. Tell her that I cut a figure in the community. Tell her that if I go to Israel, then many others will follow. Tell her to come too!" Mrs Bauman, in despair, said no more.

Observed by neither relative nor friend, they boarded the train for Vienna at the Gadanski Station and, with nothing but the guard's whistle to mark their passage, departed from Warsaw for ever. From Austria they flew not to Lod – as both the Polish authorities and Papa Zelinsky assumed they would – but to Arlanda.

* * *

The relationship between the Jews and the Poles may have been generally antagonistic, but it was also symbiotic. Take, for example, the Yiddish word *shmatta* which has its origins in the Polish *szmata*, meaning a rag or a scrap of tatty cloth. I'm willing to bet that there was not a single Swede in the whole of Arlanda who could say for certain whether the two new arrivals were dressed in *shmattas* or *szmatas*, whether they were Jews or Poles. But Hinde knew all right. My God, she thought as Papa Zelinsky and Mrs Bauman emerged from the baggage hall wheeling their worldly goods, what a pair of *schlocks*! They couldn't have been more obvious about their Jewishness if they were dancing the *hora*. She cringed with embarrassment and considered fleeing before they spotted her. Just look at that Bauman woman! She was wearing a threadbare green cardigan, a shapeless blue skirt, beige stockings and a pair of scuffed shoes. As for her father! He was stumbling around like a drunkard who had spent the previous night in a police cell; his plimsolls were laced with string and his trousers held aloft with a tie instead of a belt. Who could blame their fellow passengers for keeping well away? Would you want to be the next land-fall for a family of migrating fleas?

Mrs Bauman paused, leaned on the trolley and, looking around, pointed excitedly at Hinde, who was compelled to offer a discreet wave in return. Watching their painfully slow progress she was forcibly reminded why she had declined to attend her mother's funeral, and why she had steadfastly refused to visit her father. She had kept her distance because she knew that she would otherwise have risked being sucked into the maw of their miserable existences, from which she might never have emerged to lead a life of her own. She had a dread of reverting to type, of forfeiting the sophistication that came with her

Swedish husbands and her brand new nationality.

Over the years Hinde had come to regard herself as a Swede of dubious origins. Although she had never actually lied about these origins (as Strindberg will confirm), she did not boast about them either. She was of the opinion, secretly held, that her father had been ostracized by the Poles not because he was Jewish, but because he had flouted unspoken social conventions and ostentatiously displayed that Jewishness. In particular his eternal mourning (not to mention his hopeless vigil at the window) must have seemed like a constant rebuke to his neighbours who, understandably, wanted to see the back of him.

Facing him now, for the first time since her elopement with Mr Nilsson, she reluctantly acknowledged the enormity of changing him, of turning him into a Swede. Nonetheless, he remained her father and, as she hugged him, her heart softened and she wept. "It is a miracle," said Papa Zelinsky. Then he knelt and kissed the ground. "Why is he doing that?" asked his daughter. "Because he thinks he is in Israel," said Mrs Bauman.

Hinde's neighbours in Riddarholm nodded sympathetically when she informed them that her father, a poor refugee from Poland, was coming to live with her, and courteously enquired about his exact relationship to her former lodger, Mr Lagercrantz; initially her cousin, then her husband, and now hardly in evidence. She explained that the two men had never met, that Mr Lagercrantz (a Swede) was a distant relative on her mother's side.

Needless to say, Papa Zelinsky was devastated when he eventually realized that he had been duped, that he had ended up in the Far North rather than the Middle East. He had assumed that there were at least two trustworthy people in the world: his daughter and his housekeeper. Now, it seemed, even they had lied to him. Thus his depression was compounded by disillusion and, refusing to arise from his daughter's marriage bed, he resolved to take the anorexic route to Azrael's arms. Hinde, in desperation, threw tantrums at the bedside and – when these proved unavailing – threw plates of food at her obstinate father. "No wonder your husband divorced you," said Papa Zelinsky by way of retribution. "As it happens," replied Hinde, "we are not divorced."

This was correct. Augustus Rex could not bring himself to initiate proceedings against his wife. He rationalized it thus: a man in my position cannot afford to present himself as a cuckold. Or, if that failed to convince, he argued that he was too busy, too preoccupied with the eternal verities to be bothered with the trivial technicalities of marriage. He had outgrown such things, he assured himself; his problems were now neither personal nor artistic, they were all *political*. The truth of the matter was this: Strindberg was still infatuated with Hinde, could not bear the possibility that another person might possess her.

In order to ensure that no man did, he sent his landlord, the eunuch of Egyptology, on occasional forays to Riddarholm; ostensibly to collect an indispensable book or an irreplaceable document, but actually to spy upon his wife.

Thus it happened that he turned up a few days after Papa Zelinsky's arrival, right in the middle of a spat over the old man's suicidal fast. Hinde was in the bedroom trying, without success, to force-feed her father when her administrations were interrupted by the false cheer of the front-door bell. All she needed was a visitor! "Mrs Bauman," she called. There was no reply because Mrs Bauman was out in pursuance of her new hobby; shopping. "I'll have to see who it is," she said. In response Papa Zelinsky at last opened his mouth, breaking the white duodenal paste that sealed his lips. "Good," he said, exploring his stubble with a furry tongue. "Go! Leave me in peace." He looked at Hinde with his red-rimmed and rheumy eyes. "My daughter the Nazi," he said. This was too much for Hinde. "Don't eat the fucking thing," she cried, tossing the runny eggs on to the eiderdown, "I don't care." The under-done dish disintegrated upon impact and the fragments proceeded to slither down the slopes of the rumpled bed-clothes like yellow slugs.

Hinde watched their progress with some regret, for it once had been a perfect omelette. She took great pleasure in cooking, and had no sympathy at all for her father's extended Yom Kippur. There was only one category of food Hinde would not touch; shellfish. Faced with a plateful of the boiled baby-pink creatures she was truly her father's daughter. This outlandish aversion caused her many social problems during the endless days of mid-summer when her indigenous companions gorged themselves on kräfta, unkosher denizens of Sweden's internal waters. Perhaps this atavistic aversion to crustacea was the proper explanation for her instinctive dislike of the unfortunate Professor Terenius. Not only was the poor fellow's gait unmistakeably crab-like, but his arms also darted out in the manner of claws when he unexpectedly pulled a volume off the shelf, and as for his eyes – well, they were in constant motion, swivelling at the slightest sound as if they were on stalks. The fishy distortions of the flat's peep-hole did nothing to improve his appearance; on the contrary, Hinde was deluded into thinking that her visitor was a mock-turtle with a thyroid condition and was almost sick on the spot.

"What have you come for this time?" she snapped as she opened the door. "August needs a book," he replied, startled by her bloodless complexion. "And how is my husband?" asked Hinde (as if she cared!). "Working hard," replied the Professor. "So," said Hinde ungraciously, "get what you came for." He found his own way to Strindberg's study. It was there, while searching the stacks for a likely book, that he unexpectedly heard a man's voice coming from the bedroom. He paused and listened carefully. Alas, there was no mistake.

At which point it should be noted that Papa Zelinsky was not the only obstinate member of the household. From the moment of their reunion at Arlanda, Hinde had refused absolutely to converse in Polish. This meant that they had to talk to one another in Hebrew (which Hinde had all but forgotten) or Swedish (which Papa Zelinsky vaguely recalled from his war-time sojourn at Wahrendorffsgatan).

In the beginning Papa Zelinsky used only Hebrew, under the assumption that it was the local lingua franca, until he made the humiliating discovery that he was actually in Scandinavia; thereafter he only communicated with his daughter in Swedish. Hinde was well aware that this was a slap in the face, a manifestation of the coldness he felt towards her, but she willingly accepted the insult in the hope that it was the first step towards assimilation. Mrs Bauman he forgave more easily. He generally addressed her in Polish. Sometimes, however, they conversed in Yiddish. This was when they wished to open their hearts, to share their deepest secrets. In short, Hinde was treated as a social contact, whereas Mrs Bauman retained the role of confidante. A further (though not insignificant) consequence of this complicated exercise in linguistic etiquette was that Professor Terenius could comprehend the exchange in the bedroom.

"What a mess," the man was saying, "it'll serve you right if it makes permanent stains on the sheets." Professor Terenius was naive, but not *that* naive. Even he knew what stained sheets! He groaned at the implications. Strindberg would demand detail upon detail. At the very least he would expect a full description of the malefactor. The

Professor wept with frustration. Why couldn't he simply forget what he had heard, why couldn't he write the intruder out of history? Because there was always the possibility that Strindberg would discover the truth for himself (who knew the limits of that man's powers?) — that's why!

Professor Terenius had degrees and doctorates (not to mention a chair at Uppsala), but he couldn't think of a thing to say by way of explanation once he had burst into the bedroom and caught Hinde and her beau in medias res. And he couldn't conceive of entering without that excuse (even with it he anticipated embarrassment for all concerned).

What am I doing here? he asked himself. How has it come to this? Strindberg was to have been the means of his elevation to Parnassus, not the cause of his descent into the gutter. I am a scholar, he thought, not a seedy private detective. My place is in the museum, among books and cadavers, not in some seraglio, crawling with naked flesh and its unsavoury emissions. It boiled down to this, my dears: he wanted to leave with his dignity intact, but he dared not leave without some facts. The story of humanity, so to speak.

Professor Terenius decided upon a compromise; he would obtain the necessary data by accident, as it were. Clutching *Kingship and the Gods* by Henri Frankfort he clattered along the corridor in the hope that Hinde, upon hearing him, would emerge from the bedroom to bid him farewell, thus allowing him a fleeting glimpse of the usurper within.

It didn't work, leaving him with no choice but self-abnegation. Utterly humiliated he opened the bedroom door, peered in, and said . . . Well, he had intended to say, "I'm going now," but the figure in the bed rendered him speechless. You see, he actually thought he was looking at

148

Strindberg! For a moment he truly believed that Augustus Rex had returned to claim his consort.

To be fair, the false identification was excusable. At first glance there *was* a superficial likeness, in that both men had white hair that, when uncombed, was like the crown of a cockatoo. But there were also many deeper resemblances. Both men had been reborn, as it were. Strindberg (you'll recall) returned to Riddarholm straight from the grave; Papa Zelinsky came from another cemetery – called Poland. Both owed their renaissance to a miracle, and their continued vitality (such as it was in the latter's case) to its golden after-glow. Both had rejected the obsessive idealism of their earlier years, during which the one conjured up characters at his desk while the other desperately tried to do the same at his window. And last but not least, both were emotionally dependent upon Hinde. There the resemblances ended and gave way to a greater difference; Strindberg saw himself as the Swedish Rameses, while Papa Zelinsky fancied that he was the Polish Moses. It was a difference I intended to exploit.

Closer inspection quickly convinced the Professor that he was looking at the face of a stranger, the strained features of a man still recovering from the unaccustomed exertions of a strenuous night (if the numerous slimy blemishes on the bed-spread were a reliable guide). Gaping at the intruder, the dumbfounded rake suddenly began to shake as though feverish thoughts were tormenting his body. He whimpered like a dog (and may even have wet the bed). My God, thought Terenius, he is under the impression that I am Strindberg! What irony! it was only with difficulty that he managed to restrain his laughter. The coward, as guilty as sin, was obviously anticipating the blows that were about to rain upon him! His apparent terror almost restored the Professor's self-respect; he was beginning to enjoy the role of the vengeful husband, the bringer of fear. However, a glance in Hinde's direction quickly dispelled

149

that comforting illusion; she was staring at him with all the contempt he knew he deserved. "Who gave you permission to enter my bedroom?" she hissed. "Just look what distress your unwelcome presence has caused my ..." She was about to say "father," when a demon whispered in her ear and she was persuaded to utter a falsehood, persuaded to say, ". . . my new boyfriend."

*　　*　　*

Professor Terenius returned to Uppsala sick with foreboding. Why? Why was there not a spring in his step? Surely the news he carried was to his advantage, in that it would finally persuade Strindberg to formalize the estrangement and divorce Hinde, thereby freeing his mind for metaphysical pursuits. Some hopes! Professor Terenius was no judge of character – not living ones, at any rate – but he knew Strindberg better than that. He knew perfectly well that Strindberg would never wash his hands of Hinde in such circumstances; no, no, he would rather plunge them up to the elbows in the bile of jealousy. And, worse – far worse! – force the Professor to do likewise.

The train rushed towards Uppsala; through Marsta and Knivsta. With each passing station his dreams of scholarly acclaim receded, until he clearly saw the fate that awaited him. He would be forced, by Strindberg's over-powering obsession, to frequent Hinde's lodgings in search of her secrets, as though he were nothing but a latter-day tomb robber.

He ascended the wide staircase of 27 Kyrkogårdsgatan with a heavy heart, entered the quiet apartment and, as was usual after all such excursions, made his way straight to Strindberg's laboratory where he would – God help him – have to reveal Hinde's long-anticipated infidelity. To his

150

relief he saw, upon opening the door, that he had been reprieved. For Strindberg was not alone.

Leaning over the glimmering athanor was the Kemikum Institut's resident heart-throb, insouciantly dressed in a summer suit of crumpled white cotton, while his latest conquest sat in the corner, cross-legged upon a stool, leafing through the Italian edition of *Vogue*. If only Strindberg could be more like Max Bonnier, thought Professor Terenius. Why can't he be satisfied with the temporary possession of a woman's private parts, why does he need to own her eternally, body and soul?

Strindberg, pressing Bonnier's spotless sleeve to sustain the caesura in their conversation, turned his attention to Terenius, and saw immediately that something untoward had occurred. "Good God," he said, "if I were a director who had asked you to express shock and you appeared on my stage looking like that, I'd kick you off for over-acting." Terenius, taken aback, tried to relax, but found himself even more discomforted by the curious stare of the unknown woman in the corner. "Well," said Strindberg, "what have you got to say for yourself? We're all ears." "It's a private matter," Terenius whispered, "concerning your wife."

"I am Augustus Rex," thundered Strindberg, "I do not have a private life!" He strode across the room towards the Professor.

"There was a man in her bed," mumbled Terenius. Bonnier winked at his dark-haired companion. It was a gesture of reassurance, an attempt to assert their position as outsiders, as mere spectators in the drama that was unexpectedly unfolding. "Am I to understand," said Strindberg, "that I have been cuckolded?" "I believe so," replied Terenius. "I will not embarrass our guests by asking for your evidence," said Strindberg, "but I would appreciate a description of the unscrupulous young man who has taken such full advantage of my wife's whorish nature."

At those words the shame that had been dogging the Professor suddenly vanished, and its place was occupied by profound gratitude. Had he been elsewhere he would surely have knelt. Thank you God! Thank you for giving me the courage to enter Hinde's bedroom! "He was not *young*," he said, looking boldly at Strindberg, "on the contrary, I mistook him for you."

Professor Terenius regarded his audience as though anticipating applause for the excellent delivery of this punchline. But his triumph went unnoticed, for all eyes were already on Strindberg who, though portly, was performing a jig worthy of Charlie Chaplin. The news that his wife was consorting with his doppelgänger filled him with unexpected joy. "The dear girl still loves me," he murmured, "despite everything." How could he feel jealousy when his rival was not an individual but a mere substitute for himself? "You must meet my wife," he said, turning towards Max Bonnier, "you and your friend."

It took some time for Professor Terenius to grasp the true extent of his reversal. One of Strindberg's rages would have been bad enough, but this astonishing elation was actually even worse, being the portent of a reconciliation, a resumption of married life which would place the revenant, once again, beyond the Professor's grasp. It was true that Terenius had been unable to take advantage of his privileged position, was more of a dog's-body than a Prime Minister, but he had never lost faith in the old adage, had continued to believe that, like every other dog, he would eventually have his day.

"The resemblance was superficial, a trick of the light," he said, hoping to disqualify his previous statement. "A more considered look revealed a total stranger." To no avail. "First impressions are frequently the most accurate," replied Strindberg. "Is your wife that fickle?" asked Terenius. "Do you really expect her to welcome you back? And what of her new beau? Won't he have any say in the matter?" "He will disappear just as a shadow vanishes when the sun reaches its zenith," replied Strindberg.

* * *

Hinde was expecting him. She did not know what possessed her to mislead Professor Crustacea so maliciously but, having done so, she did not repent of her whopper. Let the old bastard stew in his own juices, she thought. Her malicious glee notwithstanding, she awaited the consequences with some nervousness. They arrived on a hot day in mid-July like the tail of a comet. The comet itself was Strindberg, of course.

Although he still had a key to the apartment he chose to seek admittance as if he were a guest. Hinde, wearing a silk kimono, opened the door and said, "Oh!" She had not seen her husband since that dreadful autumn, four years earlier, during which he had forced her to strip and poured acid over the discarded under-garments. Had he mellowed in the meantime? It did not seem likely, for nothing else about him had noticeably altered. If anything he appeared stronger, sterner. But time had been kind to Hinde too. Her robe was uttering a mantra; *look at me, look at me, look at me*. It clung to her body like a second-skin, revealing that her voluptuous curves were still firm. Her face was full, with only the merest hint of a double-chin. "Please," she said, "come in."

As he entered a strange woman departed; she looked like a peasant who had just looted a lady's wardrobe; in particular her rough hands seemed far too abrasive to slip into those delicate lace gloves. "Don't worry, I've got the list up here," she said, tapping her head; "butter, eggs, beef etcetera." The words were Swedish, but the accent was that of an ignorant Pole.

Strindberg kissed his wife upon the cheek. Had Hinde not known better she would have thought this a charming gesture, the tentative act of a genuinely shy man. His plump fingers remained upon her shoulders like a pair of epaulettes. He did not want to let her go. He liked the smell of her hair, still damp from the shower, he liked the proximity of her radiant flesh. His sensuality, dormant for so long, rose like the moon. It took all his will-power not to possess her on the spot. Hinde, who had been anticipating fireworks, was completely disarmed by Strindberg's undisguised desire.

She led him into the living-room wondering anew at his protean moods. There they sat side-by-side on the sofa like a courting couple. Strindberg had been an attractive man when he had first won Hinde's heart, but now he was irresistible. His enthusiasm and his fiery energy acted as an aphrodisiac upon her. She could feel her kimono parting of its own accord and made no move to preserve her modesty. Strindberg, observing the lavender coloured silk slowly open like curtains upon the whiteness of her naked thighs, felt the palms of his hands begin to tingle. He was about to reclaim his lost love. Hinde, surprised by her jealous husband's new-found loving-kindness, and amazed by the easy acquiescence of her body to unexpected desire, turned to kiss him.

Unluckily, Hinde's preoccupation with her visitor had made her deaf to the entreaties emanating from the bedroom. And so Papa Zelinsky, exasperated by his daughter's repeated failure to respond to his summons, arose from his bed and blundered into the living-room even as their lips were about to meet, thereby ending his internal exile. He was wearing a pair of flannel pyjamas that Strindberg, looking up, immediately recognised as his own. He also recognised the accuracy of the Professor's description; at first glance he could have been staring at his own reflection (albeit circa 1912). While the original was ruddy and robust, the facsimile was pale and gaunt, hardly worthy of Strindberg's jealousy. "So this is your new love?" he said mockingly.

Hinde, goaded by the unspoken sneer, arose abruptly and immodestly embraced Papa Zelinsky, loosening her wrap even more as she did so. "I think I've always loved this man," she said, "but yes, in a way you are right, for we have only recently rediscovered one another." Strindberg was unsettled by this response. How could she have *always* loved this man, he reasoned, if the *only* basis of their relationship was his resemblance to me? "You may think you love *him*," he said, "but you really love *me*. Indeed, the very fact that you *think* you love him actually *proves* beyond doubt that you love me."

"Who is this man?" asked Papa Zelinsky nervously (at the back of his mind lurked the fear of deportation). "My husband," replied Hinde. "I know who you are," said Strindberg, pointing an accusing finger at Papa Zelinsky. Such an assertion, so confidently delivered, confirmed the poor man's paranoia. He clutched his daughter's arm, seeking her protection. Strindberg, misinterpreting the gesture as proprietorial, laughed. "You pathetic old fool," he said, "do you really think that a red-blooded girl like Hinde will be satisfied by the *shadow* when she knows that she can have the *substance*?"

"What is he talking about?" asked Papa Zelinsky, aghast at the implication. "Tell this gentleman who I am." "She doesn't have to," replied Strindberg, "as far as I am concerned you are nobody. Now go!" Papa Zelinsky did not move a muscle. "It seems that you are going to have to dismiss him," Strindberg said to Hinde. "Please inform him that you love me, that you never loved him, even for a moment." "I'm afraid that wouldn't be true," said Hinde with mock solemnity. She paused for a moment to prolong and better enjoy her husband's discomfort. But seeing him so puzzled, so *crestfallen*, excited her pity and she decided to put him out of his misery, little knowing that their fragile reconciliation was based entirely upon the misapprehension that he was dealing with her *lover*.

"Mr Lagercrantz," she said, addressing Strindberg, "meet Papa Zelinsky." Strindberg seemed none the wiser. "Papa Zelinsky," repeated Hinde, "my *father*!" Strindberg blushed like a schoolboy.

"And who did you think he was?" asked Hinde, shaking with laughter, thinking that Strindberg, out of sheer relief, would share the joke – even though it was at his own expense. Hinde laughed so much that she did not notice the change in her husband's complexion, from red to apoplectic purple, laughed so much that her lavender kimono flew open. Whereupon Papa Zelinsky, demonstrating the real nature of his relationship, censoriously covered his daughter's naked breasts. "Your *father*!" screamed Strindberg, and was gone without a further word.

* * *

"Terenius!" he shouted. "Terenius! You are an imbecile. The man was her father not her lover." He had been angry when he had boarded the train in Stockholm, now he was furious. He had gone to Riddarholm with an undefended heart, ready to forgive, even prepared to resume married life. And what had happened? He had been humiliated by a shameless hussy. She had dug him a trap and he had fallen headlong into it. What a fool he had been to believe that

156

she still loved him. As if she ever did! It was he who had been the substitute, not vice versa. Hinde had obviously only married him in the first place because of *his* passing similarity to her father.

Strindberg had heard and half-believed the theory that the image of the murderer remains fixed upon the retina of the victim. At any rate he could not rid himself of the sight of Hinde laughing so hysterically that her wet hair scattered droplets and her body shed its single garment. He closed his eyes and what did he see? Her bare breasts dancing with glee! And what did he hear? The rushing of his blood? Oh no. He heard the same provocative duo singing a mischievous ditty in little-girly voices: *What beauties, what cuties, what a pity you can't touch, what a pity you can't have us.* They wiggled lasciviously. *What a pity*, they giggled, *what a pity*. "Terenius!" he shouted. "Where the devil are you? There is no point in hiding."

The only question that now required resolution was what part the Professor had played in the affair; had he been one of the plotters, or a helpless dupe like himself? Strindberg stationed himself in the centre of the living-room. Although it was late there were no electric lights in the apartment, but then it was mid-summer and the cloudless day seemed to have stopped decaying at twilight. *Why?* he asked himself. *Why would Terenius do such a thing to me?* Ah, if only he could look into the human heart as easily as the scientists in the Observatory across the road could penetrate the heavens. "Terenius!" he yelled. "Come here."

Eventually Terenius appeared. He seemed more angry than guilty, though (as Strindberg well knew) anger is often an effective disguise of guilt. "What is the matter?" the Professor snapped impatiently. "I am not a servant employed to do your bidding, you know. This is *my* apartment, and I too have important work to do

157

within its walls. As a matter of interest I was trying to decipher some newly acquired papyri when you broke my concentration. What is it you want?" No, Terenius is not that good an actor, thought Strindberg, his annoyance is certainly genuine.

Wrong again, August! The Professor's testy mood was indeed a defence mechanism adopted to better absorb the bitter disappointment that would surely attend upon Strindberg's return. But instead of the expected evil tidings came a diatribe; a mish-mash of curses and accusations, which Terenius endured with secret joy, for it seemed that Strindberg would be staying in Uppsala after all. Alas, my dears, the Professor's relief was as short-lived as a mayfly.

Before the week was out he was back in Stockholm. For three days he pretended to fish in the Mälaren, so as to be able to keep an eye on Hinde's apartment without arousing suspicion. He positioned himself on a long wooden platform, rocking mildly in the summer swell, and so became a temporary member of an odd community. His immediate neighbour, naked to the waist, was a middle-aged lothario with precisely waved grey hair and a black pencil moustache. Professor Terenius, who knew nothing about fishing, studiously averted his gaze, in order to ensure that no conversation developed between them. He need not have worried for it transpired that the piscatorial libertine was no more interested in the fish than Terenius, as became apparent when he was joined by a group of fellow conspirators who, whistling at all the passing women, behaved more like Italians than Swedes.

Fortunately the only other permanent resident was so dedicated to his task that he didn't even notice the Professor. He was an elderly gentleman attired in an anachronistic fashion; a tweed jacket and beige plus-fours. Terenius had borrowed his method from Huckleberry Finn, a piece of string and a bent pin, whereas this obvious expert held a nylon thread decked out with golden hooks and silver weights. It seemed that the glittering hooks were sufficient to snare the foolish sprats. Indeed, so many of them fell for this simple trick that the line was frequently pulled out of the water with three, four or even five fish shivering like silver leaves on a storm-tossed branch. The old gent calmly detached these and stuffed them, still living, into a polythene bag. Terenius, growing goggle-eyed, knew just how they felt.

Early on the fourth day Papa Zelinsky emerged, accompanied by a plain woman in extravagant clothes. Grateful Terenius quickly discarded his fishing tackle and trailed after them through the cobbled streets of Gamla Sta'n to a little cafe on Västerlåggatan. In olden days, when King Karl XV sat upon the throne of Sweden, it had been an apothecary shop, a fact the present owner chose to advertise by retaining the golden pestle and mortar that hung above the window, itself full of long-necked bulbous bottles that looked like a flock of multi-coloured Strasbourg geese.

The customers, however, were all Polish Jews. Moreover, the prevailing smell within was the dark and piquant aroma of roasting coffee, instead of the misleading dulcitude of formaldehyde or some other disinfectant. The proprietor, though Jewish, was Iraqi rather than Polish, having fled to Sweden with his family after the bloody events of 1958.

Terenius, addressing him in Arabic, ordered a cup of coffee and enquired what pastries were available. The proprietor, pleasantly surprised to hear the unfamiliar language of home, pressed a switch and the neon strip above the glass-fronted cabinet flickered before finally casting its light upon a tray of sweets that, being gilded with syrup and honey, resembled fabulous jewels. When I saw them I all but swooned, so over-powering was their sweetness. This pastry-cook had surely learned his art from the devil.

"As you see we have *baklava* and *konafa*," he said, as though reciting a litany, "we have *sanbusak bil loz* and *assabih bi loz*, we have *ghorayebah* that will melt in your mouth, we have *ma'amoul* or, if you prefer something creamy, we have *karabij*." "Do you, by chance, have any *trovados*?" enquired Terenius. The proprietor clapped his hands. "Sir, you are a mind-reader!" he exclaimed. "Only this morning my dear wife prepared a batch of *trovados* for a family wedding. She will be overjoyed if you sample one or two and receive a share of our happiness." Terenius was grateful for this warm welcome, otherwise he (the only Scandinavian in the room!) would have felt like an *utlänningar* in his own land, amid that continuous babble of Yiddish, Polish and unconventional Swedish.

The speakers sat upon pouffes or divans at tables that were round and marble-topped, or at tables that were long and wooden. The former were placed in shadowy alcoves, where couples – illicit or otherwise – could converse in privacy. Terenius settled into the vacant niche beside that occupied by Papa Zelinsky and his companion and listened in the hope of satisfying Strindberg's obsessive need for details. Fortunately the Professor's familiarity with German allowed him to understand all but the more arcane phrases of their alien tongue.

It was tantalization taken to the point of torture for sweet-toothed Beelzebub to remain unsatiated in that place; but I could not risk being seen, for I too wished to take heed of the conversation. I needed the help, albeit unwitting, of that immigrant couple. Twice already, whether by accident or design I do not know, I had failed to entrap Strindberg: as Mr Lagercrantz he had declined to murder his wife, even though it was the logical consequence of his misogyny; as Augustus Rex he had refused to be corrupted by power,

160

had not become the anticipated tyrant, although it was the logical consequence of his megalomania. There remained but one weakness to probe and to worry, in the hope that it at least would fester and bloom.

Years before, when Henrik Ibsen had declared that the Jews were "the nobility of the world," Strindberg had not disputed the sentiment, he had merely chosen to interpret *nobility* differently. He understood it to mean "people who are not manual workers," and thereby turned a well-intentioned compliment into a stick with which to beat the Jews. They were not born to mine gold, he argued, only to count it. And so, when capitalism arose, they became its natural aristocrats, the nobility of the new world, the natural enemies of the common people, of Augustus Rex and his loyal subjects (not to mention *Baal-zebul*). Of course it would have been perfect had Terenius stumbled upon a nest of conspirators, a Swedish cell of the Elders of Zion, but alas you inhabit an imperfect world and – like the Israelites of old – Beelzebub would have to do his best with what came to hand.

"I do not understand my hoity-toity daughter," Papa Zelinsky said, shakily raising a cup of coffee to his lips. "It's as though she were ashamed of me, her own father, not because I am a doddering old man, which I could forgive, but simply because *I dress like a Jew.* Do you know what she said to me the other day? 'Papa, you are so ostentatious. Don't you think you would be a lot safer if you didn't attract so much attention? One has to adapt oneself, does one not?' *Does one not?* Pah! I knew what lay behind those fancy words. She was saying it was *our* fault – what happened over there. If only we hadn't made the antisemites so mad by continuing to exist, by continuing to honour our traditions, then they wouldn't have persecuted us and killed us after all. She is only terrified that one of her neighbours will look at me and see an *ostjuden*. Do you understand what I'm saying, Mrs Bauman? I don't want to assimilate. *I don't want to become like her.*" He paused. "Be honest with me, Mrs Bauman. Can you really see this old Polish Jew turning into a Viking?"

Terenius missed Mrs Bauman's reply because other demands were made upon his attention by the beaming proprietor, who appeared bearing a small silver tray upon which were a cup of black coffee and the *trovados*. "With my wife's compliments," he said, as he placed the pastries before the Professor. "You must taste them immediately," he added, "she is very anxious to impress her relatives and fears that they might not be worthy. She refuses to believe me when I tell her how good they are. But you, a stranger, she will believe."

The cafe owner hovered expectantly while Terenius picked up a little fork and broke into one of the puffy bronze-coloured crescents, all of which were immobilised in syrup like insects in amber. Believe me, my dears, the damned in hell do not suffer worse torments than were my lot at that moment. Perfumes absconded from the broken cake as does the soul from the body, perfumes of rose water and of almond, ravishing scents that were followed by the luxurious flavours of sweet red wine and soft marzipan. "My wife calls them sticky kisses," said the proprietor. "Well," said Terenius, astonished by his audacity, "if she makes love as well as she bakes then you are surely the most fortunate man on earth." "Claudia," cried the patron, springing across his cafe like a gazelle, "Claudia, just wait till I tell you what the man said!" Professor Terenius smiled for the first time in many days. Here was a marriage that was no dance of death but a genuine pas de deux. Strindberg should be told. But he would not be interested; there was no drama in happiness.

All he wanted to know about was his father-in-law (God help the pair of them). So obedient Terenius listened and endeavoured to remember the conversation in the adjoining cubicle. "You are talking nonsense as usual," Mrs Bauman was saying, "no one expects you to behave like Eric Bloodaxe." "No," agreed Papa Zelinsky, "but they expect me to become a Swede. Well, I accept that I can become a Swedish *citizen* – a man prepared to pay taxes, salute the flag, and obey the laws of the land – and for that opportunity I go on my knees and give thanks to this country. Perhaps I will learn to say 'I come from Sweden,' but even if I live to be 120 I will not *feel* properly *Swedish*." He took another sip of his lukewarm coffee. "It has never been my habit to dance around a pole at midsummer," he said by way of conclusion, "and I do not intend to start now, at my time of life."

"More rubbish, and you know it," said Mrs Bauman. "Who has asked you to dance at midsummer? Has Hindele? Of course not! You are finding problems where none exist; such customs as you describe are no longer honoured in this land. Who knows? Perhaps that is why the Swedes are such a tolerant people. Papa Zelinsky, this is a good country, a very good country. They want us to stay. So why shouldn't we? Would it be such a terrible fate? Despite what you say, here we will be able to express our Jewishness without fear, unlike in the *alter medina*."

"Mrs Bauman," replied Papa Zelinsky, "as you know very well the majority of my family perished in the Holocaust. Because of them the whole of Jewish history is now gathered in my heart. The Poles couldn't empty it, and nor can my daughter. I am immune to her entreaties. But what of her children, my grandchildren? 'Of course I would like my children to feel Jewish,' she has said, 'but it would be much easier for them if they did not. I would not like them to suffer as you have done.' Tell me, Mrs Bauman, what was the point of our suffering and our survival if not to preserve our faith? No, don't say anything yet, there is worse to come. If my daughter had only turned her back on her people that would have been bad enough, but to deny her own flesh and blood as she has done is unforgiveable. I have searched every shelf and every drawer in her apartment for a photograph of my dead wife, may her dear soul rest in peace, but all in vain. Hinde does not possess a single portrait of her mother. Mrs Bauman, this cold land has frozen her Jewish heart. That is why we must go to Israel without delay, you and I. Lest we too suffer the same fate."

"I have held my tongue for long enough," cried Mrs Bauman, "I will not sit here any longer and listen to you tell such stories about Hindele. She loved her mother, and she loves you. If you want my opinion, they should give her the Nobel Prize for the way she has provided for you all these years, you ungrateful old wretch." Whereupon Mrs Bauman departed, pursued by Papa Zelinsky. Terenius handed the proprietor ten kroner and chased after them realizing, only then, that neither had paid their bill.

This incidental detail fascinated Strindberg. "That was no accident," he said, and ordered the Professor to continue the surveillance. Strindberg's intuition bore fruit. Such behaviour, as the Professor soon learned, was the norm. Though not exactly in the class of Bonnie and Clyde, Mrs Bauman and Papa Zelinsky had developed a criminal double-act of some style. On a subsequent outing Professor Terenius followed them into a large department store (Åhléns, if I remember correctly) and watched, with growing incredulity, as they set about their work.

They walked rapidly through the food hall, the crockery and cutlery departments (where Terenius thought he saw Mrs Bauman pocket a set of spoons, though that may only have been a trick of the light), until they reached a counter that overflowed with silk and chiffon scarves, as if it were a waterfall caught by the sun. Beside the neck-wear were ranks of elegant leather gloves, whose eloquent gestures could be variously interpreted as a signal to halt or an

164

appeal for alms. They also resembled (as it happens) the amulets that, in former years, were carved upon the tombstones of those lucky Jews who died peacefully in Central Europe. Here they separated.

Papa Zelinsky approached the shop assistant smiling shyly. "Dear lady," the Professor heard him say, "my only daughter's birthday is approaching and I have yet to buy her a present, a task formerly undertaken by my late wife, may she rest in peace. You are clearly a woman of taste, whose judgement I can trust. What do you suggest I buy?" The silly woman, charmed by this small talk, eagerly attempted to satisfy the old gentleman. Meanwhile Mrs Bauman unobtrusively filled her bulging bag with booty.

* * *

The revelation that Papa Zelinsky was a kleptomaniac heartened Strindberg. "What does the old fool want with such stuff?" he mused. "Can he really believe that material possessions will bring him security? I'll give him security!" So saying he picked up the telephone and (speaking anonymously) shopped his father-in-law to the authorities. This led to an unpleasant scene in Riddarholm, which concluded with the arrest of Papa Zelinsky and Mrs Bauman. "Murderers!" screamed Hinde as the official Volvo drove away with the guilty parties. Terenius was despatched to observe at their trial.

"Well," asked Strindberg, when his surrogate returned, "did they deport the bastards?" "On the contrary," replied Terenius, "they were acquitted." "Acquitted!" wailed Strindberg. "Why? Was the judge a Yid?" Terenius shook his head. "No," he said, "a team of eminent psychiatrists convinced him that the couple's anti-social behaviour should be pitied rather than punished, being a direct consequence of their past history – which had clearly traumatized them, probably for ever." "I haven't heard such nonsense since Dreyfus the spy was released," exclaimed Strindberg. "Does that soft-headed magistrate not realize what he has done? Is he not aware that his injudicious words will cause every Jew to believe that he can come to Sweden and behave as if he were a justified sinner?" He poured himself a glass of aquavit. "They may be able to get away with murder in Stockholm," he said, "but in Uppsala Augustus Rex takes a more robust view of justice." Alas, such an empty boast merely served to remind him of his impotence.

"My life is nothing but a sham!" he cried as he downed yet another glass of eau de vie. "I am nobody," he moaned, "a mere publisher of woes, a collector of other people's autobiographies." True enough, they queued to contribute to his anthology of miserabilia; the poor and the dispossessed, the unlucky and the unhealthy. They came by the dozen to Strindberg's apartments. One by one they were ushered into his presence by Terenius and recompensed for their hard-luck stories with gold, on the understanding that they did not disclose its source to the authorities. I must admit that I was not impressed either; when you have set a man up for damnation you expect him to commit greater crimes than tax evasion.

At first Strindberg had relished the excessive displays of gratitude, but latterly he had come to regard those fawning gestures as a travesty, a mock pageant performed by the King of the Beggars and his vassals. He was tired of play-acting, of being a monarch manqué; he longed to appear on a wider stage, to perform *great* deeds not *good* works. It depressed him to think that his name had currency only in the sewers of the city, that he was loved only by the lowly beneficiaries of his munificence. That was why he was drinking, because he was a lonely and a lovelorn man; because he was not a real king, because he had lost his queen.

Unable to bear the emotional constraints of his gilded cage, he bade farewell to Terenius, snatched his favourite jacket from the wardrobe, and quit the apartment. Where was he going? His jacket provided a clue; he always wore raffish velvet when he attended his Life Class at the Konsistoriehus. He went to those classes as another man might go to a brothel, he went to satisfy his sexual needs. Was he a voyeur? Not exactly. Voyeurs seek to be inconspicuous, whereas Strindberg chuckled continuously while he drew. At whom was he laughing? The models? No. He was laughing at their husbands and their lovers. Didn't they realize that while they were boozing elsewhere he was *possessing* their loved ones with his pencil, his *little penis*, possessing them body and soul? Only there, in the Konsistoriehus, did he feel truly *in character*; the sultan in his seraglio.

Entering the street he was almost blinded by the summer light. Blinking furiously, he staggered down St Olofsgatan passing, in this order, a barking labrador, the Universiteshus, the Cathedral, the Gustavianum and the fading portrait of a dead cyclist (whose name I have long-since forgotten). Strindberg accidentally stepped over the outline as he crossed the road and shuddered, as though he had just received a post-card from oblivion. His sketches of women were specific aide-memoires, but this crude likeness of everyman had become a general memento mori, a negative image of life. Did he therefore sink to his knees and thank Beelzebub for saving him from the universal fate? You must be joking! He perversely identified with the deceased. He felt anonymous, no better than a ghost wandering through the city streets. "Augustus Rex does not exist," he said to all who cared to listen, "his name is written on the wind."

The Konsistoriehus, an austere building, was located

in a cobbled plaza, the Domkyrkoplan, that ran from the Cathedral to the Fyris. Here, where the river was at its swiftest, stood an old mill with white-washed walls. Strindberg, still afflicted with self-pity, regarded them with the same hostility he used to reserve for blank paper. They were a deliberate affront, a reminder of his impotence, both artistic and political; they proclaimed, in a mocking voice, *Behold the mighty works of Augustus Rex*. He dug his hands into his pockets and unexpectedly felt the stubby remains of a black crayon, obtained from the Konsistoriehus. He rolled it between his fingers, until it felt warm and ready for use; at the same time some of his former confidence returned to him. Perhaps he was not impotent after all?

Behind him the red bricks of the ancient Cathedral seemed to be absorbing light, so brightly did they glow. Above them the clover-leaf windows, which extended from top to bottom of the twin spires, glittered like stars; clear indication that inspirational thoughts were being transmitted. Strindberg felt them wash over him like an invisible wave.

Having ensured that he was unobserved he approached the dazzling tabula rasa like a man with strabismus and, whipping out the crayon, quickly scribbled the words *Augustus Rex Rules*. I laughed out loud. "Who's there?" cried Strindberg.

In reality, it was not inspiration that had swept over Strindberg, but a million bluebottles, whose wings were fanning the warm air. The swarm passed over his head and alighted upon the wall before him, forming a metallic blue rectangle that shimmered in the sunlight. Strindberg watched in astonishment as countless yellow-backed beetles descended upon the flies, establishing a triangle and a disc within the larger shape. "Behold," I said, "the personal colours of Uppland's first monarch. Allow me to explicate the symbols. The triangle is obviously a mountain, a visual pun upon *berg*, though it could also be interpreted as a pyramid. The disc is the sun, the all-seeing eye. Between you and me, the pair can also be seen as the male and female parts displayed in their proper conjunction, with the triangle *penetrating* the disc."

"*Uppland*?" said Strindberg, still befuddled with booze. "Certainly," I said. "You have arisen from the grave, you have transmuted lead into gold, so why shouldn't you consolidate your power and transform the city of Uppsala into the independent kingdom of Uppland? It would make an ideal statelet containing, as it does, a royal palace, a national library, an ancient university, a cathedral and – on its outskirts – Gamla Uppsala, the country's pagan heart."

I could see that Strindberg liked the idea. "It is a good flag," he said. "I have every confidence that it will soon be flying from the topmost tower of the Castle," I replied, "unless Max Bonnier should happen to raise his first." "Max Bonnier?" said Strindberg. "What has he got to do with it?"

"I am astonished," I exclaimed. "Do you really not know that he is plotting against you? What did you think would happen after you allowed him access to the philosopher's stone? Did you honestly believe that he would be able to resist his genetic inheritance and not manufacture gold for his own purposes? Are you so naive, so unfamiliar with the habits of the Jews? Think of Papa Zelinsky. He is not an exception. He is the rule. Give the Jews an inch and they will take a mile. Already Max Bonnier is spending freely, the better to impress the beauties of the city, the better to buy their love. Thanks to your vanity, your need for *respectability*, you have created a dangerous rival who will – given half a chance – take-over your suzerainty and run you out of town.

169

The town that should, by rights, be yours!"

"What must I do?" he cried. "You must initiate divorce proceedings," I said, "and then stake your own claim to the disputed territory." Thus did Augustus Rex turn his back upon his life class and return to Kyrkogårdsgatan, driven by wild dreams of greatness.

*　*　*

Strindberg recollected our meeting as though it had been a vision or a waking dream. Either way he was inspired. He sat at his desk and quickly covered a sheet of fine cartridge paper with neatly drawn squares, rectangles and triangles, each of which was precisely framed by a perforated white border. Within these borders Strindberg subsequently painted the icons of Uppland; the prehistoric mounds at Gamla Uppsala, the Gustavianum, the Viking helmet from Vendel, the head of Augustus Rex. Having designed the stamps, he set to work on the coinage. That done, he set about the flag itself, and was applying the cobalt blue when Terenius surprised him by announcing that it was nine o'clock, time to turn on the Bang & Olufsen.

"Today I appreciate how the Palestinians must feel," Strindberg announced, wiping the blue ink from his fingers with a dirty cloth, while watching a report from the Middle East, "for I have come to understand that the only obstacle between my dream of Uppland and its establishment is a Jew – or rather, the Jews. They must be got rid of. Don't look so aghast, Terenius, I don't mean *killed* – I just want them transferred elsewhere. We must serve them their divorce papers, and ask them to leave the family home. I am well aware that Papa Zelinsky's dearest wish is to settle in the land of his ancestors. Very well, let all his people go there (better they steal from the Palestinians than from us); I mean *all of them*, not only those who want to go, but also those who think of themselves as Swedes. These invisible Jews are the most dangerous, the ones who have done the most harm to our society. Hinde, for example, always believed that in order to become a Swede it was necessary to adopt every one of our national prejudices. Flattered by such imitation the Swedes themselves have sunk into all kinds of decrepitudes, have produced a country stagnant with self-idolatry."

Suddenly his voice broke. "Pity me, Terenius, pity me, for as the Jews are to Sweden, so was Hinde to Strindberg; a false friend. She *pretended* to love me, as they *pretend* to love their adopted country." He covered his face with his hands.

Terenius did not reply. Minutes passed. At last Strindberg removed his hands and Terenius saw, to his astonishment, that Augustus Rex had been weeping. His cheeks were wet with tears and smudged with ink from his fingers. He looked primitive, wild, like Crazy Horse on the warpath. There was a malevolent gleam in his eye. "I will not permit them to spoil Uppland as they have spoiled Sweden," he said. "How will I stop them? With a cunning equal to their own, that's how. I will call my people together and describe to them how Papa Zelinsky sits in his little cafe in Stockholm and laughs at their most cherished beliefs. I will explain that this is the true face behind the urbane mask of Max Bonnier, who struts around Uppsala as if he owned the place. My eyes will be brimming with tears. Hand on heart I'll assure my audience that the bones of their mothers will lie uneasy so long as they fear for the welfare of their nation. 'What can we do?' they will cry. And I will tell them to go forth and rid the body politic of this alien bacillus!"

Professor Terenius was flabbergasted, not so much by the

sentiments (which he largely shared), but by the immortal scribbler's delusions of grandeur. It was one thing to buy the loyalty of fools with gold, it was quite another to exercise power over them. Besides the Swedes, the lower orders included, had surely grown too tolerant to conduct a pogrom – even if they really did hate the immigrants. However, he did not dare voice his doubts, he merely shook his head. Strindberg just laughed. "Oh, Terenius," he said, "this is a fine part I have conceived for myself, one of my finest. In the first place I will have the satisfaction of seeing Hinde humiliated. But – and this is the beauty of my scenario – this *personal* reward will merely be the *side-effect* of a much greater *political* achievement. Not only Hinde, but also Bonnier! Yes, my friend, irrational hatred of the Jews will be the passion that binds my little Upplanders, turns them from a miserable rabble into one people, one people under one leader. Having established unity in such a crude manner I will then be able to reveal my true colours and, through example and education, transform my subjects from pathetic ancestor worshippers into proud citizens of the modern world! Terenius, have faith, rejoice, for Augustus Rex is about to claim his birthright."

* * *

There are three royal burial mounds at Gamla Uppsala. These grassy hillocks, which bear a passing resemblance to the pyramids at Giza, contain the mortal remains of King Aun, King Egil and King Adils. There is a fourth mound, the Tingshögen, upon which stood the ancient ting or parliament (hence its alternative name, Justice Hill). I am Beelzebub, I know such things. Here it was that the aforementioned monarchs and their descendants used to address their subjects, though none had done so since the days of Gustav Vasa – none, that is, until

172

Augustus Rex ascended to the throne.

It was mid-summer's eve and the fields of gold that surrounded Gamla Uppsala, two miles north of the city proper, were filled with picnickers. They spread their chequered cloths upon the gleaming buttercups and dandelions, leaving bees to suck what nectar they could from undisturbed clusters of clover and snake's head fritillary. There is a legend which would have us believe that the fritillary first blossomed upon the battlefield of Fyrisvall, one purple bloom for every fallen Viking. Seeing the bees drain their nectar put me in mind of Samson's famous riddle: *Out of the strong came forth sweetness*. Out of the strong – the *Vikings* – came forth sweetness – i.e. *honey*. Leonine Strindberg (heedless of the riddle's hidden agenda) travelled to Fyrisvall like a Viking, bloated with dreams of glory. If everything went according to Beelzebub's plan he was destined to depart as the lowest of the low.

The bees continued to ravish the flora while other insects smacked their mandibles at the sight of so many fleshy intruders; the mosquito, the horse-fly and the bluebottle, whose idea of a midnight feast is to suck blood or sup upon the fragrant juices of over-maturity. At first the picnickers tried to protect their flesh (both the raw and the cooked) with energetic hand movements, but gradually they were overcome with lassitude and took fewer and fewer measures against the persistent drone; until the only sign of life in the great gathering was the rise and fall of a lackadaisical arm.

And so the nocturnal sun continued to shine upon the bread, the sausage, the beer and the cheese; upon the bare heads of the diners, upon their shirts and their summer frocks. Their bodies felt full and warm, ripe and ready to respond to the demands of the season.

One amongst them sipped champagne instead of beer,

173

ate avocado and cold salmon in place of simpler fare. Max Bonnier had come to Gamla Uppsala out of curiosity, anxious to see what other marvels the old alchemist had to offer. His new amante was younger than ever. Her dark hair was bobbed. She looked like a schoolgirl in a gymslip. She was . . . jailbait. Max poured her some sparkling wine to calm her nerves. She had just glimpsed her father, a religious fanatic, famous locally for the severity of his chastisements. "If he sees me here he'll kill us both," she wailed. "I'm not exaggerating, the last time daddy caught me with a man he punched him so hard that he broke his nose." "Don't worry," said Bonnier, stroking her hair, "we'll soon be lost in the crowd." She looked around and saw that he was probably right, the upturned faces were as innumerable and as indistinguishable as curds of cottage cheese. She stretched like a cat, gulped her champagne and, convinced of her anonymity, permitted Max access to her breasts for the first time.

Not everyone had chosen to eat al fresco. Hundreds of others wandered around the Mounds of the Kings and over the other graves in the vicinity. Had they really all come to bend the knee to Augustus Rex? Strindberg thought so. Professor Terenius, however, knew differently. Initially he had followed orders and passed the word that Augustus Rex had decided to address his subjects at Gamla Uppsala on a matter of international importance. The response to this announcement had been complete indifference, so Professor Terenius resorted to bribery and let it be known that a limitless supply of gold would be made available to all worthy claimants. However, he declined to inform Strindberg of this tactical manoeuvre – out of cowardice rather than malice, I would guess. As a result of this negligence Strindberg delivered his antisimetic oration completely blind to the fact that, so far as I was able to tell, the only one among the multitude who had not come for material gain, who had made the journey in the genuine

174

hope of enlightenment, was none other than Bonnier the Jew.

When Strindberg arrived, Professor Terenius, taking upon himself the role of fulsome acolyte, handed him a drinking horn filled with mead and, as the would-be monarch sipped the honey-sweet liquor, signalled to a barber's shop quartet (especially hired for the occasion) that it was time to commence their unaccompanied rendition of the famous song: "The Goths of old drank from the horn." On all other nights Strindberg would have snorted with derision at this unseemly show of nostalgia for a mythical past, but on that fateful night he had entered the character of Augustus Rex so fully that he was devoid of self-consciousness. He had achieved what most actors can only dream of; complete identification with his part.

Without relinquishing his hold on the horn he pushed his way through the throng and ascended the mound called Tingshögen. From the summit he looked down upon a sea of faces, all of whom (he still thought) had come to hear his words. "Today Gamla Uppsala!" he cried, testing the megaphone (stolen, by Terenius, from the gymnasium). "Tomorrow the city itself!" No one knew what he was talking about, but they cheered anyway. Strindberg, made vainglorious by the spontaneous acclaim, puffed out his chest and waved to his devoted subjects. Across the plain the spires of the Cathedral could still be seen, looking like a distant ship at anchor. He began his speech.

"And the children of Israel were fruitful, and increased abundantly, and multiplied, and waxed exceeding mighty; *and the land was filled with them.* Now there arose up a new king over Egypt, which knew not Joseph. And he said unto his people, even as Augustus Rex is saying unto his, 'Behold, the people of the children of Israel are more and mightier than we: come on, let us deal wisely with them; lest they multiply, and it come to pass, that, when there falleth out any war, they join also unto our enemies, and

175

fight against us, and so get them up out of the land.' But the Egyptians put aside those good intentions and made their lives bitter with hard bondage, in mortar, and in brick. Would that we could succeed where they failed and set them to rebuild here, upon the very mounds of Gamla Uppsala."

Strindberg ceased, as though overwhelmed by a Great Idea. "It remains a holy place," he continued. "*Here* in days to come let us bury our great departed. *Here* let us assemble to pray at moments of national distress. *Here* let us assemble to rejoice in times of great success. The place will be called the Temple of Memory, and the trees that surround it will be known as the Grove of Life. Yes, my friends, we need a Pantheon! But we will never get a Pantheon, the enemies of our people will see to that."

He paused. "I mean the Jews. They regard themselves as a noble race. I agree with them, they are a noble race, a chosen people, a people who look down upon those who are forced to dirty their hands with heavy labour. Believe me, my friends, they will not lift a finger to assist us in our endeavour. Oh, they will encourage us with fancy words, but all the while – behind those ingratiating smiles – they will be planning to rob us blind – as they robbed the Egyptians in the end. You may be sure that when the last brick of the Pantheon has been laid, the Jews will turn around and, picking up the keys, thank us for rebuilding *their* Temple in Uppsala's green and pleasant land. *All* Jews are of a likeness, my friends. I speak to you now from bitter experience. My wife is a Jewess and, through betrayal, has tried to rob me of my manhood. Her father mocks me, as he surely mocks you. Worst of all, I revealed the greatest secret of alchemy to a Jew. And how has he repaid me? By setting himself up as my rival. And will the honourable Max Bonnier, *Professor* Max Bonnier, share his gold with you, my friends? Of course he will, *so long as your member is circumcised.*

176

"But in their greed the Jews seem to have forgotten the iron laws of supply and demand; they have flooded the market with gold, thereby compromising its rarity and devaluing my own substantial treasury. My friends, while the Jews remain among us nothing is safe, neither our virility nor our patrimony, neither our blood nor our gold!"

At last he was using words the people could understand, words like *gold*! But what was he saying? Was he really saying that there was no more gold? Terenius, fearing that they would quickly come to this obvious conclusion, held his head in his hands and awaited the bloody riot. He heard the collective growl of outrage and, with shivering limbs, awaited his dismemberment. The people had been cheated, of that they had no doubt. But by whom? Surely not Augustus Rex? He was a windbag, but he was on their side. No, they believed him when he said that the real culprit was Max Bonnier, Max Bonnier the Jew.

Strindberg continued speaking, but already he had said enough to send the aforementioned semite running for cover. He found it among the more modest tumuli that pitted the ground some distance from the last of the royal mounds. Here he found a fine and private place, an unoccupied grave, the very thing in which to enjoy a furtive embrace. "Wow," he said to the girl as he unbuttoned her, "to think that I offered public approbation to that monster! There were signs, sure enough, but in my enthusiasm for the numinous I considered them immaterial." The girl, now naked to the waist, was too tipsy to recollect her earlier inhibitions. She raised her backside and allowed him to lift off her tiny skirt. Then she fell back, moaning softly. Her white panties gleamed like a film star's false smile in that shadowy hollow. The message was obvious; it stated, *I want you to love me*. Other sensory signals confirmed this sentiment as the pants were lowered. Bonnier the roué knew that the girl's apparent passivity was not indifference but an assumed pose; he sensed that she was making him a gift of her priceless body and he thanked her in his heart. He disrobed unhurriedly, carefully folding his socks, trousers and shirt. When he finally entered her he did so cautiously, anticipating virginal resistance, but finding only ease of passage.

My dears, I have no idea why rational human beings (as you certainly are) consider it so exciting to behave like the beasts of the field in such matters. Forget the indignity, what about the discomfort (especially for the woman)? Surely Bonnier and his young mistress would have been far more comfortable copulating on a mattress in his office, where there would have been little danger of discovery? Not that either of them seemed the least bit concerned about that possibility, judging by the groans, the grunts and the incessant demands for affirmative action.

Meanwhile, there was growing disturbance among the assemblage as more and more among them began to realize that no gold whatsoever would be forthcoming that night. A side-effect of the mental disquiet was a renewed awareness of bodily discomfort; suddenly, as though a spell had been broken, everyone began to scratch their volcanic mosquito bites, to stretch their cramped and aching limbs, and to relieve bladders distended by too many bottles of Åbro. Most of the men wandered to the perimeter of the crowd where they turned their backs and pissed directly into the open fields. Others, more modest, sought secluded locations.

One of these unsteady walkers was sufficiently careless to trip over the outstretched foot of Beelzebub and fall headlong into a bottomless pit (or so he thought in that moment of panic). Opening his eyes he saw what you and I already know; the pit contained a moveable bottom and it belonged to Max Bonnier.

Bonnier looked up, observed the uninvited guest, and whispered: "Fuck off." The man, too embarrassed to belly-

178

ache about manners, was about to meekly comply when he heard a familiar voice make the following complaint: "Max, why have you stopped?" He felt sick and dizzy and reached out to the grassy banks in order to steady himself. Cautiously he leaned forward and confirmed the reality of every father's nightmare; the abandoned girl, presently exhibiting the final throes of ecstacy, was indeed his own daughter, his only daughter, whom he loved in his way.

He could not contain himself and vomited; the beer and the sausage, the kräfta and the potato salad, the prawns and the pumpernickel, all spewed forth upon Max Bonnier's unprotected back and buttocks at exactly the same moment as his own seed was projected into the girl's belly. I don't think Bonnier realized what had happened until the stink penetrated his post-orgasmic daze, and by then it was too late; the man had seized him by the scruff of the neck. "Right, Maxie," he said, raising the potential Nobel prize-winner with his horny hand, "let's have a look at you." Bonnier instinctively assumed the worst; that he was about to be murdered and his erstwhile partner ravished over his dead body. It struck him as an absurd and unworthy fate; this was 1968, extra-marital sex was no longer supposed to be a capital offence. But who will tell that to this demented avenger?

Only when the girl screamed, "Daddy!", did he recognise the true nature of the situation. He was so relieved that he actually laughed. He had often wondered what would happen if he were cornered by the husband of a recent conquest, but he had never considered the possibility of capture by an outraged father – surely a lesser evil. "My dear fellow," he said, "I realize that you have just had a terrible shock, for which I am truly sorry. But in all honesty that is all I have to apologise for. Your daughter is above the age of consent, and she consented." "No I didn't," she whispered from her supine position.

Bonnier — who realized what accusation would inevitably follow — regarded his transducer with a look of utter astonishment. He thought: What harm have I ever done her to deserve such treatment? The answer, *none*, hardly needs stating. She was, of course, merely trying to save her own skin. "Daddy," she said, "I have just been raped by this man."

Now it was Bonnier's turn to experience trauma (it being one thing to expect certain words, another to hear them). Her father inspected the alleged violator, as if searching for scratches, but found instead more damning evidence; a shiny prick, glazed with a cocktail of semen and vaginal fluids, a prick that was unmistakeably circumcised. "Well, Maxie," said the man, with artificial bonhomie, "It seems that you're a Jew." Bonnier didn't like the phrase *it seems*, which implied (with menaces) that he had been hoping to conceal the fact (which thereby became incriminating). However, he liked what came next even less.

"His name isn't Maxie," cried the terrified girl, throwing herself upon the mercy of the citizens' court, "it's Max, Max Bonnier!" "Cover yourself, slut," replied her father, by way of thanks. Bonnier attempted to do likewise, but did not get very far. "Not you," said the man. "you can stay as you are." The girl slowly arose, plucked a few blades of grass from between her damp buttocks, and picked up the scrap of white cotton that still bore the markings of desire. "Before you put those on," said her father, "make sure you wipe the Yid's sperm from your legs." She dried herself with a kleenex and dressed in silence.

Then the three of them began their odd procession through the prehistoric cemetery, proceeding uneventfully until they reached the first circle of Bonnier's private hell. Here he was introduced to his first tormentors thus: "This is Max Bonnier the Jew. He may have robbed you, but he has raped my daughter." The word passed through the crowd like an advance guard, so that everywhere they walked Bonnier's crime was already known. Many were the outraged souls who stabbed at him with forks and cheese knives, lacerating his legs and feet which began to drip with blood. So many flies congregated upon these fresh wounds and upon his back, where the vomit was slowly drying, that he seemed to be covered with a pelt of mobile body hair. Otherwise he remained naked. Demanding vengeance they dumped him unceremoniously at the base of the Tingshögen.

Strindberg, who remained ignorant as to why the groundlings were so agitated, naturally assumed that they were responding to his oratory. Therefore, when every man and woman unexpectedly fell to their knees, he almost burst with self-satisfaction. How was he to know that they were actually responding to *my* artistry, to the collective vision that had suddenly been visited upon them by Beelzebub? I wanted to ensure that they would accept nothing less than a mid-summer sacrifice.

Now I don't suppose that many of you were aware that a considerable portion of Strindberg's oration — in particular that part dealing with the Pantheon — was pilfered from an essay written by his erstwhile comrade-in-arms, Carl Larsson, sixty years previously. Larsson, you may recall, was the man to whom Strindberg addressed his individualistic portrayal of the Sphinx. Their relationship had commenced in the 1870s, when the hot-blooded young artist had carelessly impregnated a serving girl. Strindberg immediately consoled him with the thought that such ill-conceived children often die and advised him thus: "Next time you fuck those girls, put something in between!" This intimate friendship, thus consolidated, lasted for over a quarter of a century until Strindberg abruptly terminated it by declaring that Larsson was a synthetic person who had grease-paint permanently fused with his skin. Even his beard, which was real, looked false. Larsson, for his part, rushed off brandishing an ornate knife to despatch "the revolting skunk." The murder never took place, not a drop of blood was spilled, but the dagger with the golden hilt reappeared, concealed behind the back of a red-robed priest, in Larsson's monumental *Midvinterblot*.

It was this painting made animate that everyone saw when they turned their attention to the top of the Tingshögen. Augustus Rex was still there, but he was no longer a singular figure on a lonely hillock. Now he was a true monarch, clothed in raiments of silk, amid a scene of mythical splendour. The crowd gasped, for it was as he said it should be. A marble-fronted Pantheon, decorated with rampant lions of gold, stood there gleaming in the eternal light. It was flanked by fir trees which bore the bleached skulls of wild beasts in place of conifers. Augustus Rex himself stood dead centre, before the temple gates. Beside him was a throne wrought from solid gold. He was flanked by a pair of goats. To the right were helmeted warriors with spears and shields, to the left were musicians blowing into long trumpets and curling horns. Their notes resounded, thrilling the crowd, which pressed closer and closer to the Hill of Justice. Some began to chant, others to dance. Still others formed a circle around the red-robed priest and his captive, naked save for the wolf-skin that hung from his shoulders. The father of the mendacious girl forced his way through the human chain and pressed a knife into the hand of the priest. "Do the deed with this!" he demanded. The priest said nothing but turned away and, with crab-like steps, slowly led the prisoner up the slope of the Tingshögen. They did not cease until they reached their appointed places in front of the throne of Augustus Rex. There the red-robed priest faced the king and presented his captive, while the restless crowd below whistled and bayed for his blood.

Strindberg looked upon the great scientist and was horror struck. Despite his incendiary rhetoric he was genuinely averse to the sight of human suffering; his ultimate target had always been the achievement of imaginary triumphs, not the physical elimination of his enemies. When he said of someone, "I hope he dies," he was merely wishing *theatrical* failure upon him. His whole life was really a series of happenings, each designed to bring about a dramatic catharsis, from which all were supposed to recover and – with many a thespian hug – to take their curtain call. Not for him the irrevocable judgements of real life. His weltanschauung could be summed up thus: "All the world's a stage, and all the men and women merely players."

This unworldly philosophy explains the profound shock he felt upon recognising the fact that – this time – the blood on the boards was the real thing. However, he did not panic, even when he recognised that Max Bonnier was in mortal danger. He was confident (not unreasonably, given his limited view of events) that, having got him into this predicament, he could also talk him out of it. Fully consistent with his conviction that the quotidian was essentially theatrical was his belief in the logos, in the power of language to create new worlds.

You know that he eventually succeeded in manufacturing gold only because of my intervention, but try telling that to Strindberg. He remained of the opinion that it had all come about simply because he had uttered the magic words *fiat aurum* with sufficient vigour. Likewise he had no doubt that he could calm the troublesome crowd as easily as God smoothed the turbulent waters on the first day of creation. But God did not have Beelzebub to contend with – not then at any rate.

"I am Augustus Rex," he thundered, "only I have the power of life and death in Uppland." To my astonishment the forward motion of the crowd automatically ceased as if its constituent parts had all been turned to stone. Strindberg smiled at Bonnier. "You will be safe now," he announced.

However, his confidence was misplaced, the assurance premature. The masses had been stopped in their tracks not by his commanding voice but by the simple need to reconcile his words – which suggested a stay of execution – with the whole mise en scène *as they saw it* – which allowed for nothing but sacrifice. Having done so (by naively disregarding the former) their surge recommenced with even greater momentum.

It swept them to the summit of the Tingshögen, into the very heartland of their nation's history. They were there when Sweden, the land of the Svea, was young; when the people lived in fear of the sun that would set and never rise, of the seed that would be scattered and fail, of the death that would take them all. Unless the deities could be propitiated with a blood sacrifice. And who was more appropriate than Bonnier the Jew, the stealer of treasure and the ravisher of daughters, the stranger whose very presence was so offensive to their gods? Thus was Max Bonnier transformed from criminal to scapegoat and placed beyond the help of rational defence.

At the same time the rabble, suddenly conscious of its divine purpose, became anxious to act in accordance with time-honoured procedures. The people debated the matter of Bonnier's hands. Should they be bound? Should his head be anointed with holy oil? Who knew about such things nowadays? Eventually some firebrands lost patience with the niceties and two of their number stepped forward and seized Bonnier's arms, while a third grabbed a handful of his wavy hair and jerked his head back, thereby baring his throat for the blade. "What next, Mr Lagercrantz?"

he gasped. Hearing this, Terenius (who was, poor thing, holding the knife) began to show signs of hysteria. "Mr Lagercrantz! *Mr Lagercrantz!*" he cried mockingly. "Do you really not know who this is?" "Be quiet, Terenius," snapped Strindberg, sensing what was to come. "Why maintain this stupid secrecy?" demanded Terenius. "The man will be dead in less than a minute. He has a right to know who killed him."

These words brought Bonnier a moment of reprieve, as the awesome responsibility of their undertaking suddenly oppressed the multitude – this wasn't a charade, they really were going to do it, really were going to take a human life. Within the next sixty seconds a great taboo would be breached, a sacred commandment broken, all in the name of dimly remembered superstitions.

Being the scion of a different tradition Bonnier prayed for a ram to take his place; but of course none was forthcoming. Angry with himself for resorting to such irrational remedies Bonnier sought an escape elsewhere. He began to ponder, with increasing desperation, the aforementioned fact that was being denied him. Would it make a difference? He knew that King Aun, presently beneath an adjacent mound, had the unfatherly habit of sacrificing one of his sons to Odin every ninth year, just so as to lengthen his own life. Could he be the victim of a madman who thought himself the reincarnation of that monster? Or was he merely the unfortunate subject of another pseudo-scientific experiment, a human version of a laboratory animal, about to be despatched for the sake of a madcap theory concerning immortality?

Aware of the hesitation wrought by his cri de coeur Terenius decided to make public his knowledge – for the second and last time – in the forlorn hope that it would finally bring the people to their senses. "My friends," he shouted, "do not proceed with this madness. You have

185

been led astray – as I have been – by the forces of evil, by a revenant from beyond the grave. This demagogue, who calls himself Lagercrantz at some times and Augustus Rex at others, is actually . . . is actually August Strindberg."

Strindberg's conceit was greater than his anger; instead of demolishing Terenius with a furious blow, he scrutinized the audience so as to measure its response to this sensational revelation; he looked in vain, there was none. In fact only one person had paid any attention to Professor Terenius: Max Bonnier. *Oh God*, he thought, *they are as mad as each other*. However, having no other option he decided to address their insanity.

"You are a scoundrel and a coward," the naked scientist whispered to the ersatz monarch, "you have mesmerized these thugs so that they will perform the deed you dare not do. You are not a *man*!" Augustus Rex, already humbled, was *enraged*. He snatched the razor-sharp weapon from that waverer Terenius and, swinging it wildly, charged a harmless flock of greenfinches feeding upon a cluster of ripening grass-seeds. As they took off he slashed at them and *accidentally* decapitated a straggler. The headless finch dropped to the ground where, for a few ghastly moments, the unlucky bird attempted to continue its journey by beating the ground with its wings.

Bonnier's understandable horror led him to a false assumption; that the finch was not a substitute – as the ram had been in the akedah – but an hors d'oeuvre, a tit-bit to whet the general blood-lust. "Kill me too! Kill me!" he yelled at Augustus Rex. "You have proved that you can butcher an innocent creature without a qualm. Now I'm convinced that you *really* want to see my blood and my brains on the chopping block. You are a *meshuggener*, the sort that drinks out of skulls, and feasts upon hearts roasted whole."

"Don't take any notice of him," pleaded Terenius. "You have drawn the first blood, and the people will respect you and follow you because of it. You are Augustus Rex! You are Horus, our latter-day Pharaoh! All you have to do is give the order and he will be saved."

What happened next remains the subject of controversy. Some of the investigating officers prefer to believe that Augustus Rex did his best to spare the priapic genius, notwithstanding the latter's insulting behaviour. In short, they put the blame on mass hysteria. Others maintain that his ire was aroused by Bonnier's misguided provocations, and that the fatal blow was therefore his and his alone. They are right. He slit Bonnier's throat from ear to ear.

Swish went the knife, as though a curtain were opening upon the final act. The spectators gasped as the flesh parted and thick streams of blood spurted from the severed arteries. A look of astonishment crossed Bonnier's face when he realized that his death was upon him. He thought with infinite regret of the universal secrets he had perceived but failed to penetrate, of the women he had desired but not fucked, of the Nobel prizes he had dreamed of but would never win. He remembered his beautiful wife and wept.

Tears streamed down his cheeks as he struggled to retain his consciousness, fought desperately to sustain his awareness of self; believe me, my dears, if will alone were sufficient he would have stayed alive. But his life-blood was flowing from him, and the boundaries between his body and the world were diminishing by the moment; he tried to speak but all he could emit were unfamiliar sounds over which he had no control. He was unable to order his thoughts. He only knew that he had to resist the overwhelming demands of his innards. No, no, no, no. YES! A final gush of blood marked his unconditional surrender. It was succeeded by a trickle. Bonnier's heart had stopped pumping. Only then did they let him fall.

Why did Strindberg do it? Had madness finally overtaken him? Or did he believe that Beelzebub would somehow intervene between the deed and the dying, and make Bonnier the same offer that he had made to him? A glance at the flies and other verminous insects now dining freely upon the gore, quickly disabused him of that fallacious presumption – their so-called Lord was clearly *not* in the vicinity. No, on this occasion I was happy to leave the carcass to Azrael's tender mercies, and accept the consolation prize of Strindberg's soul.

It was then that I chose to send ten thousand mosquitoes to arouse the entire population of Uppland from its hypnotic slumber. They awoke from their nostalgic dream into a midsummer nightmare. Their leader, Augustus Rex, was standing before them with a smoking dagger in his hand. At his feet was a naked corpse. Each man looked to his neighbour and saw a good, a tolerant, and an honest Swede. How could they have allowed such a thing to happen, in their country of all places? Then they recollected the words of Terenius and knew that he was right. *They had been led astray.* Accordingly they booed Augustus Rex and, still hissing, turned their backs upon him. Before long only three people remained at Gamla Uppsala; of these one was already dead, a second was contemplating suicide, and the third was raving mad.

Strindberg dropped to the ground like a great tree that had been felled and, abandoned by all, rested there until the dew had drenched him. When he arose his heart was changed from that of a man to that of an animal. He ate grass like the oxen. As the months passed his nails grew like the bird's claws and his hair was matted like an eagle's feathers. And so he lived among the beasts of the field and the beasts of the forest until nearly all had forgotten there had been such a one as Augustus Rex.

EPILOGUE : 1975

For seven years August Strindberg roamed the wild lands like a moonstruck calf.

From Uppsala he went directly north to Österbybruk and Lövstabruk, where the red-hot fires of the ancient iron foundries made weary Beelzebub homesick. After fire came water. He tramped along the crowded beaches from Rullsand to Gävle, but there he did not linger. The road pointed north and he took it. On and on he went until, at Sundsvall, he quit the rocky coastline and turned west toward the old town of Östersund. How did he live? Kind people took pity on him, especially when the nights grew colder. They offered him a hot meal and a bed; and in return he entertained them with a story. A simple tale, or so it seemed at first. However, long before the narrative was complete the listeners began to shift uncomfortably in their seats, having recognised in it their own most secret fears and desires. Thus did our wanderer gain the reputation of a seer, of a holy fool.

He left Östersund and crossed the Jämtland peaks and the plains beyond until, months later, he came to Luleå at the northern end of the Gulf of Bothnia. Here he was befriended by a cobbler – a dealer in soles, like me – who offered him a new pair of boots in return for an afternoon's entertainment. The man was an artist, the Rodin of reindeer hide. Kneeling before Strindberg he

189

laced the buttery boots from ankle to knee. Properly protected, Strindberg set off for Boden. Beyond Boden the settlements were few and far between; oases of light in the dark, dark forest. The inhabitants were generous but quiet; they asked no questions and received no replies. Before long it was generally assumed that Strindberg was dumb.

Still he kept walking. The trees thinned out. Heather flourished in their absence. The ground was boggy. He was alone, save for the reindeer, which bolted at the sight of him. After many days the terrain changed and reddish rocks erupted from the tundra, as though the planet were suffering from acne. One morning, when Strindberg emerged from his wayfarer's cabin, he saw that the bare ground was laced with snow. He was not deterred. The rocks became mountains. The snow grew deeper. Soon it was the season of perpetual night. He was approaching the Arctic Circle. He crossed it near Jokkmokk and reached Kiruna, not without difficulty, on the last day of 1968. He rested there, in the shadow of the iron mountain, for a week or so, then took the train to Abisko, near the frontier with Norway. Lake Torneträsk was frozen.

The locals, who should know, have a golden rule: under no circumstances should anyone hike alone. Strindberg ignored it. He set off down the Kungsleden, the Royal Trail, without a map or a compass, let alone a guide. When he neither returned nor showed up at the various shelters en route, a search party was assigned the task of finding him. It failed. There was no trace, not even a footprint in the snow. He was written off, left for dead.

So there was something of a sensation when he suddenly appeared at the Trail's end many years later. Although a diet of lingonberries had dyed his beard blue, and the elements had tanned his skin until it was the colour of mahogany, there was no doubting his identity. A visit to the barber merely confirmed it. He was . . . the missing man! Great was the curiosity. Many were the questions. What was his name? Where had he been? On what had he lived? Why had no one seen him? Was he a hermit? A misanthrope? A pantheist? An anthropomorphist? Had he been cared for by animals? Was he any the wiser? To which he gave not a single reply. He simply turned his back on the good people of Tärnaby and set off down the long road to Umea and the coast.

The harbour was full of boats; he had no destination in mind, so he stowed away on the nearest one. It happened to be bound for Stockholm. For two nights he slept on the deck, in a gap between crates. At dawn on the third day, as the boat sailed slowly through the archipelago, he arose and beheld a cream-coloured lighthouse erect upon a rocky outcrop. Normally the light shone from its head like the shafts of a slowly revolving propeller, but not today. Today it threw out light in a radiant circle; for its integral luminescence had been augmented by the reflected glory of the rising sun. Strindberg had witnessed all manner of celestial wonders – eclipses of sun and moon, shooting stars, meteors, comets, rainbows, not to mention the aurora borealis – but this vision moved him more than all of them. For the light had penetrated his darkness, flooded even the most obscure recesses of his memory. The longer he looked at the lighthouse the stronger became his sense of déjà vu, until he was fully convinced that he had experienced a comparable illumination years before. And he was right!

"I woke up and went up on deck," he had written in the *Occult Diary*; "didn't know where we were; saw the lighthouse at Korsö in the light of sunrise. Felt ecstatic and saw some perspective on the future, connected with the lighthouse! Many times in my life I have remembered that moment, one of the most wonderful in my life." Well, he remembered it again that April morning, it came upon him as a revelation. *I am that lighthouse*, he thought, *le phare, c'est moi.* After seven years of existing only in the here and now Strindberg once again had some *perspective on the future.*

* * *

As is well known, it is harder for a camel to pass through the eye of a needle than for the uninvited guest to enter a Swedish apartment. Since Strindberg's unpremeditated flight the front door of 27 Kyrkogårdsgatan had been fitted with a digital lock, the combination of which was known only to the residents, their loved ones, and the postman. It was a shocking discovery.

Strindberg had expected to re-enter his former life as naturally as a ship returns to its home port after a long voyage. His plan was to sneak unannounced into the laboratory, restart the production line, and then amaze Professor Terenius with his presence. His failure even to enter the building therefore filled him with foreboding.

In an attempt to diminish these intimations of disaster he turned the corner into St Johannesgatan, browsed through some recent editions of his correspondence in the second-hand bookshop, and ordered a cup of black coffee in the nearby cafe. Sipping it, he decided that he should return to his former residence and, the day being warm, patiently await the emergence of Terenius or at least a neighbour prepared to admit him.

He was fortunate. Within a few minutes the old lady whose valuable biblioteque had burned so brightly all those years ago could be seen approaching slowly, carrier bags from Åhléns in either hand. Strindberg had no difficulty in recognising her though, if anything, she looked younger. (No, my dears, I was not responsible. She had not disposed of her soul. It was simply that she had been leading a far healthier life since the destruction of her library – less reading and worry, more fresh air and exercise etcetera.)

"*God morgon,*" she said, when she was close enough to identify Strindberg's features. "Am I to deduce that you remember me?" he enquired. "I'm hardly likely to forget you," replied the lady. "The police must have shown me your photograph a hundred times." "The police?" asked Strindberg. "Of course," she said, "there was the little matter of Professor Bonnier's death and your simultaneous flight. It was a very suspicious thing to do. I know for a fact that they would have charged you with his murder if it hadn't been for Professor Terenius."

"Professor Terenius," said Strindberg, "what did he do?" The woman dropped one of her bags and put her hand to her mouth. "Oh," she said, "don't you know?" "Know what?" asked Strindberg. "Poor Professor Terenius did away with himself," she announced. "Did away with himself?" gasped Strindberg, almost at a loss for words. "Oh, there's no doubt about it," she said cheerfully. "They found a note. Of course no one's supposed to have any idea of its contents. But you know how people are, somehow the word spread. Apparently Professor Terenius heard voices; the most prominent being that of August Strindberg – to whom you bear an uncanny resemblance, if you don't mind me saying. Anyway, although there was never any real proof, the police decided that the best thing for all concerned would be to blame the murder on a deceased madman and forget about it. Which is what they did."

"How did he do it?" he asked. "What, the murder?" she enquired. "No," he said, "how did he kill himself?" "Oh," said the woman, "that was the most bizarre aspect

193

of all. It seems that he had been hoarding the kernels of peach stones for ages. Just like a squirrel. They are very poisonous, you know. Deadly, in fact. Anyway, he ate a whole bowl, enough to demolish an elephant. Those who saw the body say his face was contorted by pain, hideously so."

The lady punched out her number on the lock, causing the door to buzz and swing open. She smiled at Strindberg. "Would you care for some tea, Mr Lagercrantz?" she enquired. Strindberg shook his head and fled. "What's your hurry?" she called. "Wouldn't you like to meet the delightful couple who have taken over your old rooms?"

* * *

Where else could he turn but to Riddarholm? Of course he no longer knew if Hinde was still living there, it being probable that she had taken up with another man and moved elsewhere. Nor did he know what had become of Papa Zelinsky. Perhaps his final oration at Gamla Uppsala had borne other fruit; perhaps the old man had been driven from Sweden by antisemites, or perhaps he had died and been buried, as is the fashion among the elderly. Even if their circumstances had not altered dramatically it remained highly unlikely that he would receive a cordial reception from either one. If he knew Hinde she would first spit in his face and slam the door upon him. Accordingly he did not approach his former residence directly, but made for the same floating platform once occupied by the late Professor Terenius.

As you may recall, the Professor was compelled to counterfeit an interest in marine life so as to justify his continuing presence in the neighbourhood. Strindberg found a more comfortable hide-out in the hull of a Viking longship which had been moored thereabouts in the intervening years. At its prow was the head of a dragon that breathed real fire, at its stern was an erect tail that concluded in a whorl. Fearsome young men strode its deck; their beards were blond and flowing, their helmets were horned. Swords were strapped around their waists. But in their hands, which should have been whirling mighty hatchets, were notebooks and plastic trays. These emasculated Norsemen took the orders of tourists and weary fishermen to whom they subsequently delivered steaming bowls of ärter och fläsk, or plates of köttbullar and blodpudding, not to mention innumerable cups of coffee – many of which were destined for Strindberg's little table, whence he was able to keep much of Riddarholm under constant surveillance.

It was a fine Sunday morning in May. A few families walked briskly to church but most, being cheerful agnostics, strolled aimlessly along the waterfront. A poodle barked, a child laughed. Lovers clasped hands, men purchased roses for their mistresses. Images of sex and death filled Strindberg's mind as he watched the parade; he wondered about the genitals of the men and women, he pictured their frenzies, and named the illnesses and accidents that would kill them all. He could not help but regard the normal flow of life with a certain schadenfreude; it being his revenge for the brief interludes of pleasure that were denied to him. He considered it a curious paradox that those who feared death the most could still experience joy, whereas he who had no need to count his days was a stranger to quotidian happiness.

Why had his four marriages all been such disasters? Why had he failed to find peace with Hinde? He viewed that final relationship with judicial calm, not flinching even when it came to the matter of sexual congress. There had been problems; not of potency, but of engagement. Strindberg had been unable to put himself in the picture, as it were, to conceive of himself as an object in the third dimension. And if *he* was not present during fornication it followed that Hinde was actually making love to *another*. No wonder he had been compelled to leave a woman who had practised infidelity with her own husband! He considered the premise that he was constitutionally unsuited to marriage and did not find it wanting. It was hardly the ideal state for a man who was both eternally present – as observer – and eternally absent – as participant.

The obvious solution was to eschew sexual intercourse altogether, to concentrate exclusively upon the life of the mind. He congratulated himself upon the excellent beginning he had already made, exemplified by his ability to envision Hinde's private parts without any concomitant reaction in his own. The undeniable truth, to which he had so long been blind, was that intellectual ability rather than sexual prowess or vulgar popularity distinguished him from the crowd. If he genuinely wished to perpetuate his fame he would do well to forget Mrs Lagercrantz and Augustus Rex and to concentrate all his energies upon adding to the works of August Strindberg.

The appearance of Hinde abruptly terminated these well-meant meditations. There she was, across the gilded water, arm-in-arm with her father! Strindberg turned pale. His heart raced. Worse, there was evidence of spontaneous tumescence in his pantaloons. So much for his scientific detachment! He turned his face away, deeply ashamed of his obvious susceptibility. Despite her innumerable betrayals it seemed that he still desired his false wife! How could he ever hope to take control of his destiny when he couldn't even master his own prick? Strindberg knew in his bones that he should let her go; but it was equally clear that he never would. He settled his account and charged after her as the Egyptian chariots had pursued the fleeing Israelites.

Apparently Hinde and Papa Zelinsky were in no hurry,

though they were not without purpose. Why else would they have entered the New Town via the Strömbron, the most distant of the available bridges? This took them directly to the Kungsträdgårdsgatan, which should ring a bell, it being the location of Hinde's lost childhood. Could this be an attempt to retrace those halcyon days? It seemed so, for they soon turned right into Wahrendorffsgatan. Keeping his distance Strindberg did likewise, expecting them to enter the synagogue.

They didn't; instead they bisected a small park, passed the Dramatiska Teatern (which was advertising a new production of *The Dance of Death* starring Erland Josephson), and marched along Nybrogatan until they came to the Jewish Centre, which proved to be their real destination. A large poster on the door proclaimed – in bold blue letters – the commencement of the Judisk Kulturvecka. What had happened to Hinde that she should be interested in such things? Had Papa Zelinsky turned the tables and, having kicked the idea of assimilation out of the window, forced his daughter to become an Israelite? Or had she fallen under the spell of a co-religionist who insisted that she be re-koshered? There was, of course, an easy way to find out.

Strindberg opened the iron door, quietly ascended the stairs, and entered a crowded hall on the second-floor. He found an empty seat near the back. A symposium of sorts was in progress.

"And now, my dear comrade," said the prematurely bald chairman to one of the participants, "perhaps you could open the proceedings by explaining why you became a writer."

"Oh, for the very best of reasons," he replied, "Freudian ones. I wanted to attract women, and found I operated better at a distance. My first attempts were therefore letters.

197

Then I surmised that the recipients would be even more impressed if I could get these efforts published. Only much later did it occur to me that my ambitions were somewhat limited. Now I want to seduce the world." He looked around the room and smiled ingratiatingly. "Though I'll settle for the audience this morning," he concluded.

Strindberg (once again the dandy) examined his prospective bed-fellow and realized that he must have given some thought to his dowdy outfit of corduroy and tweed, as much as you could expect from an Englishman at any rate. However, it was as nothing in comparison to that devoted to *his* by the gentleman beside him – but Emmanuel Adler was a *philosopher*. His clothes were doubtless selected to best represent his manichean world view, being black and white, though what the upturned collar on his shirt signified was beyond understanding.

Strindberg had been ready to loathe the man from the moment he first saw his name on the poster downstairs. It is true that Adler (Eagle in German) was not an uncommon name, but that gave no comfort to Strindberg. In the 1870s he had often utilised *Örnen* (or *The* Eagle) as a pseudonym, and therefore regarded the use of the same by another writer as a personal slight and an undoubted challenge. He liked Adler even less in the flesh, when he saw that he was over six feet tall and had thick black hair which he habitually combed with his artistic fingers. His features were sharp, the sort that appealed to French film directors and promiscuous women like Hinde.

Emmanuel Adler was not only a philosopher, he was also an orator. More than that; he was a *personification*. Thus, when called upon to speak by the chairman, he began by announcing: "We were Maoists, we were Leninists, and those of us who were Jews were Sartrean Jews." *We* did not indicate some royal delusion, but referred to the generation of '68. What did he mean? Well, a Sartrean Jew was one who was dependent upon antisemitism for his identity. Judaism was therefore regarded by the generation of '68 (as personified by Emmanuel Adler) as a real hindrance to self-expression. Or so our hero believed when he sat down to write his first philosophical text. It went swimmingly until it came to my pet subject, the subject of evil. "That chapter proved impossible to write," he explained. "Each day I tied it up, and each night it undid itself." It was a problem he eventually solved, not with modern philosophy, but with ancient Hebrew texts. Yes, Emmanuel Adler was a *baltshuve*, a born-again Jew; though, because he was a philosopher, it was his thought process rather than his behaviour that had been altered. He continued to *act* like a Frenchman. Hence the presence, in the front row, of his blonde and willowy mistress.

The third member of the panel was none other than Mrs Bauman, whose dispassionate account of life in the Warsaw Ghetto had become a best-seller in Sweden. Her Swedish, though fluent, still betrayed her late arrival. Otherwise she seemed a well-adjusted woman, afflicted with nothing worse than outrageous taste in clothes and nicotine addiction.

Although she was present on account of her memoirs she had not assumed the role of professional survivor, nor had she adopted the pulpit-patter that usually accompanied it. Her subject was the universal application of the Holocaust experience. Unlike some of her contemporaries (whom she chose not to name) she refused to dwell upon the moral superiority of the Jew. Actually the English writer did name Elie Wiesel, and not to pay him compliments. This enraged Emmanuel Adler, who looked upon Wiesel as a saint. He maintained that it was the duty of *all* Jewish writers to memorialize the victims of the Nazis whom Wiesel (another personification) spoke for. The Englishman was accused, in no uncertain terms, of wanting to forget about the Holocaust. This, in turn, enraged him. "I said that I didn't feel inclined to *describe* the Holocaust," he replied, "not that I didn't want to *know* about it. You are a thinker, you are supposed to be aware that there is a big difference between fiction and history. The former being *lies*. You should also know that it is possible to write about the Holocaust without seeming to."

Being an antisemite Strindberg saw no merit in either argument, but the remainder of the audience was beginning to take sides. The men seemed evenly divided but most of the women, alas, only had eyes for Emmanuel Adler. And what those moist orbs expressed was not hostility. Some women even arose and expressed their support vocally. Among these, I regret to say, was Hinde, who claimed to have been so moved by Mani (*Mani?*) Adler's confessions that she wished to share her recent dreams with the entire assembly.

"Like Mani and many others of my generation I was *not* galvanized by the triumph of '67," Hinde explained to the hushed room. "It seemed so . . . so atavistic, so *biblical*, so out of keeping with modern times. Ah, those modern times! I was not a Sartrean Jew, like Mani, but a Jewish Swede. Same difference! It was the Yom Kippur War which changed me, as I am sure it changed Mani Adler. Once again it seemed that our brave new world – our *modern* world – was prepared to stand idly by while the Jews were annihilated. Since those terrible days I have been tormented by dreams that speak of a bad conscience."

Whereupon she paused, apparently uncertain whether to continue with her psychic strip-tease; though Strindberg, an old pro, recognised that she was merely tantalizing the audience, inviting it to beg for her to do so. "Don't stop now," said one. "Tell us," demanded another.

"Well," continued Hinde obligingly, "I dream, for example, that I am a little girl in a party frock. As is well known, all cute little girls want nothing more than to please their fathers. Not this little girl. She longed to please her new teacher. She painted pictures to please him, she read books to please him. Which they did. But when she showed her work to her Papa he did not praise it. Instead he plucked out his eyes. The girl screamed. Her father clutched his ears. He opened his mouth to speak, but he could only utter strange words that she did not understand. She ran to her teacher. 'How can I help Papa?' she wailed. 'You cannot help him,' he replied. 'You must forget him.' And she did as he advised. The years pass quickly, as happens in dreams. By now the little girl is a woman. She finds herself in a dark wood. She has lost the right path. She has been abandoned by her teacher. She is alone. 'Papa,' she cries. 'Save me! Show me the proper way.' Night after night I am plagued by similar dreams. According to my analyst there has been of late an epidemic of such dreams in Stockholm and elsewhere. Jungian archetypes, he tells me, are all the rage. You ignore them at your peril. Therefore I beg you to follow the path of enlightenment, the path of our elders and our betters, as Mani Adler has done in his own way!"

Hinde sat down to general applause as Papa Zelinsky arose to claim the final word. Unluckily for his daughter he was Aaron reincarnate, and his way was the way of idolatory. He worshipped Eretz Yisroel, the land of Israel, and blessed its eternal capital, Jerusalem the Golden. He therefore cursed its enemies, the Arabs, whom he saw as nothing but Nazis in djibbas. "Every Jew should be an Elie Wiesel," he said, "constantly reminding the world what it once did to us and, only recently, tried to do again." The old complaint! The English writer looked crestfallen; Strindberg, however, was apoplectic with rage. He had counted *at least* five separate references to Emmanuel Adler in Hinde's contribution; as if that wasn't bad enough she had frequent recourse to the diminutive form, which suggested more than a passing intimacy with the oleaginous *Mani*. What further proof did he require? The

201

Frenchman was obviously her lover.

At last he could envision a denouement to the drama of their marriage. The three of them would be in a crowded room. He would observe how they behaved when they met, witness the exchange of petty intimacies and then, in a smaller space, would expose his wife in the very act of adultery. However, this presented certain practical difficulties, the most obvious being that his presence (the sine qua non of the scene) would inevitably alter the course of events. It was a problem that tested his artistry. Surely even Hinde, shameless as she was, wouldn't fuck another in front of her husband?

Strindberg's concentration was rudely disturbed by the woman on his right who suddenly leaned forward and said to the woman on his left: "Looks like I need to have a serious rethink about my costume for tonight, now that I've actually seen *him*." To which the other replied: "I already have, I already have. I'm going to wear that tight little dress with no back and precious little front. If nothing else it will make my dear hubby insanely jealous." *Thus spake Messalina*, thought Strindberg, *thus speaks everywoman*. And of what were they speaking? An orgy in the forum? No. They were simply discussing the celebratory meal which was to be served that night in the library of the Great Synagogue. Strindberg was sure that Hinde would be present, a willing handmaiden to her new god. In his desperation he turned to me. *Dear Beelzebub*, he thought, *I want to be there too*. How could I resist such a well-mannered request?

And so I did what I had always planned to do; I turned him into a fly, a greenbottle to be precise. That's right, my dears, August Strindberg went to dinner clad in the bright green livery of *lucilia caesar*. Appropriate, eh? It took him some time to become accustomed to his unusual condition,

which he had initially ascribed to bad vodka and a particularly unforgiving bout of delirium tremens, but gradually he came to accept the reality of his situation (which he obviously regarded as a temporary expedient) and even to relish his novel accomplishments (not to mention his brand-new bottle-green blazer).

The more conventional guests, in their lounge suits and sexy gowns, continued to discuss the controversies of that morning's symposium, even as they were ushered into the long room lined with dark wood and books. Strindberg simply flew over their heads, buzzing everyone who had the temerity to speak well of Emmanuel Adler. What a lark!

For some the main course was fish roll in cream sauce, but for most – notably the speaker himself – it was Mani's after-dinner lecture. Neither he nor his mistress took a mouthful of food, indeed they left the table and repaired to a small room, wherein he prepared himself. When he returned it was in the guise of a romantic hero; his dark hair was swept back, his dazzling white shirt unbuttoned to the *pupik*. His adoring co-star clung to his arm, transmitting an unambiguous message: this man is hot stuff. "Look," said Hinde to Mrs Bauman, "even the flies are attracted to him." Strindberg, circling around his enemy's dark mane, caught sight of her glowing face out of the corner of his many-faceted eye and knew instinctively that the blonde stick was merely a decoy, an amorous under-study. But how many others in that room could pick out the real star; could see through her artful innocence, and appreciate the true brilliance of her performance? None but the two eagles!

"Do you know the first question he asked me when I collected him at Arlanda?" whispered the rabbi, referring to the one in human form. "How many reporters are coming to my lecture?" Emmanuel Adler need not have worried. The adjacent hall, which seated 250, was packed with writers, journalists, artists and starry-eyed women. Outside people were being turned away. "His bag was filled with twenty-five kilos of papers," added the rabbi admiringly, "just so that he could carry on with his book in Stockholm. It was so heavy I could hardly lift it." If those were the volumes he required for a couple of days in a foreign capital, who could take the true measure of his mind, now well into its third decade? He must have devoured more books than were housed in the Great Synagogue, library and all. Indeed, he quoted from most of them as erudition poured from his tongue like molten lava.

He leaned upon the lectern, and spoke in confidential tones (as he had done that morning) of his past mistakes (Mao, Lenin, Sartre), until he knew that his audience had once again forgiven him. Then he told of his repentance, of his Jewish renaissance. Finally, with a smile, he concluded that literature itself, by dint of its talmud-like nature, was essentially *Jewish*. The audience went crazy! Strindberg, though offended by Adler's overblown semitic imperialism, was forced to agree that it had been a formidable achievement, a veritable tour de force; to have spoken so fluently (in a foreign tongue!) with so few notes to guide him.

Emmanuel Adler was now reclining Chopin-like against the grand piano, absorbing the adoration. In his closing remarks the bald chairman offered the French philosopher's chameleon ability to change his convictions from day to day as proof positive of his genius. This was too much for Strindberg, who prized constancy in thought as in women. "You are so impressed to have this colossus as a friend that you have obviously lost whatever sense of judgement you once possessed," he hissed, having settled in his ear. "You are like a lion tamer in a circus who boasts, 'Ladies and gentlemen, here is a wild beast I have pacified for you,' and then proceeds to put the animal through its paces. And naturally Monsieur Adler obliges." Alas, Strindberg was wasting his breath. The chairman, hearing nothing but a tiresome drone, heedlessly brushed the troublesome fly away with his hand.

Meanwhile Emmanuel Adler's mistress flung herself upon her lover and delivered a congratulatory kiss. Adler stroked the rump of her leather culottes and then, with a condescending pat, pushed her aside. She departed cheerfully and, finding the rabbi unattended, engaged him in conversation. Her former position beside the lady-killer was filled by candidate after candidate who melted away in their turn until – at last! – there came the event for which Strindberg had waited so long, had endured so much; the final confirmation that his instinctive distrust of the female was definitely not a paranoid fantasy.

Voila! Hinde was talking to Adler! Of what were they speaking? Of the Jewish God? Of the manifold tragedies that had befallen His people? Of starvation and poverty? Of munitions and disarmament? Of the random injustices of suffering? Of death? I doubt it. Just look at Hinde! Is that the sort of dress a woman wears when she wants to discuss philosophy? Even Socrates would have found it a test to concentrate upon the discourse at hand, when so much other flesh was on display. Why, her breasts were all but bare!

Strindberg, unable to resist the pale curvature of those delicate globes, dropped upon their northern slopes. Hinde ignored him, enabling him to remain a temporary ornament upon her heart, a mobile beauty spot. Although he had six feet in situ, they somehow failed to convey the expected stimuli to his brain. Where were the transports of delight? Instead he received strange impulses, all of them negative; he had been misdirected by his eyes, here was no suppuration nor any decay to nourish the larvae, this flesh

206

was too firm, too fresh. He was about to take off for more advantageous sites – those grubby plates on the table in the library looked most desirable – when the increasing vibrations from her voice-box attracted his attention.

He folded his wings, and listened to his wife. "Tell me," she was murmuring, "how do you reconcile your obvious commitment to Judaism with the fact that you have a *mistress* who is so *transparently* of a different persuasion?" She moistened her lips with the tip of her strawberry-red tongue, not the action of a participant in a typical platonic exchange. This was clearly no cerebral dialogue but a prelude to rutting, a wanton display of availability. Strindberg, being an expert in such matters, sniffed out the hidden meaning in less time than it takes a pig to find a truffle. Do I really need to spell out that the underlying purpose of Hinde's silly provocation was not to bring about Adler's intellectual capitulation, but to hint at the possibility of her own? Yes, my dears, Strindberg was on the right track for once; she *was* promising the Frenchman a kosher fuck.

Being well-versed in linguistics and semiotics, Adler also understood that all sentences have subtexts, was no slouch himself when it came to discerning the licentious underwear that lay beneath their strict rules of grammar and style. He quickly grasped what his voluptuous interlocutor was proposing and could think of no good reason to reject her offer. "As you say, Kate is a *shiksa*," he replied. "She is also anorexic," he added, as though the two states were inevitable complements, like salt and pepper. "You, I perceive, are neither. Such a woman, provided she were of a charitable disposition, might want to help me mend my ways. It would be a *mitzvah*, I assure you."

They retired and ascended the spiral staircase that led to the rabbi's bolt-hole above the Ark of the Covenant where, earlier that evening, Adler had rehearsed his performance with his mistress. Neither noticed the third party that accompanied them; a rather agitated greenbottle. Adler shut the door and began to unbutton his shirt. Hinde, however, remained immobile in a dark corner. *What is she playing at?* thought Strindberg, buzzing with frustration.

"I should warn you that I am a little out of practise at this," she said, "I have been faithful to my husband for more years than I care to count." "There is no need to be embarrassed," said Adler, now wearing nothing but a little black posing pouch, "many women feel the urge to experience a different lover after a prolonged period of monogamy, and then become apprehensive at the last moment." "You do not understand," said Hinde, "I have not fucked *anyone* in more than a decade. That is how long I have been an *aguna*, a deserted wife."

Strindberg looked at Adler and saw, to his astonishment, that the great philosopher was taken in. The sucker believed her! Hinde *chaste?* So much for the Frenchie's insight into the female heart. At the same time Strindberg was forced to admire his wife's consistency; she hardly knew the man and she was already lying to him. Duplicity thy name is Hinde! Why else was she doing it? She had no idea that her husband was in attendance and therefore had no need to comfort the poor cuckold with false boasts of fidelity. No, telling lies to men was simply an unbreakable habit, an addiction.

Hinde continued to hesitate, until even Strindberg began to doubt that she would ever remove her dress. *Do it*, he thought, *do it, you bitch!* Eventually she did, but only after she had modestly turned her back upon the rampant Frenchman. *The pants*, screamed Strindberg, *take them off! Now you see us*, they whispered obligingly, *now you don't.* Hinde was naked, but none could enjoy her save the woodworm in the old panelling. Strindberg knew that when she revealed herself to Adler it would make a reconciliation between them impossible – yet here he was, urging her to do just that. "If you would prefer," said the Frenchman, stroking her backside, "I'll take you from behind, like a Bulgarian." "Not this time," said Hinde, facing him at last.

Now that she had finally committed herself she became an enthusiastic participant, kissing Adler passionately and groaning loudly whenever he touched her between the thighs. "Oh God, Mani," she said, "I'm so wet." "So warm and so wet," he said, "and so ready for me." "Yes," she said, "I'm ready for you."

Adler lowered her gently to the floor and parted her legs so that her desire for him was manifest. Whereupon a greenbottle, apparently attracted by the rank and meaty secretions of Hinde's cunt, buzzed wildly around that glistening orifice, seriously impeding Adler's own advance. I doubt that even Strindberg, maddened as he was, knew whether he wanted to enter Hinde himself or merely to hinder Adler. As it happened, being only a *fly*, he could do neither. He could only watch helplessly as another man burgled his wife.

Once the couple had established a steady rhythm, Strindberg calmed down. Why the fuss? After all he had no desire to curtail the action; all he really wanted was to pass judgement upon it. But how? Buzzing around Hinde's sweaty brow, however annoying it might be to her, was a poor substitute for a ringing denunciation of her flagrant sin. Had he not been a fly he would have wept with frustration. Here he was, at the dramatic climax of his career, utterly incapable of responding to his cue, of delivering the coup de théâtre. Instead of being the dramatis persona par excellence he had been reduced to the insignificant status of a verminous extra.

As soon as the guilty couple had taken their bows and departed, Strindberg summoned me in the expectation that I would come and restore him (somewhat belatedly) to his proper form, but I did not respond. Nor will I ever. My work was done. Not without reluctance I abandoned Strindberg to his eternal fate. For all I know he is still hurling himself at the heavy door of the rabbi's windowless room.

Alas, poor Strindberg! All his dreams of winged creatures have come down to this. Poe's raven, Jupiter's eagle, the falcon of Horus — every one a sham and a delusion! His true destiny was to be just another of Beelzebub's flies; yet another greenbottle among the billions of house-flies, horse-flies, flesh-flies, dung-flies, robber-flies, hover-flies, crane-flies, drone-flies, bluebottles, mosquitoes, gnats, midges and all the other diptera — many of them, like Strindberg, household names. All of them snared in their singular hell. Pity poor Strindberg trapped in his; sans voice, sans fingers, sans everything. Only you can release him from this eternal torment, dear reader; but first you have to know which fly to swat.